Time was running out.

The three menacing men marched close. Dark glasses hid their eyes, but their dark suits did little to hide the bulges of their gun holsters.

Addison surveyed the layout of the train station. "C'mon." He jogged up a flight of steps, two at a time. He crossed the overpass —a footbridge directly over the waiting train.

Eddie scurried nervously after him. A growing knot in his gut told him that Addison was hatching something. "Talk to me, Addison. What are you thinking?"

"Eddie, what's the worst idea I've ever had?"

"The time we tried swimming across an alligator-infested river in Colombia?" guessed Eddie.

"The time we stole Colonel Ragar's limousine in Ecuador?" tried Raj.

"The time you entered us in the Mongolian national horse race with four stolen horses?" Molly volunteered.

"Right, well . . ." said Addison. "This idea is worse than all those."

Two of the armed men hustled up the steps behind them on the walkway. The other man dashed up the far side, shutting off any escape.

Addison looked down on the train. He swung one leg, and then the other, over the metal railing of the footbridge. He judged the drop to be a good eight feet, but then again, he had never been particularly good at judging distances. He heard the train doors hiss closed. The dark-suited men, sensing his purpose, sprang toward him.

There was nothing for it but to jump.

THE ADDISON COOKE SERIES

THE THRIFTY GUIDES

ADDISON COOKE

AND THE
RING
OF
DESTINY

JONATHAN W. STOKES

PUFFIN BOOKS

PUFFIN BOOKS
An imprint of Penguin Random House LLC, New York

First published in the United States of America by Philomel Books,
an imprint of Penguin Random House LLC, 2019
Published by Puffin Books, an imprint of Penguin Random House LLC, 2020

Visit us online at penguinrandomhouse.com

THE LIBRARY OF CONGRESS HAS CATALOGED THE PHILOMEL BOOKS EDITION AS FOLLOWS:
Names: Stokes, Jonathan W., author.
Title: Addison Cooke and the ring of destiny / Jonathan W. Stokes.
Description: New York : Philomel Books, [2019] | Sequel to: Addison Cooke and
the tomb of the Khan. | Summary: "Addison and the team travel to Paris, Istanbul,
Cyprus, and beyond to stop the enemy Malazar and find the treasured Ring of
Destiny"—Provided by publisher. Includes notes on Knights Templar.
Identifiers: LCCN 2019012751| ISBN 9780399173790 (hardback) |
ISBN 9780698189300 (ebook)
Subjects: | CYAC: Adventure and adventurers—Fiction. | Secrets—Fiction. |
Buried treasure—Fiction. | Antiquities—Fiction. | Mystery and detective stories. |
BISAC: JUVENILE FICTION / Action & Adventure / Survival Stories. |
JUVENILE FICTION / Humorous Stories. | JUVENILE FICTION / Historical /
Ancient Civilizations.
Classification: LCC PZ7.1.S753 Acr 2019 | DDC [Fic]—dc23
LC record available at https://lccn.loc.gov/2019012751

Puffin Books ISBN 9780147515650

Printed in the United States of America

3 5 7 9 10 8 6 4 2

Edited by Cheryl Eissing.
Text set in 11-point Garth Graphic Std.

For my father

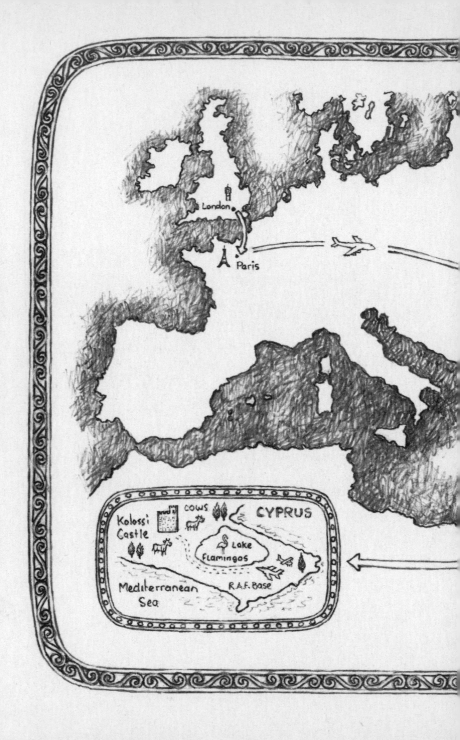

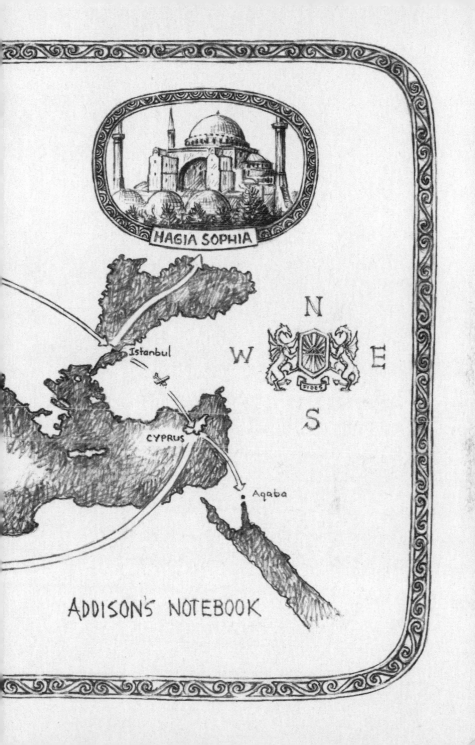

I

THE

TEMPLAR
KEY

Chapter One

The Ferret and the Yorker

ADDISON COOKE WAS DOWN on his luck. Rain clouds had been following him around for months, though to be fair, he was in England. Whatever switch controlled the British weather was permanently stuck on Rain. Addison imagined that if archaeology didn't work out for him, he could always enjoy an extremely easy career as an English weatherman.

Today's weather was even more dismal than normal, and the same could safely be said for Addison's mood. He was, in a word, miffed.

His troubles had begun, as troubles often do, when

his aunt and uncle were thrown from a cliff in Outer Mongolia. This unfortunate act had been perpetrated by a dangerous man named Vrolok Malazar, known in criminal circles as the Shadow.

Fearing for Addison's life, Addison's uncle Jasper had sent him into hiding at the Dimpleforth School in the town of Weebly-on-Hammerstead. The boarding school was founded by King Edward III more than six hundred years ago, and as far as Addison could tell, no one had yet updated the plumbing.

Dimpleforth was a rambling estate filled with rambling professors and blue-eyed, blue-blooded students with family names older than the ivy-covered buildings. The daily dress code at Dimpleforth was a black tailcoat, a starched white collar, and pinstripe trousers. "Trousers," Addison had discovered, was the British word for pants, and "pants" was the British word for underwear. Addison learned this the hard way on his first day of school, when he innocently asked his professor if the dress code required him to wear pants to lunch.

This mistake earned Addison his first trip to the headmaster's office, where he was sentenced to sit quietly for two hours after dinner. And this, in turn, was how Addison learned that "dinner" was in fact the British word for lunch, and "tea" was the British word for dinner. Thus, Addison showed up for his detention at dinnertime, or rather teatime, and missed lunch, that is to say, dinner, entirely. And so Addison earned his second detention right on top of the first. Try as he might, Addison could not seem to get the hang of England.

Now here he was, stuck playing a game of cricket in a spitting drizzle. The two team captains happened to be the two meanest boys at Dimpleforth: Weston Whitley from Upper Nobbly, and Randall Twigg, a scholarship student from Lower Nobbly. They took infinite pleasure in teasing Addison for his complete lack of understanding of the British game.

Cricket, Addison had discovered, was much like baseball, if baseball had been designed by a vast committee of bureaucrats paid by the hour. The game of cricket was four hundred years old, and no wonder: a single match lasted thirty hours over the course of an entire week. Weston Whitley's team was currently beating Addison's team by a staggering three hundred points.

Addison trudged across the muddy grass to take his place in the outfield. He had no idea which position to play. "Where should I stand?"

Randall Twigg squinted at Addison in disgust. "Just stand at cow corner so the ball will never come to you."

"Which way is cow corner?"

"It's next to deep midwicket, you grotty ferret. Unless . . ." Randall added thoughtfully, "unless we move to attacking field, in which case you'll move up to midwicket."

Addison shook his head and sighed. He trotted to the farthest corner of the playing field and stood next to his roommate, Wilberforce Sinclair, the one person in school who would bother to answer his questions. Addison had no friends to turn to. "Wilber, why do they call me a ferret?"

Wilberforce pushed his foggy glasses higher on his narrow nose. "Because a ferret is a rabbit, you see."

"How," asked Addison as patiently as he could, "is a ferret a rabbit?"

"In cricket they're much the same thing. A rabbit is someone who scores zero points. And in cricket, zero points is called a duck."

"So a ferret is a rabbit with a duck."

Wilberforce clapped Addison on the shoulder. "Now you're getting it."

Addison found this all so dumb that he found he was dumbfounded. It was one thing to have a nickname. But it was another thing to have a nickname that made no earthly sense.

After watching the grass grow in the outfield for a good half hour, it was finally Addison's turn to go to bat. "Any advice?" he asked Wilberforce.

Wilberforce polished his glasses on his white cable-knit sweater. "It's easy, really. Don't swing at anything off stump, block any yorkers, and cut the bouncers. Unless . . ." he added helpfully, "unless you play off the back foot, in which case pull the bouncers."

"Thanks," said Addison, thoroughly confused. He trotted to the stump, hefted the cricket bat over his shoulder, and wound up like a baseball player. This resulted in Weston Whitley toppling to the ground in laughter. Addison gripped his bat, unsure whether he wanted to hit the ball or just take a run at Weston's kneecaps.

"Ferret," said Weston, "in cricket, we bat underhanded, like swinging a golf club."

Addison adjusted his grip accordingly. "Just pitch me the ball." He wanted to get this over with.

"Oh, ferret," Weston guffawed again. "You don't 'pitch' a cricket ball, you *bowl* it."

Addison was bowled over. To him, bowling involved wooden lanes, rented shoes, and a loose acquaintance's interminable birthday party. "Fine, just throw it to me."

Weston Whitley wound up and pitched the ball directly at Addison's head. It smacked into Addison's jaw, sending stars across his vision. Addison took two dizzy steps backward and crumpled to a seat in the wet grass.

Randall Twigg, Addison's team captain, was furious. He marched to stand chest to chest with Weston Whitley. "You can't bowl a beamer at a bloke! That was a bean ball bowled at the batsman's brains!"

"It weren't never a beamer," Weston retorted. "It was a fine googly, and a dibbly-dobbly at that."

Addison tuned them out. When he had lived in a cramped apartment in New York City, he had often grown quite sick of it. But now he found he was homesick for the very home he was once sick of. He loved England's history, he loved England's culture, but he could not seem to fit in at Dimpleforth.

While the boys argued, Addison stood up and left the field. The patting drizzle turned to a pelting downpour. He had never felt so alone. Addison limped back to his dormitory, feeling every bit like a ferret who'd been beamed by a yorker.

Chapter Two

The Earl of Runnymede

IT WAS LATE DECEMBER, and the students were packing up to leave for the winter holiday. Already, there was an abandoned feel to the dorms. Addison, drenched from the rain, dragged himself up the steps of his dormitory, Talfryn Brimble Hall. For centuries the famous hall had produced prime ministers and captains of industry, though primarily, Addison noticed, the aging hall produced mold, moths, and mice.

Addison's roommate, the aforementioned Wilberforce Sinclair, held an unofficial school record for consecutive days without showering. Wilberforce seemed to be dedicated to several hobbies with a fervor that bordered on mania. These included pressing spiderwebs in a photo album, cutting his toenails in the common area, and feeding the pet garter snake he stowed in a shoebox under his bed. The garter snake, Teddy, required a steady diet of earthworms that Wilberforce purchased from a local pet store. Addison had no great love for the garter snake, though at least it had the decency to chew with its mouth closed and didn't constantly borrow Addison's hairbrush without asking. Addison had endured poison ivy rashes that were better company than Wilberforce.

Despite all this, it was Addison, and not Wilberforce, who was the least popular kid in his grade. Ever since his aunt and uncle had gone missing, Addison could not seem to pull his life together. He was tortured by guilt, wondering if there was anything he could have done to help them. At night, he couldn't sleep. During the day, he couldn't stay awake.

Since he could not bury his aunt and uncle, Addison buried himself in his studies. He considered history to be his strong suit, but all the other students knew more than he did about British history. Addison needed a tutor to teach him about the Tudors. His crusty Greek and Latin teachers seemed older than the languages they taught. The one course Addison enjoyed was ancient history, where he devoured tales about the Assyrian Empire, the Queen of Sheba, and the kingdom of Solomon.

His exams done, Addison now packed up his suitcase to go home to Uncle Jasper's for the winter holiday.

Wilberforce looked up from feeding his garter snake. "Addison, I hope your holiday is wickedly good fun."

Addison had noticed that British people often spiced up their sentences by saying, "It's *awfully* good to meet you," "It's *terribly* nice of you," or "This is *frightfully* decent pudding." Addison had tried to get the hang of this, telling the dining hall cook that his jellied eels were *disgustingly* tasty and *nauseatingly* appetizing. It had earned him another trip to the headmaster. All in all, Addison was glad to be rid of the school, rid of Wilberforce, and rid of everything in between.

"Wilberforce," he said, by way of goodbye, "I shall miss you. *Terribly.*"

· · · · · ·

Addison took the two-hour train ride back to Surrey and walked the last half mile to his uncle's manor house, a sprawling estate called Runnymede Hall. It was only a few months earlier that Addison had discovered that his eccentric, gambling-obsessed uncle Jasper was, of all things, the Seventeenth Earl of Runnymede. Uncle Jasper insisted this title was nothing special, there being no fewer than 212 earls in the country of England, not to mention all the dukes, marquesses, viscounts, and barons. "All nobility means," his uncle had explained, "is that if you break the law, you have the right to be hanged by a silk rope."

Addison left his bags with the butler, Jennings, in the grand entrance hall of the manor house. He changed into his gym clothes, grabbed a snack from the kitchen, and headed for the secret bookcase in the library. The swiveling bookcase opened to a spiral stone passage that led down to a basement among the Saxon roots of the original castle.

Here, Uncle Jasper kept a hidden training facility. He insisted that on weekends and school vacations, Addison and his little sister, Molly, learn the skills of gentlemen: horseback riding, shooting, boxing, and even swordsmanship. Generally, Addison was a bookish type who endorsed being indoors. But after nearly being killed on several continents in the past year, he saw the value in learning to defend himself.

Addison crossed behind the balance beam, the sword rack, and the practice dummies pricked full of knife wounds. He ducked under the rope-climbing course where he worked on overcoming his fear of heights. Addison reached his locker and began strapping on his sparring gear: a mask and protective padding.

Molly was already warming up on a punching bag, riddling it with roundhouse kicks.

Her short hair had recently grown long enough to be swept back in a ponytail, so it no longer fell in her eyes. She was twelve now, and attended the Wyckingham Swithy School for Girls. Molly had a natural knack for the martial arts, and had skyrocketed through the sparring ranks of her local dojo. Since the disappearance of Aunt Delia and Uncle Nigel, Molly had poured all of her energy into training. If Addison buried his grief in his studies, Molly buried her feelings in the faces of her opponents.

Uncle Jasper spotted Addison and clasped his hands together. "You've joined us at last. Addison, choose your weapon and meet Molly on the sparring mat."

Addison crossed to the weapons rack and picked out his favorite wooden practice knife.

Molly's weapon of choice was her sling. She unwrapped the leather pouch and stuffed it with a wooden peg that was only slightly less lethal than its normal lead slug.

The siblings took off their shoes, squared off on the practice mat, and bowed.

Molly was Addison's partner for everything. When they weren't sparring, they even had to take ballroom dance lessons together. Uncle Jasper insisted that the foxtrot would help with their balance for fencing and fighting.

Molly started her sling swinging and charged Addison, walloping him on the upper arm.

He yelped in pain and dug the flat edge of his wooden practice knife into the side of his sister's neck. This, for Addison, was a typical Friday.

Uncle Jasper clapped his hands once, stopping the match. "What went wrong there?"

"He got lucky," said Molly.

"No, you chose the wrong weapon." Uncle Jasper crossed the mat and took a knee between Molly and Addison. "Molly, I know you love your sling, but it's not a weapon for close quarters. You'll barely get it spinning before an attacker has you on the ground. Besides," he added, "it is not a gentleman's weapon."

"I'm not a gentleman," said Molly. "I'm a gentlelady."

"Not that gentle," said Addison, ruefully rubbing his arm. His first time seeing his sister for the winter holiday, and this was how she greeted him.

Uncle Jasper sighed, weary lines showing on his forehead. "Molly Cooke, there are people who want you dead. Grown men twice your height, twice your weight, who've been fighting twice as long as you've been alive."

Molly lowered her head and nodded.

"Here, I've got something for you." Uncle Jasper handed her a small can marked PEPPER SPRAY. "It's the same stuff as the tear gas police use to break up riots. It will make a grown man cry in pain. Keep it with you at all times." He pointed to the trigger by the spray nozzle. "If you ever get in a pinch, pinch this button."

Addison unstrapped his protective mask. "When are you going to tell us why these people are after our family? We know we're somehow related to the Knights Templar. We know there's some secret prophecy that involves wiping out anyone unlucky enough to be born a Cooke. But who is Malazar? Why has he declared open season on us?"

Molly joined in. "When are you going to tell us our family's Templar history?"

Uncle Jasper shut his eyes and swiveled his head from side to side. "When you come of age."

"What does that even mean?" asked Molly.

"I can't answer that," said Uncle Jasper, "until you come of age."

Addison reached under his shirt and drew out the Templar medallion that had once belonged to his uncle Nigel. The bronze disk was embossed with the symbol of an eye in the center of a dazzling sun. Surrounding it were the Latin words for teamwork, knowledge, faith, perseverance, and courage: all the Templar virtues. "It's funny," said Addison. "I don't see a word on here about keeping secrets."

Uncle Jasper folded his arms and sighed. "Just for that, you'll be doing an extra hour of running tonight."

• • • • • • •

Addison's muscles were sore when he went down for breakfast in the morning. The manor house had a dining room big enough to comfortably seat a college marching band, but Uncle Jasper found it cozier to eat in the kitchen.

The uncle in question greeted Addison with a friendly wave of his toast and jam.

Addison attempted a cheerful wave, but today was a day he'd been dreading for months.

Molly was already dressed head to toe in black. She poured milk into her cereal. "Why are we even having a funeral? Aunt Delia and Uncle Nigel have only been missing five months. They could still be out there."

Uncle Jasper took a sip of tea and set his cup down in the saucer. "It's time, Molly. By declaring them dead I can wrap up their affairs. We can sell off their things; we can empty your New York apartment. And I can begin the process of legally adopting you."

Addison had watched his aunt and uncle be pushed off the cliff in Mongolia. He knew his uncle was doing the necessary thing. He just didn't want to admit it. "What will you bury in their coffins?"

"There won't be any coffins," said Uncle Jasper. "Only headstones. Like your parents."

Addison nodded.

Molly ate her cereal in silence.

On the other side of the house, the doorbell chimed. Uncle Jasper brightened. "Addison and Molly, I know this is a difficult day for you, so I do have one pleasant surprise . . ."

Jennings appeared in the kitchen doorway in his immaculate suit and starched white gloves. "Pardon me, Addison and Molly. We have guests in the main hall for you. A Mr. Edward Chang and a Mr. Raj Bhandari."

Chapter Three

The Merchant of Baghdad

ADDISON FLEW TO THE front door as if blasted from a cannon. It was the first unfiltered happiness he had felt in many months, and it nearly overwhelmed him. He realized that he hadn't had friends for a very long time. Addison clasped Eddie and Raj in a three-way hug.

"Addison," said Eddie, eyeing the grand staircase and the crystal chandelier above, "how did you talk your way into this castle?"

"I didn't have to trick anyone," said Addison. "It's my uncle Jasper's."

"Does it have a dungeon?" asked Raj. "Or any hidden rooms?"

Addison pursed his lips, unsure whether to mention the training facility. "There's a hayloft in the stable. That's sort of hidden."

"Awesome."

Addison took in his friends' appearances. Eddie looked even taller and ganglier than he had the previous summer in Mongolia. It was as if someone had taken a regular-sized boy, laid him out on a baking sheet, and gone over him with a rolling pin.

Raj looked more wiry and strong. His hair was wild and disheveled like a mad scientist's, possibly from sleeping on the overnight flight from New York.

Addison wondered if he appeared different to them as well. He ushered his friends through the foyer. "Thank you for coming here on your winter break. Jennings will get your suitcases, but I'll show you to the kitchen. You must be starving after your flight."

Eddie nodded emphatically.

"Eddie, there's a piano in the great room you can practice on." Addison pointed down the east wing hallway as they passed it.

"I stopped taking piano lessons," Eddie said quietly.

Addison halted, turned, and gaped.

"I'm in eighth grade now," Eddie explained. "The pieces got way harder. I started getting stage fright at recitals. I'd sweat. My hands would shake. My teeth would chatter. It got so bad, my parents said it'd be okay if I took a break.

The upside is, I've had way more time to practice my lock picking."

Eddie had discovered a real gift for lock picking during their adventure in Mongolia, and Addison was pleased Eddie was pursuing this talent. Still, it didn't sit right with him that Eddie was abandoning music. Eddie loved piano and was phenomenal at it. "Eddie, when did your stage fright begin?"

Eddie shrugged. "After everything that happened in Mongolia, I guess."

Addison led the way into the kitchen, shaking his head.

"A lot changed after that trip," said Raj. "I dropped out of Boy Scouts."

Now Addison had heard everything. "Impossible! Last time I saw you, you were on a bullet train to making Eagle Scout!"

Raj looked sheepish. "When my mom heard what happened to your aunt and uncle, she made me drop out of Scouts. This survival stuff isn't just fun and games: people can get hurt and die. She wants me to focus on school. I'm not even allowed to go to survival camp anymore. It's a miracle she let me come visit you."

Jennings laid out an English breakfast, and Eddie and Raj demolished it. Molly joined the table and filled Eddie and Raj in on her past few months at the Wyckingham

Swithy School for Girls. Addison didn't get much speaking in during breakfast. He let the conversation bubble around him. He felt responsible for what had happened to his aunt and uncle. And now he could see that Mongolia had affected the lives of his two best friends as well. He felt, in other words, wretched.

......

The funeral was in the afternoon. Uncle Jasper led everyone to the family funeral plot near the wishing well in the orchard. The vicar from the local parish revved into a long speech about the importance of faith in times of adversity.

Addison gazed at the desolate winter garden; the wisteria hanging from the trellis was withered and brown, the rose garden pruned to the nubs. He stared down at the granite headstones of his mother and father, set in the cold earth. He knew there was nothing buried there— his parents' bodies had never been found. Now his aunt and uncle would have empty graves as well. Someday, Addison thought, archaeologists might try to dig up all these archaeologists, and they would find nothing.

His eye wandered across the headstones of all the old Cookes going back seven hundred years. The farthest grave belonged to Adam Cooke, who spent his fortune building Runnymede on the ruins of a Saxon castle in 1309. It must have been a hefty job, because he promptly died in 1310. Addison wondered at how little he truly knew about these men and women, their faded, ivy-grown headstones all marked by the family crest—two dragons supporting a Templar shield, and that simple motto: *fides*. Faith.

Addison watched the vicar soldier on with his solemn speech. Eddie and Raj looked jet-lagged but hung their heads in respectful silence. Jennings the butler shed tears. Everybody loved Aunt Delia and Uncle Nigel.

Addison knew the earth rotated at about a thousand miles an hour. He reckoned that over the course of the funeral, the world spun seven hundred miles.

He felt every mile of it.

······

Afterward, a small gathering of Uncle Jasper's friends and acquaintances drifted back to the house, where Jennings served tea and biscuits. Addison stayed behind in the garden, still gazing at the headstones. He pulled the medallion from his neck and turned it over in his hands, his thumb tracing the Latin words.

After a few moments, he realized Uncle Jasper was still with him.

"Archaeologists," said Uncle Jasper. "We spend our lives digging things out of the ground, and in the end, that's where we end up."

Addison shook his head. "Aunt Delia and Uncle Nigel aren't in the ground. Not here, anyway."

Uncle Jasper nodded.

Addison took a deep breath. "I've spent my whole life trying to forget my mom and dad, so I can move on. Now I have to get to work forgetting Aunt D and Uncle N as well."

Uncle Jasper frowned. "You mustn't forget them, Addison. Archaeologists honor the past. It teaches us about our present and future."

Addison blinked a few times, a lump in his throat like a cricket ball. "Digging through the past got my aunt and uncle killed. Whatever this prophecy is, it's not worth it. I'll give up archaeology if it means keeping everyone safe."

"Then you would let Malazar win?"

Addison said nothing.

"Archaeology is in your blood, Addison. You would turn your back on your calling?" Uncle Jasper knelt down by the headstones. He took a few of the fresh white lilies from Aunt Delia's and Uncle Nigel's grave markers and placed them on the graves of Addison's parents. "Have you read W. Somerset Maugham? He lived not far from here."

"I mostly read nonfiction."

Uncle Jasper looked up at Addison. Even on this sad day he had a glint of humor in his cobalt-blue eyes. "A merchant in Baghdad sees Death beckoning to him in the marketplace. Terrified, the merchant flees to Samarra to hide. That night, he again meets Death in the street. Death says to the merchant, 'I was surprised to see you in Baghdad this morning . . . since I had this appointment with you tonight in Samarra.'"

Uncle Jasper rose to his feet and set a hand on Addison's shoulder. "The harder you run from your destiny, Addison, the faster you will run right into it." He patted Addison's shoulder a few times, then turned and strolled along the gravel path, back toward the manor house.

Addison fingered the medallion in his hands and stared at the headstones for a long time. Something in his life was going to need to change.

Chapter Four
The Secret Will

THE FIRST THING NEXT morning, Uncle Jasper shuffled off to his lawyers' offices in Twickenham to commence paperwork on becoming Addison and Molly's legal guardian. He would be gone the entire day, he announced, donning his derby hat, and this had absolutely nothing to do with the fact that Twickenham just happened to be across the river from the Moulsey Hurst horse racetrack.

This left Addison and Molly with complete run of the estate for the day. They came downstairs to find Eddie watching Raj guzzle water directly from the kitchen tap.

Addison observed the spectacle for a few moments in silence. "All right, I'll bite," he said finally. "Raj, what are you doing?"

Raj came up for air, chin dripping. "Drinking lots of water can help you get over jet lag."

Molly squinted skeptically. "Is that a survival tip from Babatunde Okonjo?"

She was familiar with Raj's obsession with the famous survival author.

"It's just a theory I'm working on," said Raj, panting for breath. "I might write my own survival book someday."

"I'll try anything," said Eddie, rubbing his tired eyes. He took over Raj's position, slurping water from the tap.

Jennings materialized in his usual way as if from thin air and offered Eddie and Raj water glasses.

The conversation turned to forming a plan for the day. Raj, who had conceived a love for horses while in Mongolia, was dead set on visiting the stables. Addison, however, knew that Runnymede's rickety old stable buildings were on the verge of collapse. They were unstable stables.

Addison proposed discussing their plans in the sitting room.

"What do you do in a sitting room?" asked Eddie.

"Sit." Addison shrugged.

"You can do that in any room!"

"It seems like a waste to sit in any old room," Addison countered, "when you have a perfectly good sitting room that no one is sitting in."

••••••

Jennings obliged them by serving breakfast in the sitting room. Addison indulged himself in a tall glass of Arnold Palmer. His aunt Delia had always objected to him drinking that much sugar first thing in the morning, but after a semester of blood sausage and boiled tomatoes in the Dimpleforth dining hall, he felt he had earned a decent breakfast.

Addison sifted through the assortment of London newspapers Jennings had arrayed on a silver tray.

Jennings coughed politely. "A letter arrived for you and Molly in the post this morning."

"Really?" Addison set down his copy of *The Daily Telegraph*. He had never received mail at Runnymede before, owing to the fact that he and Molly were supposed to be in hiding.

With one white-gloved hand, Jennings handed Addison a letter from the Law Offices of Pinfield & Hipwistle, Esquires. "With your aunt and uncle officially buried, sir, I believe you are receiving their will."

"Whoa," said Eddie. "Your inheritance!"

"I wonder if you'll inherit the stables," said Raj excitedly.

Addison frowned and tore open the envelope. Inside were two letters: one from Aunt Delia and one from Uncle Nigel.

Raj stared in awe. "A message from beyond the grave!"

"What's it say?" asked Molly.

Addison cleared his throat and read the first letter aloud.

London, January 3

Dear Addison and Molly,

If you are reading this, then your aunt and I have passed away. Hopefully from eating too much linguine while cruising the Mediterranean in a hundred-foot yacht. Or possibly from some sort of chocolate-related overdose at Trastevere Restaurant on 47th Street. Either way, I'm sorry we're gone, and sorry we've entrusted you both with such a grave responsibility.

Please take good care of your inheritance. You must stay strong and have faith. Always remember, it is our characters that determine our destiny. Your aunt and I love you both. We know you can handle this.

Yours always,
Uncle Nigel

Addison was overwhelmed to read something written in his uncle's hand, less than one day after planting his gravestone. Before Addison's emotions ran away from him, Eddie and Raj pelted him with questions.

"What's the inheritance?" asked Eddie.

"Yeah," said Raj. "What's the grave responsibility? How could he not explain that part?"

"Read Aunt Delia's letter," said Molly. "Maybe she explains."

Addison still felt a bit rattled from reading Uncle Nigel's letter. But he took a sip of his Arnold Palmer, steadied his voice, and read on . . .

January 3

Dear A & M,

We are in the lawyer's office as I scribble this, and they are charging us every fifteen minutes. So, well, sorry we died and all that. I'll write something more thoughtful when we're not on the lawyer's clock. Your uncle Jasper insisted we should write up a proper will, but between flight delays and a long lecture at the museum, we haven't the time today, so we'll fix this later. Until then, Addison, don't drink Arnold Palmers for breakfast. Molly, if he does, punch him on the arm.

Cheers!

Aunt D

Molly punched Addison on the arm.

"Ow!" Addison rubbed his twice-bruised upper arm

and grimaced. He was pleased that Molly was getting so good at kung fu, but not when he was the target. He stared at Aunt Delia's letter and chewed his lip. "This letter raises more questions than it answers."

"It doesn't answer anything!" Eddie cried. "You call that a will? Why would your aunt and uncle go through all the trouble of paying lawyers just to send you those two flimsy letters? They didn't seem to leave you anything."

"They must have," said Molly. "Uncle Nigel says he left us a grave responsibility."

"That's just what I've always wanted," said Raj. And he seemed to really mean it.

Eddie shook the envelope to see if they were missing anything.

A single key clattered onto the table.

"Neville Chamberlain!" Addison exclaimed. He had been made to memorize the names of British prime ministers while at Dimpleforth, and he liked to employ them in moments of shock, pain, or emotional distress.

The four friends all leaned in so quickly, they would have clunked heads if the coffee table hadn't been so large.

Addison picked up the key and weighed it in his hands. It was small, silver, and as light as a penny. "Some inheritance." He handed it to Eddie. "You're the expert with locks and keys. What does it open?"

Eddie held the tiny key up to the light and read the manufacturer's number engraved along its side. "This is called a five-pin key. And you can tell from the size . . . it's a bank key."

"We inherited a bank?" asked Molly.

"Well, a safe deposit box."

"What's a safe deposit box?"

"It's where you keep something so valuable you can't keep it in a house," said Eddie.

"So you lock it in a box inside a bank vault."

"Which bank?" asked Addison.

Eddie shrugged. "It could be anywhere."

Addison picked up the torn envelope from the Law Offices of Pinfield & Hipwistle, Esquires, and read the address aloud. "47 Piccadilly, St. James's, London." He fished in his hip pocket, retrieved his well-thumbed copy of *Fiddleton's World Atlas*, and opened the crumpled map of London.

Molly moved to his side of the sofa. "You're thinking Aunt Delia and Uncle Nigel chose a bank on their way to the lawyer's office?"

"That's a leap of faith," said Eddie.

"It's a place to start," said Addison, using his felt-tip pen to circle a bank on the map near Trafalgar Square.

Dialing Uncle Jasper's ancient candlestick phone, Addison began calling banks, inquiring after the safe deposit box. He lowered his voice and did his best impression of Uncle Nigel's twee British accent.

Eddie and Raj kept downing glasses of water.

"Don't expect to find the bank," said Eddie.

Molly frowned. "Why would you say that, Eddie?"

"I'm a pessimist. That's my philosophy in life. If I always expect to be disappointed, then when I get disappointed, I'm not disappointed."

Molly squinted and slowly nodded.

Eddie and Raj finished the entire water pitcher and took an emergency bathroom break. By the time they returned, Addison was calling his sixth London bank. He called three more before he found the one where his uncle owned a safe deposit box.

Addison jotted down the bank address and hung up the phone. "Aunt Delia and Uncle Nigel opened a bank account five years ago. On January third."

Molly gasped. "That's the same day they wrote the will!"

"Well," Addison said, buttoning up his blazer. "Who still wants to go to the stables?"

Chapter Five

The Bank Vault

ADDISON KNEW THE TRAIN routes from his regular pilgrimages to London's world-class archaeology museums. Train fare was not an issue, because he had won a monthly train pass off his roommate Wilberforce in a dice game. He didn't tell Wilber that his uncle Jasper had taught him from an early age how to memorize the odds and never fade an any-seven bet. Addison felt no remorse, however; Wilberforce rarely left their dorm room and was more likely to use a bar of soap than his monthly train pass.

Addison's group alighted at the Charing Cross Railway Station and waded into the crowded streets of downtown London. The prime minister's residence at 10 Downing Street was just to the south. Buckingham Palace was just to the west. And it was just two days before Christmas, so all the shop windows were hung with twinkling holiday lights. Wreaths brightened the lampposts. Festive holly boughs, festooned with bells, adorned the fence posts along St. James's Square.

"I like London," said Molly. She turned in a slow circle, admiring the scenic charm. "Let's try not to get kicked out of this city."

"I shall do my best," said Addison.

●●●●●●

It was nearly lunchtime when they arrived outside the Blandfordshire Bank at 1 West Chiselton Place. Eddie announced his burning desire to visit one of London's famous Indian restaurants, but Addison insisted they stick to business and visit the bank first.

Addison stared up at the imposing doors of the ancient bank building. He turned to survey his team. "We need to look respectable. Aunt D and Uncle N's will is a little on the vague side. This bank is not obligated to open their vault for any random bloke, bloater, or blighter who wanders in off the street, especially a gaggle of thirteen-year-olds. So let's all look our sharpest."

He straightened his navy-blue blazer, smoothed the collar of his dress shirt, and lined up his team for inspection.

Molly wore sneakers and khaki cargo pants with extra pockets. Their father's leather survival bag was slung across one shoulder. Addison thought she looked more like a war correspondent than a respectable bank customer, but it couldn't be helped.

Raj looked even more out of place in the ritzy Mayfair neighborhood. He wore a black T-shirt and his favorite camouflage pants, and topped it off with his signature red bandana. Addison imagined Raj's entire closet was filled with nothing but red bandanas and camo pants, but he respected a person whose clothing made a statement.

It was Eddie's attire that Addison found unacceptable. Eddie dressed like a person who had only narrowly outrun a tornado. His public school blazer was hopelessly wrinkled from his transatlantic flight. His tie looked like it had been square-knotted by a drunken sailor. And his pants were so short around Eddie's long legs that if a flash flood swept the London streets, his cuffs would stay perfectly dry.

Addison pulled and prodded Eddie's blazer, trying to wring out the wrinkles. "Eddie, you look frumpled!"

"Is 'frumpled' even a word?"

"It should be. It describes you perfectly."

Eddie squirmed and fidgeted. "Addison, we're visiting a bank, not the White House."

A cowlick of hair stood up on the top of Eddie's head

like a deep-space antenna. Addison figured the cowlick could only be cured with a buzz saw. He stopped fussing over Eddie's jacket creases and sighed. "Well, it will have to do."

He led the team up the stone steps of the bank.

"Guys, I've been working on my situational awareness," said Raj. "You know, checking for sniper positions before entering a building—that sort of thing."

Addison paused at the front doors and stared at Raj quizzically. "And?"

Using only his eyes, Raj indicated a black SUV parked on the far side of the street. "We're being watched."

Addison's eyebrows lowered to their bottom floor. Turning slowly, he feigned interest in a passing double-decker bus and risked a glance at the black SUV. Inside were four large men wearing dark suits, dark sunglasses, and dark expressions. Addison would lay ten-to-one odds they were staring directly at him from behind their black shades. It did not give him a rosy feeling. "Interesting," he said thoughtfully. He heaved open the door for his group, and they filtered into the bank.

••••••

They stood in the high-ceilinged bank lobby, gaping at the magnificent splendor. Every surface was polished marble, maple, or mahogany. Addison crossed to a narrow window and drew aside the curtain an inch. Peering onto the street, he saw that the suspicious men were already gone. Before he could reflect too deeply on this, he was approached by a rather snooty-looking bank manager.

"I'm sorry, the restrooms are for bank customers only." The manager wore a two-button jacket with his three-piece suit; the four-carat diamond on his tiepin flickered like a five-alarm fire.

"We don't need the restrooms," said Addison.

"I do," said Eddie.

"Same here," said Raj, hopping from foot to foot. They had each guzzled down two bottles of water on the train.

Addison quieted them with a stern look and returned his most pleasant smile to the manager. "We are bank customers. I would like to see your vault."

The bank manager's eyes widened at Addison's bedraggled group. He gazed all the way down his long nose to view this spectacle through his spectacles. "This bank possesses a very distinguished clientele. I know every customer personally. I have never laid eyes on any of you before."

Addison felt he had lost his mojo. Not so long ago, he could have smooth-talked his way past this oozing blister of a man without even breaking his stride. But ever since Aunt Delia and Uncle Nigel had vanished over the side of that cliff in Mongolia, Addison had been second-, third-, and fourth-guessing his every move. Life had bumped him off his seat, and he could not get his feet back on the pedals. "I have a safe deposit box," he said simply.

"Impossible. We do not rent safe deposit boxes to minors." The manager waved to a guard across the floor. "Security!"

"The box belongs to my family. My aunt and uncle." Addison produced the key from his pocket. "And they've given the key to me."

"Oh really?" said the bank manager, his voice dripping with several fluid ounces of condescension. "Who are you? And who, pray tell, is your uncle?"

Addison sighed. He drew himself up to his full height. "I am Addison H. Cooke, son of Addison Cooke, brother of Lord Jasper Cooke, the Seventeenth Earl of Runnymede."

Addison could not have changed the bank manager's expression more if he had flattened the man's face with a frying pan. The gaping manager cycled from abject shock to abject humiliation. Addison usually got out of situations by claiming to be someone he was not, rather than someone he actually was. He found he could quite get used to this.

"A thousand apologies," the bank manager gushed. "Please, forgive me, Mr. Cooke! I shall lead you to the bank vault personally. Is there anything I can offer you? Perhaps tea, or a cooling beverage?"

"I need the bathroom," said Eddie.

"Of course," said the bank manager.

Addison read the burnished metal name tag on the manager's lapel. Leopold Dalton. "Waters for my friends, Leo. With slices of lemon."

"And for you, sir?"

Addison straightened the cuffs of his blazer. "Do you know how to make an Arnold Palmer?"

••••••

Leopold Dalton ushered the group down marble steps, through the basement, and into the spacious bank vault. It was decorated like a plush Victorian living room, with cozy leather sofas, a hat rack, and an umbrella stand. Addison found a coaster and set his Arnold Palmer down on the oak coffee table. Eddie and Raj, fresh from the bathroom, showed up looking quite relieved.

Eddie rapped his knuckles against the vault wall and admired its sturdy door. "You're looking at a twenty-four-bolt vault door. Steel-reinforced concrete. Twelve-inch-thick walls. Forty-five-thousand-pound door. Dual-control time lock." Eddie sniffed and hitched up his pants. "Yeah, she's a beauty."

Leopold raised one manicured eyebrow precisely seven millimeters. "If I didn't know any better, I would say you were casing the joint."

Eddie shrugged, his face the portrait of innocence. He

had spent the previous five months learning his way around safes the way he knew his way around a grand piano.

Leopold showed Addison to his safe deposit box and hovered eagerly over his shoulder. It was evident that he had spent years wondering what the Cookes hid inside their vault.

Addison inserted the tiny key in its lock and glanced up at Leopold. "May we have some privacy?"

"But of course." His face a mask of disappointment, Leopold bowed deeply and shuffled backward out of the room.

The old Victorian table lamp flickered, casting eerie shadows around the vault as Addison unlocked the box.

"Maybe it has information about our parents," said Molly.

"Maybe it's filled with cash," said Eddie.

"Maybe it's a mummified head," said Raj.

Everyone turned to stare at Raj.

"What?" said Raj. "Some people would pay a lot of money for a mummified head!"

Addison shook his nonmummified head and opened the small safe deposit box door. Inside was a single object, wrapped in frayed sackcloth. He carried the heavy object over to the coffee table and carefully unwrapped the decaying fabric.

He was astonished by what he found inside.

Chapter Six

The Ambush

IT WAS AN ANCIENT bronze tablet. The group stared at it, mystified.

"What is it, exactly?" Raj breathed.

Addison shook his head. "It's either the world's heaviest paperweight or the world's ugliest doorstop."

"Thanks, Aunt D," said Molly.

Eddie tapped it with a finger. "I think my mom would love it as a coffee table ornament."

Addison picked up the heavy tablet and held it to the flickering light of the Victorian lamp. The tablet was about the size and shape of a good-sized dictionary. The top was inscribed with a small circle filled with strange runes. Something about the ornate carvings looked centuries old.

Addison had the strange sensation that he'd seen the cryptic runes somewhere before. But where? He scrounged around in the deepest pockets of his memory, but couldn't come up with the answer.

He turned the tablet over in his hands to examine the other side. It was covered with wavy lines in no discernible pattern. If the tablet was a puzzle, it was inscrutable.

"Why did Uncle Nigel call this a grave responsibility?" asked Molly. "We don't even know what this is."

"Aunt D and Uncle N didn't give us a ton of guidance here," Addison admitted.

"Maybe that's on purpose," said Raj, his eyes widening. "Supposing you get kidnapped and tortured for information: you won't be able to tell anyone anything about the tablet."

Addison wasn't sure why Raj's mind always went straight to the darkest places. He was pretty sure his aunt and uncle hadn't explained more about the tablet because they hadn't planned to fall to their deaths in a Mongolian river gorge. They'd assumed they'd have all the time in the world to tell Addison and Molly about the tablet when they grew older.

Eddie picked the tablet up, held it to his ear, and shook it. "What if it contains a treasure?"

"Then it's better left here," said Addison. "We should lock it back up."

Molly stared at her brother, aghast. "Addison, get ahold of yourself." She had known him to toddle home carrying everything from snakeskins to eggshells to unusually large acorns. Now, faced with a genuine archaeological mystery, he was suddenly willing to turn his back.

Addison sensed her bewilderment. "I lost the golden whip in Mongolia. If this tablet is some important relic, I can't risk losing it. I shouldn't even be touching it." He wrapped the tablet back in its sackcloth. He didn't say what he truly felt . . . that if it wasn't for him, his aunt and uncle would still be alive. "Whatever this tablet is, it's not safe with me."

He made to stuff the tablet back inside the safe deposit box, but Molly barred his path.

"Aunt Delia and Uncle Nigel only left us this one thing," she said. "This is all we have from them—it must be important. They wanted us to have it—they gave us a key! Let's at least bring it back to Runnymede to show Uncle Jasper."

Addison wavered uncertainly.

Molly pressed her case. "We know so little about our family's past. Maybe this tablet can answer some of our questions."

Addison stared down at the strange hieroglyphs etched in bronze. He had to admit he was curious . . . Extremely curious. "Well, okay," he said at last. "But you have to carry it." He lifted Molly's satchel off the sofa, buckling a little under the weight. "Wow, Molly. What do you carry in here, anyway?"

Molly smiled demurely. "Just a few things I think might come in handy." As she bundled the tablet into her satchel, the Victorian light flickered and went out entirely, plunging the vault into near darkness.

"I have a bad feeling about this," said Eddie.

Molly was unperturbed. "You're a pessimist, Eddie. You have a bad feeling about everything."

......

When they had pushed their way out the front doors of the bank, Addison pushed up his collar against the gathering winter cold. "Eddie, I know you wanted Indian food, but it will have to wait. We need to get this tablet straight home to Uncle Jasper, where it'll be safe."

"Hey," said Molly, pointing across the street, "it's Leo the bank manager!"

Addison followed Molly's finger and spotted Leopold Dalton in his dazzling suit, pointing directly at them. This was surprising, to say the least. Addison realized Leo was in urgent conversation with someone in a black SUV—a rather familiar-looking black SUV. All four doors of the SUV opened simultaneously, and four unusually large men simultaneously stepped out.

A split second later, an identical black SUV skidded to a halt at the far end of West Chiselton Place, sealing it off from traffic.

"Margaret Thatcher!" Addison sputtered. Unlike Eddie, he was usually an optimist by nature. But even he didn't like where this was heading.

The four men marched across the street, closing in on Addison's crew. They wore black suits, black boots, and black sunglasses. If they were armed, Addison didn't need to guess what color their guns were.

Addison briefly considered running back inside the bank, but discarded the thought. Whatever was unfolding, Leo the bank manager was in on it.

"There's no need to panic," Addison told his team. He hurried down the bank's front steps, leading his group south on Chiselton Place, away from the black-suited hulks.

"They're after us," cried Molly.

To Addison's horror, he heard the heavy footfalls of the men bearing down on them. Addison and his crew broke into a run. "This way!" he called. He raced around the corner onto Orange Street and ground his heels to a stop. Before him were so many men in black suits, it looked like an undertakers convention. Or, perhaps, an undertakers meeting at a bodybuilders convention. Whichever the case, the crowd of giant men stared at Addison through their rows of dark glasses. And as one, the men clenched their fists and closed in.

"Okay, panic," said Addison.

Chapter Seven

Panic

FOR EDDIE, THE ROAD to panic was never very far. He could be sent into a cold sweat by an unusually fast elevator ride. The sight of a row of linebacker-sized men charging directly at him was more than enough to overload his circuits. Eddie bolted like a startled deer, his body barely keeping up with his feet. He sprinted south on Haymarket Street.

Addison, Molly, and Raj dashed after him.

"Good thinking, Eddie!" Addison shouted. "We'll split up! Meet back at the train station!"

Eddie and Raj continued straight. Addison and Molly branched east down a side street. Addison saw a half dozen of the black-suited men barreling through the crowd of holiday shoppers, charging straight toward him. Pedestrians screamed as they were shoved to the ground.

"The Right Honorable Winston Churchill!" Addison gasped. He banked hard, hurtling down an alleyway. Wherever Molly was, she was going to have to fend for herself. Addison leapt over shipping crates and knocked over garbage cans, struggling to slow down his pursuers.

He reached the wide-open plaza of Trafalgar Square and poured on the speed, racing headlong for the train station. Molly galloped in at a fast clip—she had outrun her pursuers as well.

Raj wove across street traffic, raising an angry chorus of honks. "They're closing on us!"

He merged with Addison and Molly as they burst through the nearest open door to the train station.

"I've got something that can slow them down," said Molly, dropping to a crouch and whipping open her satchel. She pulled out a large sack of marbles and poured them out in the doorway.

"Wow, you really do have a lot of stuff in there," said Raj. "Do you think this will work?"

Molly listened to the sound of footsteps pounding closer. "Definitely."

Eddie rounded the corner at full gallop, his face a portrait of panic. He skied across the marbles, his arms pinwheeling, his legs scissoring in all directions like a giraffe on an ice rink. Both feet flew out from under him, landing him on his back with a sound like a thunderclap.

"Ow!" Eddie hollered. "What did you do that for?"

"I'm sorry, Eddie!" Molly was mortified. "Are you okay? What hurts?"

Eddie rolled back and forth on his back like an overturned turtle. "My ankles!"

"Your ankles?"

"Yes, ankles. The wrists of your legs!" Eddie tried to get up, and slid down again. "Who lost their marbles?"

"Wasn't Molly," said Addison. "She lost her marbles years ago."

"Don't laugh, Addison. Get me some aspirin or something." Eddie managed to gain his feet.

"Laughter is the best medicine, Eddie."

"*Medicine* is the best medicine!"

Raj pointed at the inbound herd of men in black suits stampeding toward them. "Here they come."

Addison led the way, racing through the main concourse, his leather wingtips sliding on the polished floors. Usually Molly was much faster than him, but she was weighed down by the bronze tablet and whatever else she had hidden in her satchel. He scanned the departure board for outbound trains, but spotted nothing leaving for fifteen minutes. He searched the concourse for the familiar black-and-white uniform of a London police officer, but strangely, there wasn't a single officer to be found.

Addison was hot from running. He felt it important to dress respectably, but his blazer trapped heat like a pizza oven. Black-suited men converged from both ends of the concourse. Out of options, Addison fled across the station and escaped, terrified, onto Craven Street.

Black SUVs skidded to a stop at both ends of the block.

Addison stood on the sidewalk heaving for breath. "We're cornered."

"I have purple smoke balls," said Raj. "They're perfect for an escape."

"What," asked Addison, with all the patience he could muster, "are purple smoke balls?"

"You know, for magicians. They throw them onstage when they need purple smoke for a big exit. I bought them at a magician's supply shop in Times Square."

Addison swiveled his head, watching black-suited men circle in from all directions. "Raj, I appreciate your help, but we're going to need more than purple smoke balls. We're going to need a miracle."

"Like what?" asked Molly. She was already drawing her sling from her satchel and loading it with a metal slug.

Addison never answered. He was too busy watching a white luxury Mercedes speeding past the train station. It jumped the curb, swerved around a black SUV, and screeched to a halt directly in front of them. A young woman threw open the passenger door. She had ebony skin, with long dreadlocks piled on top of her head and tied with a scarf. When she spoke, it was with a French accent. "Get in."

Addison stared at the young woman and hesitated, wondering if this was a trap. "Absolutely not. I don't get into cars with strangers."

"You fools!" She revved the engine with impatience. The sedan lurched forward a few inches. "I said, *get in!*"

Addison heard Raj gasp, and looked up to a horrible sight. The closest men in black suits were reaching into their blazers and drawing weapons.

Addison turned back to the woman. "We have reconsidered your offer," he announced. He dove into the Mercedes.

Molly, Eddie, and Raj piled into the back seat.

Addison was astonished to hear concussions of gunfire. He felt bullets slam into the metal frame of the car. The mysterious woman floored the accelerator, rear wheels smoking, and they blasted south, black-suited men hurling themselves from their speeding path.

Chapter Eight

D'Anger

YANKING THE WHEEL, THE young woman tore a course east along the Thames River before rocketing north past the Royal Opera House. Addison realized with no small excitement that their route would take them past his favorite place in London—the British Museum—though he didn't figure they'd have time to take in an exhibit. Black SUVs were already lining up in their rear-view mirror.

Addison took in his unknown driver. He figured her for seventeen or eighteen: old enough to be allowed to drive, but not old enough to be any good at it. She lurched the Mercedes in and out of lanes, desperately trying to pack distance between her and the pursuing SUVs.

She fixed Addison with an intimidating stare and spoke rapidly in her clipped French accent. "What have you done, you foolish child?"

"Me?" said Addison. "I'm just a guy trying to use the bank. They're the ones shooting guns!"

"You took the tablet map, didn't you?" The young woman shook her head in disgust. "This is precisely the sort of galactic incompetence I would expect from the Cooke family."

Addison frowned. "I'm sorry, I don't believe we've met."

"Put on your seat belt," the woman growled. She ripped the wheel, tires screeching as they rounded a corner at Russell Square Park.

Two black sport utility vehicles kept pace, engines roaring. They jumped the sidewalk and shortcutted through the park as pedestrians shouted and leapt for cover. The SUVs were four-wheel-drive beasts that could drive up a mountain backward in an avalanche; a manicured London park was not about to slow them down. The two SUVs smashed onto Woburn Place, surrounding the Mercedes.

In the back seat, Eddie gripped his overhead strap with both hands as the Mercedes wove between cars at nail-biting speed. "This is *horrendous!*"

Raj tightened his seat belt. "Each year there are more than seventeen hundred automobile fatalities in England."

"There's going to be one more fatality if you don't pipe down." The young woman took another tire-shrieking right turn. A hubcap popped off one rear wheel. "It's okay," she told Addison. "It's a rental."

"I can't help but wonder," said Addison, as they passed the British Museum for the second time, "where are we going?"

"How should I know?" the woman grunted in her tough Gallic accent. "Do I sound like I'm from London?" She held down her horn and shot through a red light. "There's a map in the glove box."

Addison opened the glove compartment and unfolded the map. "This," he announced, "is a map of Paris."

The driver did not answer. Instead, she careened through another red light. Two London squad cars turned on their sirens and joined the chase. Addison sighed. Five minutes earlier there hadn't been any police when he needed them; now there were too many.

He pulled out his London map from *Fiddleton's Atlas* and stuffed the Paris map back into the glove compartment. As he did so, he noticed the driver's name signed on the rental car forms: *Tilda Danger*. Addison looked at the young woman with newfound respect. "Wow, your last name is Danger?"

"It's French," said the woman. "It's pronounced *d'Anger*. Tilda d'Anger. People call me T.D."

Addison's head swam with the scent of her perfume. He knew she was only four or five years older than him, but she seemed vastly more sophisticated. He suddenly felt the need to impress this woman. "Your perfume," he said in his most debonair voice. "Is that Chanel Number Five?"

T.D. furrowed her eyebrows at him. "I don't wear perfume. You're smelling my shampoo. It's called Pizzazz. It costs two ninety-nine at the grocery store."

"Well," said Addison, unruffled, "if I had been right, it would have been incredibly suave."

Molly, in the back seat, rolled her eyes. "Addison, just use your map to get us out of here!"

"No need," said T.D. "I can see the highway from here." She blasted onto the center divider and thundered past a row of cars. The police kept up their chase, their blue lights flashing.

Molly eyed T.D suspiciously through the rearview mirror. "Who are you and how did you know to find us?"

"Your uncle Jasper came home, read your aunt's letter, and figured it out. He begged me to rescue you at the bank. I was almost too late."

Molly had to shout over the wail of police sirens. "How did those guys in suits know to stake out the bank?"

"And who are they anyway?" Eddie added.

"They are not fans of yours," said T.D.

Addison felt this was a small understatement. An SUV sped close and bumped the rear of the Mercedes. The car fishtailed wildly.

T.D. gunned the engine, shifted into fourth gear, and regained control of the vehicle.

"Can you be more specific?" called Molly. "There are a lot of people who aren't fans of us."

"They are called the Collective."

Addison and Molly shared a look. Finally, someone was willing to give them answers. "What is the Collective?" asked Molly.

T.D. shook her head. "I can only tell you when you come of age."

Molly gritted her teeth.

T.D. hit a wall of traffic and slammed on the brakes. *"Mon Dieu!"* she exclaimed. "All this traffic! Having a high-speed chase in London is like trying to sprint the hundred-meter dash in a crowded elevator!"

A black SUV screamed to a stop next to the Mercedes and rolled down its windows. Guns protruded.

Addison grabbed his door handle. "Let's get out and run!"

"No!" T.D. gripped him by the arm. One-handed, she managed to steer the Mercedes behind a delivery truck, blocking any shots from the SUV. "Addison, let me put this in words you will understand. Those dark metal things in their hands—those are called guns. They fire nasty little metal things called bullets. They make you *dead*, and we prefer to be *not dead*."

Addison felt she was making a lot of sense. Still, he had to do something. He pulled her rental form from the glove box and held it up. "You paid for car insurance, right?"

"Sure."

"And English drivers are required to have car insurance?"

"It's a civilized country."

"Okay." Addison nodded. "We need to cause some traffic."

"More traffic?" asked Eddie.

Addison reached over and pulled T.D.'s steering wheel hard. The Mercedes cut off a double-decker bus that swerved across its lane and plunged into a telephone pole. Cars piled up behind the wreck like water behind a dam. The police cars were trapped.

"Are you out of your mind?" Tires shrieking, T.D. skidded the Mercedes north, heading for the highway. The two black SUVs managed to smash their way through Addison's traffic blockade. Addison jerked the steering wheel again, cutting off a dump truck. The truck mashed its brakes and spun out, colliding with both SUVs.

T.D. merged onto the highway. Not a single car was

able to follow them. Addison felt bad about causing so many accidents, but on the cosmic scale of things, escaping from bloodthirsty gang members was probably a decent enough reason to cause a few fender benders.

Tilda d'Anger glanced over her shoulder at the growing traffic jam in her wake. Hundreds of commuters were now unable to merge onto the highway from either direction. All London seemed to be one growing mass of red brake lights and a din of honking horns. She turned to her passengers. "Do you destroy every city you set foot in?"

"Not on purpose," said Molly.

T.D. regarded the black SUVs shrinking in her rearview mirror. "I am impressed."

"Scratch a Cooke and you'll find resourcefulness," said Addison. "Though you really shouldn't go around scratching Cookes," he added.

Chapter Nine
The Knight

THE MERCEDES CRUISED ALONG the highway. Addison spotted a sign for Heathrow Airport and turned to T.D. "You want us to leave the country?"

T.D. said nothing.

"All this trouble over an ugly chunk of bronze," said Addison. "We're risking our lives over this tablet, and we don't even know what it is!"

"You know it's important," said T.D. "You just saw a group of men tear down half of London trying to take it."

Addison shook his head. "I don't want anyone else to get hurt. I'm running low on family members! Can't we just hide the tablet somewhere?"

"What, a precious relic your family has guarded for

centuries?" T.D. snorted. "Sure, just stick it in your sock drawer and call it a day. No, you cannot just hide it somewhere! If you stay in London, you will get caught. The Collective will torture you and find out where you hid it. Why am I arguing with a bunch of thirteen-year-olds? Could you guys be any more clueless?"

Raj liked a challenge. "Probably."

"This is my friend Raj," said Addison. "He doesn't know that you don't have to answer rhetorical questions." He returned his attention to T.D. "Why don't you take the tablet? I don't want it. I'll only get it taken."

"My family does not handle relics. That is a Cooke job."

Addison heard the disdain in her voice. "Well, what does your family do? And how do you know so much about us anyway?"

T.D. shook her head impatiently. "The Collective is hunting you. Don't you realize that? You have been chased out of London. Your uncle and his butler have fled Surrey. With or without the tablet, there is nowhere in the world that is safe for you."

"Who are you anyway? And why do you care what happens to us?" asked Addison.

T.D. slammed the steering wheel with her fists in frustration. "Addison, you impossible Cooke! How can you not realize what I am?" She reached under her collar and pulled out a bronze medallion. An eye in the center of a bright sun was emblazoned across the front. "I am sworn to the same order as your family!"

••••••

Addison's thoughts were a fizzy cocktail: two parts shock, one part disbelief, and a twist of amazement. He had learned in Mongolia that the Cookes were descendants of the Knights Templar, a secretive order of powerful knights that vanished in the Middle Ages. Aside from his uncles, he had never met another living member. Addison was silent for a few miles while his mind teeter-tottered, trying to regain its balance. At last, he turned to T.D. "The Knights Templar. I didn't think there were any left."

"We are not extinct," said T.D. "Not yet," she added grimly. She took the exit to Heathrow Airport.

Addison already held a lofty impression of T.D., but it grew even loftier when she steered the Mercedes to a private security gate, flashed an ID badge, and drove directly onto the tarmac.

Eddie sat up straight in his seat. "Are you allowed to drive on a runway?"

"Of course I am," said T.D. "How else would we get to our private plane?" She guided the car to a Learjet, its engines warming up for takeoff.

"So the Templars are rich?" asked Molly.

"The Templars are, but you're not," said T.D. "Aside from that big, crumbling house, the Cookes care more about history books than pocketbooks. But the d'Angers still have a few coins to rub together. You'd be amazed how much a savings account can accumulate when your family is seven hundred years old."

T.D. pulled the Mercedes to a stop in front of the airstairs to the jet. She shifted the car into Park and turned her intense gaze on Addison. "I cannot answer questions about your family and who you really are. But if you wish to learn more, I can assure you, the answers are with that tablet."

Before Addison could thank her for the lift, a parade of black SUVs arrived on the tarmac. They were still several football fields away, but closing in fast.

T.D. scowled. "The Collective."

"I thought we lost them!" said Molly. "How did they find us?"

"They are infinitely resourceful," said T.D. "They can track you through satellites, traffic cameras, and informants. They own police and politicians. They can enter any building—even an airport. Wherever you go in this world, assume the Collective are coming for you. Now hurry!"

Addison's group jumped out of the Mercedes. A uniformed flight attendant stood by the airstairs, a red carpet rolled out for them on the tarmac. The group bounded up the steps. Everything about the twin-engine private jet spelled speed: its snappy winglets, its sporty body, its nose cone tapered to a sharp point.

T.D. shouted up to them over the roar of the engines. "Tell the pilot to fly you to Paris! Get to the Fortress—it's our Paris safe house. There you will find a man who can give you more answers than I!"

Addison cupped his hands to his mouth and shouted, "Who is he?"

"The Grand Master of the Templars."

The flight attendant rolled up the red carpet and jogged up the stairs.

"Wait," shouted Addison. "T.D., how do we find the Fortress?"

T.D.'s voice was faint over the howl of the engines. "Are you Cookes or not?"

The flight attendant herded Addison into the aircraft, sealing the hatch door. The plane began taxiing down the runway.

Addison rushed to a window. He watched T.D. stare down the approaching SUVs. She took something long and skinny out of the trunk and rested it across the hood of the white Mercedes. He saw her lean close to it, cupping her cheek against the stock. Addison couldn't hear anything over the blasting engines. He only saw each SUV's front tires pop in quick succession, the wheels spitting sparks as their rims hit the tarmac.

Addison blinked. His uncle Jasper had once taken him skeet shooting with an old, dusty flintlock rifle. They'd spent thirty dollars sending twenty clay pigeons into the air and hit two. If he'd seen what he thought he'd seen, T.D. was incredibly handy with a rifle.

With the SUVs slowed down, she hopped back into her car and sped away.

Only one SUV, grinding its wheel rims on its shredded tires, chased the airplane down the runway. But it was no match for the Learjet. The plane lifted off at a stomach-dropping angle, soaring high over the West London suburbs. It banked south over Sussex at five hundred miles per hour, pointing its nose for Paris.

II

THE
TEMPLAR
CODE

Chapter Ten

On the Run

ADDISON EASED HIS TIRED feet out of his wingtips. He stalked the flight cabin in his stocking feet, taking stock of his surroundings. Strange decorative symbols and artistic artifacts cluttered the wood-paneled walls. A Crusader sword hung over a faux fireplace. An ancient Slovakian spear sat on the satinwood sideboard. The design was so rustic and old fashioned, Addison briefly wondered if he had somehow stepped into a huntsman's cottage.

The private jet had an actual dining room, decked out with dinnerware, doled out on a dining room table. The only thing it lacked was an actual dinner, France being but a short flight away. Eddie scavenged some snacks from the sidebar: fresh fruit, potato chips, and even an elegant mahogany chest chock-full of chocolate. They had skipped their Indian lunch, and Eddie was ravenous. But to his chagrin, Raj insisted they ration their food for provisions, and Addison seconded the motion.

When they touched down at Charles de Gaulle Airport, the winter sun was already setting, darkening the rain-soaked tarmac. Their flight attendant escorted them to the airport terminal under a giant umbrella and bid them a cheerful *bonsoir*.

Addison strode to the main concourse and turned to his friends. "Eddie, Raj, you guys can catch a flight home to New York. Molly, you should go with them. Whatever this tablet is, it's hazardous to the health. I've buried enough family members. I'm not losing any more."

Molly shook her head firmly. "Your odds of keeping the tablet safe are better with our help."

Raj stepped forward, standing resolutely at Molly's side. "Addison, I live and die for life-or-death situations. It's what I spend my life training for!"

Eddie shrugged in reluctant agreement. "My parents are on vacation. I have nowhere to fly home to. Besides, how could we afford last-minute flights?"

Addison could see he was on the losing end of this argument.

"I want to see Paris," Molly declared. "Provided you don't find a way to burn it to the ground."

"Well, for Paris's sake, let's hope for the best," said Addison. He was already scanning the airport crowds for any sign of the Collective. A few men in suits perched on a shoeshine stand were eyeing him suspiciously. "If we're going to keep this tablet safe, we need to figure out a way to get to this Templar safe house."

"The Fortress," said Molly. "What is it and how do we get there?"

"Let's see what *Fiddleton's World Atlas* has to say on the subject." Addison flipped through the index of the Paris map. He was pleased to see that T.D. had not been speaking in riddles: there was an actual castle in the heart of Paris that was simply named "the Fortress."

"Are we positive it's the same fortress we're looking for?" asked Molly.

"According to Mr. Roland J. Fiddleton," said Addison, "the Fortress was built in the 1200s by none other than the Knights Templar."

Molly nodded. "Works for me."

......

Addison followed signs through the airport to ground transportation. His group reached the Réseau Express Régional train that could take them the fifteen miles to downtown Paris.

"Addison, we don't have any French money," said Molly.

"We don't have any money, period," said Eddie.

Addison eyed the train ticket clerk, sizing her up. Scowling and flinty eyed, she didn't look like an easy mark. He wasn't willing to wager he could sweet-talk her, particularly when he spoke no French. "Eddie, you still haven't learned French, have you?"

"I've been busy!"

Addison spotted the same three men from the shoeshine stand, stalking toward him across the station. Their shoes were beaming; their faces were not. Two airport police seemed to be eyeing him as well.

The RER train to Paris was idling just a few feet away, commuters sardining themselves aboard. It was so close and yet so far. Addison knew they could not just traipse through the turnstiles without a ticket. Nor could they jump the turnstiles with police watching. Addison needed another solution.

The three menacing men marched close. Dark glasses hid their eyes, but their dark suits did little to hide the bulges of their gun holsters.

Pressurized air hissed out of the train's brakes. Time was running out. Addison surveyed the layout of the train station. "C'mon." He jogged up a flight of steps, two at a time. He crossed the overpass—a footbridge directly over the waiting train.

Eddie scurried nervously after him. A growing knot

in his gut told him that Addison was hatching something. "Talk to me, Addison. What are you thinking?"

"Eddie, what's the worst idea I've ever had?"

"The time we tried swimming across an alligator-infested river in Colombia?" guessed Eddie.

"The time we stole Colonel Ragar's limousine in Ecuador?" tried Raj.

"The time you entered us in the Mongolian national horse race with four stolen horses?" Molly volunteered.

"Right, well . . ." said Addison. "This idea is worse than all those."

Two of the armed men hustled up the steps behind them on the walkway. The other man dashed up the far side, shutting off any escape.

Addison looked down on the RER train. He swung one leg, and then the other, over the metal railing of the footbridge. He judged the drop to be a good eight feet, but then again, he had never been particularly good at judging distances. He heard the train doors hiss closed. The dark-suited men, sensing his purpose, sprang toward him.

There was nothing for it but to jump.

••••••

Addison landed hard on the metal roof of the train. Molly and Raj clanged down next to him. The train was already moving by the time Eddie screwed up the courage to leap, foiling the black-suited man lunging to catch him by the collar.

The train quickly poured on speed. Soon, howling wind lashed their hair and whipped tears from their eyes. It threatened to yank them off the roof of the train.

Eddie hugged the roof like a dear friend. "Addison, you were right!" he called.

These words were always music to Addison's ears.

"This," Eddie continued, "is your worst idea ever!"

Raj, ten feet upwind, couldn't hear Eddie's complaints. He smiled rapturously as Paris clattered past at blistering speeds. "Addison, this is your best idea ever!"

The sharp turns in the tracks made Addison feel like he was riding on the back of a dragon. They rumbled past ragged industrial sites and tattered tenements gutted with garbled graffiti. "Stay low!" Addison called as they passed under a concrete overpass.

Eddie inched his body closer to the group, his eyes tearing in the gale. "Could this be any colder?"

Raj shouted over the bellowing train whistle. "When Admiral Peary explored the North Pole, the temperatures dropped to fifty below zero."

"Raj, remember," said Addison, between chattering teeth. "We talked about rhetorical questions."

Squinting into the icy wind, Addison saw they were approaching a tunnel. "This train's going underground! Hurry!"

The group crawled along the roof toward the head of the train car, careful not to touch the circuit breakers, converters, and couplings that drew electricity from the overhead power lines. They reached the iron ladder and scrambled down between the train cars just as the rails reached the tunnel and plunged them into total darkness.

Addison wrenched open the train door against the rushing wind and stumbled into the train car. His team followed, their hair windswept as if they'd just used a jet engine for a hair dryer. Caked in dust and grime, Addison was amazed at how filthy they were. The bewildered train passengers seemed to be pretty amazed to see them as well.

The group staggered off the train at the Gare du Nord station in the tenth *arrondissement* neighborhood of Paris. Addison proposed transferring to the Paris Métro, but Eddie—still catching his breath with his hands on his knees—refused to set foot on another train.

Chapter Eleven

The Fortress

KEEPING THEIR PROFILE AT limbo-champion lows, they trickled through the Paris streets, following Addison's map toward the Templar Fortress. Despite hunger, cold, and fear, Addison couldn't help but marvel at the beauty of the city. According to Mr. Fiddleton, Paris was one of the first cities to line its avenues with streetlamps, earning it the nickname the City of Light. With the holiday season in full bloom, there were even more lights than usual, glowing and blinking in every color.

They strolled south on the Boulevard de Magenta, winding ever closer to the Seine, that fabled river that meandered through Paris's heart and into Addison's. They passed the former home of post-Impressionist pointillist painter Georges Seurat, Addison noting with surprise that the house was not painted with tiny dots. The group dodged traffic crossing the Rue Saint-Denis, which was built by the Romans in the first century. They passed theaters and coffee shops and glimpsed the famous Canal Saint-Martin, ordered built by Napoleon in 1802. Eddie was hungry and longing for French cooking; he was tantalized by the smells of rich food wafting from the shops.

After twenty-seven minutes of tooth-grinding cold, they reached the Templar Fortress. The main tower of the castle spread its dark shadow over the old Paris neighborhood. The castle was surrounded by a twenty-four-foot wall, spiked with crenellations like the spine of a monster. The turrets were built of brown stones the color of rotting bones. These were pierced by narrow arrow slits that seemed to peer down at Addison's team with a malevolent gaze. The clouds broke with a peal of thunder, and fresh rain drenched the team.

"Well," said Eddie. "Should we find a door and knock?"

Addison quickly shook his head. "If the Collective can stake out Blandfordshire Bank, they can certainly stake out a Templar safe house. Let's scout it first."

Clinging to the shadows of the alleys and shrouded by the hissing rain, Addison's group circled the perimeter walls.

"That black SUV," said Molly, pointing to a car parked

down a side street. "It's the same model as the ones that chased us in London." The group squinted through the rain-speckled windshield at the shapes of four large men inside the car. The men appeared to be watching the front gate of the Fortress.

"It could just be a coincidence," said Eddie hopefully.

"There's another SUV down that other side street," said Raj, pointing to a second black SUV fifty yards away. "Two men in the front seats and two in the back."

Eddie sighed.

"I would never presume to tell someone how to run their criminal organization," said Addison, "but if I had to offer a word of advice, I would tell the Collective not to buy an entire fleet of the exact same car."

"Maybe they get a bulk discount," Eddie reasoned.

"I still wonder how they knew to stake out that bank in London," said Molly. "And I wonder how they knew we'd go to this exact fortress."

"I wonder why after you shut the freezer door, it's so hard to open the fridge," said Addison, ducking down a fresh alleyway, "but that's not important right now. What's important is, we need to find a way inside without attracting attention."

"Wait," said Raj, his face radiant with excitement. "Are you saying we need to break into a castle?"

Addison nodded.

"I would just like to remind you people," said Eddie, "that this heavy hunk of bronze we are lugging around seems to be important. And our job is to keep it away from those SUVs. Maybe we should try breaking into a building that *isn't* surrounded by armed criminals."

"Tilda d'Anger said we'd find answers inside this building," said Addison. "Answers from the Grand Master of the Templars—a group that went extinct seven hundred years ago. Now, we can spend your winter vacation playing hide-and-seek across Europe, or we can go get some answers."

"Hide-and-seek across Europe sounds pretty good actually," said Eddie. But the group had already followed Addison down the narrow lane.

They snaked along the alley, keeping clear of the glow of the lamplights, until they reached an oblong section of wall beyond the sight line of any of the SUVs. Addison sucked his teeth and considered the twenty-four-foot wall looming over their heads. "Raj, how did people get over castle walls in the Middle Ages?"

"Lots of ways! They'd build mines, tunneling under the wall."

"I don't think we have the time."

"They'd build catapults," Raj offered.

"You want to fling us over the wall?" asked Molly.

"Sometimes they'd build a battering ram and attack the main gate."

Addison tried to imagine four middle-schoolers charging through the streets of modern Paris with a battering ram. He couldn't quite picture them pulling it off. For one thing, where would they find a tree to saw down? Or a saw, for that matter. Besides, smashing a castle gate in downtown Paris might raise a few eyebrows with the local *gendarmes*. "Any other ideas?"

Raj frowned at the high wall and shook his head. "It's completely impossible," he conceded. "I mean, if we had a grappling hook, *maybe*."

"You mean like this one?" said Molly, opening her satchel and producing a twenty-five-foot coil of nylon rope, tipped with four iron claws.

"Wow," said Raj. "What *don't* you have in that bag? It's like Mary Poppins's purse."

"My dad gave her that survival satchel," said Addison morosely, "and all I got was his book on Genghis Khan."

"Which you left in Genghis Khan's tomb," Molly reminded him.

"I was being sentimental."

Molly sighed. "Sometimes, Addison, you put the 'mental' in sentimental."

Addison frowned but decided she had a point.

Eddie poked at Molly's satchel with a tentative finger. "Do you have any snacks in there?" he asked.

"First things first," said Molly, twirling the grappling

hook. Each of its claws was tipped with rubber for silence. Her first two throws fell short of the battlement. Her third caught the lip of the wall. Molly tugged the rope, testing its strength. It held firm. "All right. The faster we do this, the less likely we are to go to jail."

......

Addison was dreading the climb. He was no great fan of heights and he had utterly failed the rope climb test every year in gym. But to his surprise and pleasure he found that Molly's rope had knots tied every foot or so, making it much easier to scale.

One by one they reached the top and clambered over the battlement. Addison had never stormed a castle before, and he found it quite suited him. Gazing out through an arrow slit, he could picture how just fifty archers could hold this fortress against the world.

Keeping low, they raced along the rampart to a crumbling turret and found stone steps spiraling down to the ground level. Before them lay a massive courtyard with a broken well, a rotting stable, and an unappealing assortment of crumbling wooden storehouses.

"Some castle," said Eddie.

"It's a fixer-upper," Addison allowed.

"Eddie, let's leave *you* out in the rain for seven hundred years and see how good you look," said Molly.

They hustled through the pouring rain to reach the imposing oak doors of the main tower entrance. The massive doors were hung with round iron knockers the size of car tires, but Addison could see they weren't going to need them. The padlock chained across the door was smashed and one of the oak doors splintered in. Addison furrowed his brows. "What do you make of it, Raj?"

Raj knelt down to examine the sharp wooden splinters of the crushed door. "Fresh," he said. "Whoever smashed open this door did it very, very recently."

Addison slowly nodded. "Let's do this carefully." As slowly and quietly as he could, he heaved the broken door open. With nothing but a flash of lightning to glimpse his path, Addison stepped into the dark castle.

Chapter Twelve

The Dungeon Tower

ADDISON'S EYES ADJUSTED TO the gloom. Molly, Eddie, and Raj crept in after him. They were standing in a vast, high-ceilinged entrance hall. Sconces set high in the stone walls must have once held torches. Massive racks of elk antlers that had once formed an elaborate chandelier now lay shattered on the floor.

"Mr. Fiddleton says the Fortress was the European headquarters of the Knights Templar back in the 1200s," said Addison.

"I think that's the last time they decorated," said Molly.

Raj shut the splintered door behind them and set to

work dragging several large wooden planks that looked like they had once belonged to a siege weapon.

"Raj, what are you doing?" asked Addison.

"Building an elephant trap."

"You're expecting elephants?"

"That's just its name," said Raj. "It's a trap big enough to stop an elephant. We don't want anyone sneaking in behind us." Breaking a sweat, Raj dragged an old oak table in front of the door. On top of this he piled a broken chest of drawers and balanced three dining room chairs. It was all carefully rigged so that anyone pushing open the splintered door would be met with an avalanche. Addison hoped the mailman had already made his rounds for the day.

Molly crossed the cavernous entrance hall, strewn with the rubbish of centuries. "Why would the Grand Master meet us here? This place is abandoned."

"There could be a caretaker," Eddie offered.

"If there is," said Addison, stepping carefully over some pigeon droppings, "I hope they're not paying him much."

"Look!" whispered Molly, reaching the far end of the hall. "Footprints!"

At the word "footprints," Raj zipped across the room as if pulled by a magnet. He dropped to all fours to study them. "Fresh! And lots of them. A whole crowd of men charged through here."

Addison gestured for Raj to lead the way. *Quietly*, he mouthed to the group. *We don't know who's still inside the castle.*

As the rain drummed its fingers on the stone roof, the group crept deeper into the ruins. They crossed through the great hall, where hundreds of knights once dined on long oak benches. They passed an armory that still housed rusted pikes and jagged spears. Raj kept his nose bent to the footprints and led the team up the wide staircase that wound around the curve of the main tower.

He guided them through a low stone archway and into a cold, damp tower room, the wind and rain sputtering in through cracks in the mortar. It was filled with strange iron equipment.

"What is this place?" asked Eddie. His voice sounded hollow in the echoing darkness.

"The dungeon," replied Raj ecstatically. Chains and manacles hung from the walls. Sharp iron pokers sat in the fireplace. Addison, who desperately wanted to rest his weary feet, found that every chair in the room was covered in iron spikes.

Raj inspected every torture device like a kid in a candy shop. "Wow, an iron vat! That's for boiling people!" he cried. "Oooo—an iron maiden! That's for crushing people." He dashed around to a different corner. "Wow, an actual oubliette!"

"Let me guess," said Molly. "It burns people."

"Better," said Raj.

"It steams them?" asked Addison.

"Better."

"It lightly braises them with olive oil?" asked Eddie.

"It doesn't do anything," said Raj triumphantly. "You just lock a person in it and forget about them."

"So the Templars tortured people?" asked Molly.

"I don't think so," said Addison, crossing to a row of cells on the far side of the tower. "I think they were the ones being tortured." He pulled open the squeaky iron gate of the largest cell. Hundreds of names were scratched into the flaked and crumbling prison wall. Addison had scoured Uncle Jasper's library for every book he could find on the Templars, and standing here in the Fortress, he felt the history coming alive. "King Philip IV of France was deeply in debt to the Knights Templar. So he had his army arrest the Templars on Friday, October thirteenth, 1307 . . ."

Addison ran his fingers over the names that condemned men had clawed into the limestone seven hundred years earlier. "He locked the knights in this Fortress. He even captured the Templar Grand Master, Jacques de Molay, and his right-hand man, Geoffroy de Charnay. Thirty-six knights were tortured to death here. Another hundred were hanged. That's the reason why Friday the thirteenth is considered unlucky."

"So what happened to the Templars?" asked Molly.

"The king and the pope stole all of the knights' money and property. This Fortress became a prison. It's the actual site where King Louis XVI and Marie Antoinette were imprisoned before being guillotined by the French mob."

"Look!" cried Molly. "Jacques de Molay signed his name right here! And Geoffroy! They were really here."

Addison peered closely where Molly was pointing and saw that the men had also taken the time to scratch in their coats of arms. "Look at this one, Mo," he gasped. "It's our family crest!"

Molly studied the twin dragons and the pyramid with the all-seeing Templar eye. "It's identical to our crest except for the Latin motto." She pointed to two words. *Tutor Thesauri*. Any idea what that means?"

Addison shook his head.

"When I need help with a word," said Eddie, "I use a tutor . . . or a thesaurus."

Addison read the name scrawled above the crest. "Adam de Cooke, 1307." He scratched the short hairs at the back of his neck. "Mo, the Adam Cooke in our family plot built the Cooke manor in 1309 and was buried in 1310."

"Do you think he's the same guy? How did he escape this prison?"

Addison could only shake his head. He examined the coats of arms of Jacques de Molay and Geoffroy de

Charnay. They were different from Adam's, but all contained the same motto: *Tutor Thesauri*.

His eye snagged on something at his feet: splatters of red on the cell floor. He squatted down to investigate. The puddle was still wet. "Raj," he said, trying to steady his voice. "Please tell me this is just ketchup."

That was when a gut-wrenching cry of pain sounded from the attic above.

••••••

Raj took the lead as they dashed up the narrow stone steps to the top story of the tower. He followed the blood trail to a row of low-ceilinged stone cells. A bloody dagger lay on the floor.

Only one of the cells was locked. Addison gripped the window bars of the thick oak door and peered inside. An old man, cloaked in shadows, was groaning in misery. He wore a groundskeeper's outfit and a woolly beard. "The caretaker!" Addison cried. "Eddie, hurry!"

Eddie knelt and pressed his ear to the cell door. He drew a set of delicate picks from his jacket pocket and fished them into the lock. Eyes shut tight in concentration, Eddie jimmied the lock in ten seconds flat.

Addison and his team tumbled into the room. The old Frenchman, in workman's coveralls, was tied to a medieval torture rack. His feet were chained to the bottom and his wrists roped to the top. A wheel crank had been tightened so that his body was stretched to its absolute limits.

Raj loosened the crank. The old man gasped in relief. Molly and Addison set to work untying the man's ropes while Eddie unlocked the iron chains.

If the old man wasn't on death's doorstep, he was at least on the driveway. Addison helped ease the man into a sitting position. "Raj, find him some water so he can speak! Eddie, learn French!"

Raj drew a canteen from his pack, unscrewed it, and tipped it to the man's parched lips. The man sputtered and coughed, water dribbling from his beard. His weary eyes focused on Addison. When he spoke at last, his French accent was only very slight. "Addison, is that you?"

"Who are you?" Addison whispered.

"My name is Gaspard," the old man gasped. He tried sitting up on the rack and was racked with coughs. "Gaspard Gagnon."

"Have we met?"

"No," said the old man, with a shake of his head. "But I have known about you and Molly for a long time."

"How?" asked Molly.

"Because I," said the man, pushing himself up to a full sitting position and setting his feet on the ground, "am the Grand Master of the Knights Templar."

Chapter Thirteen

The Last Grand Master

"YOU ARE TOO LATE," Gaspard croaked, clutching the knife wound in his side. "The Collective is already in Paris. Addison, Molly, you must run."

"Not until we get answers," said Addison. "Besides, we can't just leave you here."

"We need to call an ambulance," said Molly. "Gaspard, is there a phone in this dump? What are you doing all by yourself in this creepy, rotten building, anyway?"

"I live here," said Gaspard.

"Oh," said Molly. "Sorry."

"Someone must stick around here to safeguard our past, no? Come, there is a phone in my quarters."

Addison and Eddie gently helped Gaspard to his feet. Raj grabbed a spare T-shirt from his backpack and pressed it to Gaspard's knife wound, stanching the bleeding. "We just have to keep pressure on it."

"Who did this to you?" asked Addison. "And why?"

"They were looking for you, of course," wheezed Gaspard.

"Us?"

"Your tablet. Luckily, T.D. will surely have made you hide it somewhere safe."

"She told us to bring it to you!" said Molly.

"*Mon Dieu*. You have brought the tablet here? Into the wolf's den? The Fortress is surrounded. The Collective is awaiting your arrival!" Gaspard frowned. "How did you get in here, anyway?"

"We climbed the wall," said Addison.

"Clever," said Gaspard.

"We're Templars," said Molly.

"No," Gaspard coughed painfully. "Not yet. First you must—"

"—come of age," said Addison, finishing his sentence. "We know."

They eased him downstairs, step by careful step. They passed abandoned storerooms now home to nesting pigeons and empty larders with caved-in roofs, soaked by the drenching rain. Blood pooled out of Gaspard's shirt and left a trail of droplets on the stone floor.

······

The old Templar directed them to his cozy, furnished quarters in a smaller tower of the castle. Eddie and Raj deposited him carefully on the sofa while Addison found a phone and dialed emergency services. Once a French voice answered, Addison handed the phone to Eddie.

"Addison, I've told you I don't speak French," Eddie squawked. "Don't you speak English?"

Addison handed the phone to Gaspard, who rattled off his address before sinking into the couch, exhausted. "The ambulance is on its way."

Gaspard's little room was decorated with the saddest, spindliest Christmas tree Addison had ever seen. The old man was shivering, so Molly wrapped him in a blanket.

Raj blew on the embers in the fireplace and stacked on fresh wood. He quickly built up a crackling fire.

"Well done, Raj," said Addison. "Treating a wound, starting a fire . . . Someone might almost mistake you for a Boy Scout."

Raj sighed and dusted off his hands on his camouflage pants. "Those days are behind me."

Molly turned to the old man. "T.D. said you would have answers about our family's past."

"You have not come of . . ." Gaspard was seized by a fit of rasping coughs that left him wheezing for breath.

Molly had heard enough of this coming-of-age business. "We've been chased all over the world. We've been threatened, stabbed, tortured, and nearly burned at the stake. All because of some prophecy no one will even tell us! If we haven't come of age yet, when will we?"

Addison chimed in. "There are hardly any Templars left. If you don't tell us what's going on, Gaspard, who will?"

Gaspard sighed, the cracks in his face showing every one of his years, like the rings of a tree. He leaned closer to the fire, the dancing light reflected in his eyes. "In the Crusades, European knights pillaged the tombs of Damascus and plundered the temples of Jerusalem. Knights robbed the cross of Josiah from Tripoli, only to have it stolen by highwaymen in Antioch. So many relics were lost or destroyed, the Templars decided to act."

He took a sip from Raj's canteen. The team leaned close to hear the old man's words. "Jacques de Molay, the Templar Grand Master, formed a secret order within the Templars—"

"A secret order within a secret order?" Raj interrupted, eyes wide.

Gaspard nodded. "A secret order to find and safeguard the treasures of history."

"*Tutores Thesauri*," said Molly.

"Yes," said the Grand Master. "We protect the treasures of the world." Gaspard clutched his blanket tighter; he was still shivering. "May I see the tablet?"

Molly drew it from her satchel, the bronze gleaming in the firelight.

Addison wondered at the strange glyph carved inside the circle emblazoned on the tablet. He again felt the strangest sensation that he had seen the design somewhere before.

"It's beautiful," said Gaspard.

"Can you tell us what it is?" asked Addison.

"I have no idea. Each Templar family guards different relics. We don't share information—it's safer that way." He ran a pale, bent finger over a flowery rune carved on the corner of the tablet. A sword in front of a scroll. "You know, I've seen this rune before. In Istanbul."

Addison leaned forward eagerly. "Where in Istanbul?"

Gaspard gazed into the fire, lost in his memories. "The most beautiful mosque in the city." The old man was shaken by another fit of coughs.

"Which mosque?" asked Addison.

Before Gaspard could answer, a terrific crash and scream erupted from the main hall of the fortress.

It was the yelp of a man whose forehead was being rapidly acquainted with an old oak table, a chest of drawers, and a large siege weapon. This yelp was immediately followed by the sound of three carefully balanced dining room chairs cracking over a man's back.

"*Mon Dieu!*" Gaspard yelped.

"It worked!" said Raj. "My elephant trap worked!"

"It's the Collective, right?" said Molly, leaping to her feet.

"Well, if that's the ambulance people," said Eddie, "that was awfully fast."

Addison's eyes darted to the crackling fire. He smacked a hand to his forehead. "The Collective must have seen the smoke from the chimney. They know we're in here."

"Time to go," said Molly.

"But," said Raj, pointing to the doorway. "My elephant trap. It did work. Right, you guys?"

•••••

"Gaspard, we need to move you," said Addison urgently.

"Impossible. Just leave me."

"This is not a negotiation." Addison was pretty sure it was his fault Gaspard had been tortured. If he hadn't removed the tablet from the Blandfordshire Bank, none of the day's events would have been set in motion. He couldn't let Gaspard fall prey to the Collective.

Raj's first aid skills kicked in. "Everyone take a corner of his blanket—we can use it as a stretcher."

With four of them lifting, the withered old man was not hard to move. Shuffling together, they maneuvered Gaspard out of the little room, upsetting only a few piles of books, some antique candlesticks, and a large glass flower vase. They made it through the narrow doorway on the third try.

"Listen!" Molly whispered.

Shouts and pounding footsteps echoed in the corridors below.

"Double time," said Addison. They jogged Gaspard's makeshift stretcher into the library. Addison nearly dropped his corner of the blanket in astonishment. This was clearly the one part of the castle that Gaspard had kept in perfect working order. The shelves were ornate wood paneling and heaped with parchment scrolls, gilt-painted manuscripts, and books so old that monks had copied them out by hand. Addison saw some of his favorite classics: *You and Your Planets* by Gail Andrews, *The Body in the Library* by Ariadne Oliver, and even *Alchemy, Ancient Art and Science* by Argo Pyrites. He could have happily spent a year in the library. But unfortunately, he got only seventeen seconds.

Boots thundered up the staircase. Three men in black suits burst into the room, quickly followed by three more. There may have been another three after that; Addison wasn't stopping to take a head count.

The group stuffed themselves through the library's rear door and slammed it shut behind them. Raj threw the bolt. In seconds the door split as a heavy boot kicked through the cherrywood. A gloved hand reached through the hole, unlocking the door.

"These guys hate doors!" Eddie shouted.

"Eddie, hurry up!" Molly did not think he was doing a good job carrying his corner of the stretcher. Gaspard swung precariously between them like he was in a hammock in a hurricane.

They trotted down a hallway lined with suits of armor. Weapons racks held pikes, lances, longbows, and all manner of swords and sabers, daggers and dirks. Addison thought about grabbing a weapon, but he didn't have any hands free.

The black-suited men barreled after them.

The group retreated into a kitchen. Raj, clutching the stretcher, kicked the kitchen door shut and slid the bolt home with a well-placed elbow.

Gaspard pointed them to a trapdoor that Molly nudged open with her toe. The group, panting for breath, teetered down spiral steps into a cold, dank wine cellar.

Eddie looked around frantically for an exit. "We're trapped!"

"No," said Gaspard. "Move aside those old wine barrels."

The group set Gaspard down on the stone floor of the basement as gently as they could. Raj and Eddie wrapped their arms around a heavy barrel and wobbled it aside. Two more barrels and they discovered a deep hole cut in the flagstone. Molly, Eddie, and Raj peered down into the hole, contemplating the drop.

Addison wheeled on Gaspard. "You still haven't told me where you saw those runes!"

"I need only tell you this." Gaspard clutched Addison's sleeve. "If I do not make it . . . tell your uncle: this is our hour of need. Spread the word. The order of the Templar must rise again. Now go!"

"What about you?" asked Addison.

High above them, the trapdoor to the wine cellar sprang open. Heavy boots pounded down the steps.

"Don't worry—they will run right past me." Gaspard crawled behind the wine barrels and pulled some old sacks down on top of himself. "At all costs, save the tablet. Jump, Addison!"

"You want me to just jump down a dark hole?"

"It's okay," cried Gaspard. "You'll land in the sewer!"

And before Addison could process that, the old man gave him a kick, knocking him into the hole.

Chapter Fourteen

The Paris Sewer

ADDISON SPLASHED INTO FREEZING water.

On the one hand, he was glad there was something to break his fall. On the other hand, here he was, in a sewer. That was the thing about life, really. One moment your biggest concern is being stuck in a wine cellar; the next you are neck-deep in sidewalk runoff.

The cold shock seized his lungs. He swam frantically, arms and feet whirring like propeller blades until he reached the far side of the sewage tunnel and climbed, gasping, onto the ledge. His team splashed into the frigid water behind him.

Eddie came up for air and filled his lungs for a shriek, but Molly clamped a hand over his mouth. "Shh!"

They paddled to the ledge where Addison was mourning his drenched blazer. "Nothing like a cooling dip to restore the spirits," he whispered as cheerfully as he could. At least it was raining in Paris, Addison reasoned, so all the water pouring down the sewage grates was fairly fresh.

The sewer tunnel was a circular tube, large enough to stand up in. A river of water flowed down the center. Safety ledges, like narrow walkways, ran along either side.

"Keep moving!" whispered Molly. "They're right behind us."

Shouts from the wine cellar above revealed that the men in black suits had found their escape hatch.

Addison's team inched down the tunnel into the pitch black.

"I have my military-grade flashlight," said Raj. "One thousand candlepower."

"That will only help them find us faster," Addison said.

"Well, we need something!" Raj exclaimed. "We're not bats that can see in the dark."

"Do not talk about bats right now," Eddie whispered.

Addison scrounged around in his messenger bag and came up with his penlight. They sidestepped faster along the ledge. He heard a giant splash behind them as one of the black-suited men cannonballed into the water. The man yowled in a language Addison did not understand. Which, Addison reflected, was nearly all languages.

More splashes were followed by more shouting. Addison tried to count the splashes, but the echoes were confusing in the tunnel.

The bright beam of a powerful flashlight lit up the group like a Broadway stage.

"They've seen us!" called Molly.

The group sprinted down the shaft, hooked a right at a junction, and banged a left deeper into the labyrinth. Finally, even Molly ran out of breath and stopped at a fork in the tunnel. "This bronze tablet is like a ship anchor." Exhausted, she handed Eddie her satchel.

It had already been an incredibly long day, and Addison, who was normally indefatigable, was finding himself quite fatigable. Faint echoes of the suited men's voices seem to waft in from several directions, like the whispers of ghosts.

Raj stood still for a moment with his hand in the air, listening. He even pressed his ear flat to the concrete ground. "They've split up, trying to track us."

"We just need to keep moving away from the voices," said Molly. She led the way down the narrower tunnel at the fork. The concrete sewer pipe ended and gave way to rocky caverns carved in the limestone.

"What is this place?" asked Eddie, staring at the rough-hewn gypsum tunnels forking in all directions.

"The Mines of Paris," said Addison, panning his penlight over the chiseled stone. "Two hundred miles of mines and hidden tunnels under the City of Light. Some of the waterways are big enough to ride a boat through. The French Resistance used them to smuggle weapons during World War Two." Addison held up his well-thumbed copy of *Fiddleton's World Atlas*. "Mr. Fiddleton may be the only person to have traveled all of the tunnels, but he chose not to publish his map in order to preserve their sense of mystery." Addison shook his head with admiration. "Just think, wherever you go in life, Roland J. Fiddleton got there first."

Eddie paused to root around in Molly's pack and distribute the food rations they had scavenged from the private jet. When he bit into a candy bar, he sighed in relief. "I feel so much better about life now."

"Eddie," said Addison calmly, "you might be interested to know there is a human skull by your left foot."

Eddie squinted at Addison, not sure whether to believe him. He decided to chance a glance. There was indeed a human skull lying next to his left foot. Eddie leapt in the air like a startled cat. "This is *horrendous!*" He pointed an accusing finger at Addison. "Would you mind explaining to me, Addison, why there is a skull in here?"

"Ah, yes, about that," said Addison. "I should have mentioned. The Paris Mines are a sort of underground graveyard."

"I'm sorry," said Eddie, who had forgotten all about his candy bar. "It almost sounded as if you said that the Paris Mines are a sort of underground graveyard."

"I did say that," said Addison. "It's nothing to be concerned about, Eddie. It's really the living people in these tunnels, and not the dead people, that we should be worried about."

"I am worried," Eddie explained, "about *becoming* one of the dead people. Can you go back to the part where you explain why there's a skull lying by my left foot?"

"What, this old thing?" Addison picked up the skull, dusted it off, and placed it in a nook in the rocks. "Paris doesn't have enough room for cemeteries. So the citizens tucked more than six million skeletons into these tunnels up ahead. They're called the Paris Catacombs."

Eddie looked gobsmacked.

Addison shrugged. "What would *you* do with six million skeletons?"

Before Eddie could formulate a response, shouted voices sounded down the tunnel behind them.

Addison shone his flashlight on the archway leading into the heart of the Paris Catacombs. It was decorated with human skulls and crossbones. "C'mon, Eddie, we're going in."

······

Addison hustled into the ossuary. The caverns that branched off on either side, as far as his flashlight could illuminate, were decorated floor to ceiling with bones. Some featured spiraling patterns of arm bones and leg bones, others contained mosaics of ribs.

Eddie loped along, lugging the satchel and fuming with anger. "Addison, why is it that every time you leave the house, you wind up taking me to a graveyard?"

"I don't see what the big deal is. I would think you'd be used to it by now." Addison scooped up an arm bone from his path and used it to wave at Eddie. "I don't suppose you find this humerus?"

Eddie switched the heavy satchel from his right shoulder to his left. "So we're just going to cross through millions of graves and hope we can find our way out?"

"We're going where the path leads us," said Addison. "Nothing's set in stone."

"Tombs are," said Eddie morosely.

The tunnel ran ever deeper. It was held up by crude pillars and archways, some of them carved with centuries-old French graffiti. They passed through a chamber decorated entirely with swirling patterns of vertebrae.

There was no sun or moon to guide them. Addison's compass seemed to be thrown off by interference from iron water shafts or perhaps iron deposits in the lime-stone. The narrowing walls seemed to press in on them. Every animal instinct in Addison's body panicked at the thought of becoming trapped underground.

"Admit it," said Eddie at last, heaving for breath. "We're completely lost. We may never escape."

Distorted by echoes, the howls of the pursuing gunmen almost seemed to be coming from the leering grins of the surrounding skulls.

"If you get lost in the forest," said Raj, "you follow a stream downhill. It will lead to a river, and the river will lead you to civilization."

"Raj, I hate to be *that guy*," said Eddie, "but we're not in the forest."

"No, Raj is right," said Addison. "We need to get back to a waterway. It will feed into larger tunnels and lead us to the River Seine."

Raj cupped his hands to his ears and rotated them like satellite dishes. Moving in absolute silence he guided the group to a trickle of water leading through a cavern. They followed it downstream. All the while, they could hear their pursuers stomping along just a few tunnels away.

At last their trickle flowed into the deep, rushing stream of a giant tunnel. "Progress!" said Addison. But he soon heard the sound of engines, building to a deafen-ing roar. Men in black suits blasted out of the darkness, arriving on three powerboats. More men raced out of the tunnel behind Addison's group, cutting off their escape. All things considered, it was not the best minute of Addison's life.

"What I want to know is, how did they get powerboats down here?" said Molly.

"What I want to know is, how do we get out of here?" said Addison.

Eddie wrung his hands. "I think we're going to die!"

"Well," said Addison smoothly, "at least we're already in a graveyard."

Chapter Fifteen

Ivan the Terrible

THE MEN IN SUITS climbed out of their powerboats and closed in on Addison's group. Addison took a step forward and did his best to look cool and confident.

Raj leaned in close behind Addison and whispered, "I have purple smoke balls."

"Not now, Raj."

The leader of the black-suited men stopped a few feet from Addison. The man's gnarled hair was long and woolly, with frayed strands poking in all directions. Addison wondered if the man's barber was blind or just mean-spirited. His goatee was tangled and greasy, like he had collected it from a shower drain. His skin was as mottled and oily as Swiss fondue. All in all, Addison had known plantar warts that were more charming.

"Let me guess," said Addison. "You're a male model."

"Let *me* guess," said the man in a gruff Slavic accent. "You are Addison Cooke."

"At your service."

"The same Addison Cooke who got Boris Ragar killed on a mountain in Mongolia."

"Speaking," said Addison.

"And the same Addison Cooke who trapped Vladimir Ragar, Zubov Rachivnek, and their whole team inside a mountain in Peru."

"How many Addison Cookes did you think there could be?"

The man glared down at Addison.

Addison stared right back. "Vladimir Ragar wasn't exactly Man of the Year. I did the world a favor."

The man continued to glare, only harder.

Addison hesitated. "I don't suppose you're Vladimir's brother or anything like that?"

"No."

Addison inwardly sighed with relief.

The man continued. "My brother was Zubov Rachivnek."

Addison experienced one of those rare moments in his life when he had no ability to speak. He emitted a sort of airy squeak, like he was hiding a mouse in his throat. He remembered Zubov all too clearly. A knife-wielding psychopath who had tracked him from

Colombia to Ecuador to Peru and nearly killed him in all three countries.

"I have looked forward to this day for a long time," said the man, in what Addison now knew to be a Russian accent.

"I always look forward to making new friends as well," said Addison. He had rapidly begun to suspect that diplomacy might be the better tack. He thrust out his hand for a shake. "And you are?"

The man ignored Addison's proffered hand. "Ivan."

"Do you have a nickname like your brother?"

"They call me," said Ivan, taking a step closer to Addison, "Ivan the Terrible."

Addison was pretty sure that epithet had already been taken by a Russian czar a few centuries ago, but then, nobody became a deranged tablet-thieving criminal because of their gift for creativity. "Well, Ivan the Terrible," said Addison with a respectful nod of his head, "I will go one further. I will call you Ivan the Absolute Worst."

Ivan squinted at Addison, perhaps wondering if this was an insult.

"We've met Vladimir Ragar and his brother Boris," Addison continued. "We've met Zubov Rachivnek and now his brother. Tell me, is stealing archaeological treasures a family business?"

Ivan nodded. "We are all part of the Collective. And we know about the prophecy."

The words chilled Addison, who was already shivering to begin with.

"Now," said Ivan, stepping dangerously close to Addison. "Which one of you broke my brother's foot?"

Addison knew the answer to this question: it was Molly. She had stomped on Zubov's foot in Colombia, though—to be fair—it was in self-defense. Addison didn't see any percentage in explaining any of this to Ivan. So he simply shrugged. "I'm afraid I don't know what you're talking about."

Ivan gripped Addison by the shoulders, pulled him close, and stomped down on his foot. This introduction made a deep and lasting impression on Addison, as well as on his shoe.

Addison howled and hopped around. He strode in a furious circle, trying to walk off the pain. The hard leather of his dress shoe had deflected much of the blow. But scuffing perfectly good oxford wingtips was stubbing the very toe of Addison's immortal soul.

Ivan, evidently amused, grabbed Addison again, preparing for round two.

Molly stepped forward. "That's enough," she said evenly.

Ivan turned to look down on Molly. She was little more

than half his height. He wrinkled up his brow. "What are you going to do?"

"I could break that nose for you," Molly offered.

Ivan's woolly eyebrows shot up his woolly hairline. He was not used to being taunted by twelve-year-olds. Still, he did not appear to have any qualms about fighting twelve-year-olds either. Ivan reached down to his belt and drew out four feet of steel chain. He wrapped half of it around the knuckles of his right fist and let the other half dangle free. He assumed a fighting stance and began twirling the heavy chain like a fan blade.

Molly could see that he was well trained. She circled him slowly. He was taller, his arm reach was longer, and he was at least twice her weight in solid muscle. Molly pulled her sling from her satchel and loaded it with a lead slug.

"Molly, are you sure?" Addison was still wincing from the stabs of pain in his foot.

Ivan smirked at Molly. "That is your weapon? You won't even get it spinning before I cut it into pieces."

Molly shrugged. Perhaps her uncle Jasper was right. She pulled the can of pepper spray from her pocket and pulled the trigger.

The jet of liquid hit Ivan full in the face. He clutched his palms to his eyes and roared.

Molly kept spraying, filling the air with a noxious cloud.

The suited men, racing to attack her, suddenly squeezed their eyes shut in a blind, panicked rage. They clutched their throats, coughing and choking, their eyes burning red and brimming with tears.

Molly, Eddie, and Raj turned and fled back into the maze of the catacombs, Addison limping after them. The cloud of pepper spray had mostly missed them, but they were still coughing. Addison, bringing up the rear, even felt his nostrils stinging like he had inhaled a lump of wasabi.

Raj turned to Molly with worship in his eyes. "Wow, Molly. That was just, wow—I mean you really, wow—that was really just—"

Addison caught up to Raj and pulled him along. "Well said, Raj. You should be a color commentator for sports."

The group had to edge sideways to squeeze through the fissure into the next tunnel. Molly called to Addison. "I used up all my pepper spray, and those guys are going to want to kill me!"

Addison hobbled to keep up, patting dust from his clothes. "You think you've got problems, my jacket is getting *filthy.*"

They raced over a bridge of bones. It led them over a muddy river of sidewalk runoff, strewn with trash. Addison shook his head as he ran. "How many brothers, uncles, nephews, and cousins do Ragar and Zubov have?

Are we going to spend the rest of our lives rushing from Russians? I have nothing against Russia—I love Russia!"

"Addison, what's our plan?" asked Eddie.

"To delay them."

"Until what?"

"Until we think of a plan."

"And how are we going to delay them?"

"By running around in this maze," said Addison.

Eddie jogged to a halt. "Easy for you to say—you're not the one carrying a tablet-shaped refrigerator in your satchel."

"I am open to suggestions," said Addison.

Molly faced the group. "How about instead of running around like nincompoops with no plan, we try *not* running around like nincompoops with no plan?"

"You may be on to something there, Mo." Addison nodded sagely. "Hold the phone—I think I've got something."

"One of your good ideas or one of your bad ideas?"

"One of my very worst," said Addison. "We need to circle back the way we came."

Molly was about to protest, but she noticed a certain gleam in Addison's eye—the sort of expression a fox might take upon discovering a wide-open henhouse door. Molly knew that in such circumstances it was usually best to go with Addison's instincts.

The group followed him back to the bridge of bones.

They found it guarded by a gigantic dark-suited man. The wings of his mustache were so thick and angular that Addison could picture it flapping a few times before flying away like a startled starling.

Eddie sized up the heavy-browed brute of a man. If he wasn't a Neanderthal, he could certainly play one on TV. Eddie dug in his heels. "I don't want to cross that bridge."

"We go backward and we may never find our way out of the catacombs," said Addison. He tried to sound braver than he felt. "The only thing worse than crossing that bridge will be not crossing that bridge."

The group bustled onto the brittle bridge.

The mustached man's eyes were red and tearing from pepper spray. It looked as though he had just finished watching a real tearjerker of a movie. It said something about the man's sheer size that he was still intimidating despite being in tears. He blinked hard and glared down at the group. In his giant hands, he clutched a crowbar. "Do you want to die?"

"No need to answer that," said Addison, turning to Raj. "It's a rhetorical question."

Addison noticed the scars mapping the man's face and scoring his knuckles. Life had clearly dealt this man some hard blows, though, Addison reflected, perhaps not hard enough.

It was Molly who stepped forward first. "I hope you

have a good doctor," she said, pulling out her can of pepper spray, "because you're going to need first aid, second aid, and third aid."

Addison knew she was bluffing—she had said herself the can was empty. Still, the thick-jawed man, blinking away tears, was so focused on Molly and her dreaded can of pepper spray that he never saw Raj coming.

Raj scuttled in low like a beetle, scrambling on all fours, and plowed into the man's shins. The man's legs buckled. He wheeled his arms in surprise and toppled off the bridge, dropping into the river of runoff. He came up for air with a mouthful of mud.

"Bitten off more than you can chew?" asked Addison. He was quite proud of himself for that one, but no one else seemed to have heard the line. He cleared his throat. "I said, have you bitten off more than—"

"Addison, quit gossiping with him and run!" Molly grabbed him by the sleeve, shoving him along toward the next tunnel.

"What about you?" asked Addison.

Molly stooped to pick up the man's crowbar from the bridge. She turned to face the mustached man, who was crawling, dripping, from the water. "I'm going to slow him down."

Addison saw Molly's determined expression and decided she had things well in hand. He loped after

Eddie and Raj, retracing their route through one final tunnel to arrive back at the powerboats.

The boats were completely unguarded. All the suited men had fanned out through the tunnels, hunting Cookes. "There!" Addison breathed a sigh of relief, pointing at the waiting boats. He beamed at Eddie and Raj triumphantly. "I told you I had a plan!"

Raj hopped into the first boat, getting a feel for the steering wheel, throttle, and clutch.

"Can you drive this thing?" asked Addison.

"Of course," said Raj. "Babatunde Okonjo's masterpiece, *Mission: Survival III*, contains an entire chapter on aquatic escapes."

Eddie bent over the ignition, drew his pick set, and went to work hotwiring the engine.

Molly raced into the cavern, beelining for the boat. Two black-suited men lumbered after her.

Addison pulled her aboard, helping her over the gunnel. "How did we do in there?"

Molly, still carrying her crowbar, grinned and gave him a thumbs-up. "I hit the man with a big mustache!"

"You should have hit him with your fist," said Addison.

The men closed in on the boat.

"Eddie, how much more time do you need?" Addison called.

"Thirty seconds!" Eddie had unscrewed a wooden

panel on the dashboard and was fiddling with the wires.

Addison flicked open his butterfly knife and started to climb out of the boat.

"No," said Molly, staying his hand. "I've got this."

"Are you sure?" asked Addison.

Molly nodded. "They're blind as bats from that pepper spray. Watch."

The two large men reached the boat, lunging for Molly. Their eyes swollen nearly shut from pepper spray, they were practically fumbling in the dark. Addison almost felt sorry for them. Molly dodged their clumsy swipes and crowbarred them both in the kneecaps. The two men collapsed, groaning.

Eddie hollered excitedly. "I got it!" The speedboat engine roared to life.

Raj shifted the boat into reverse, backing out into the center of the channel where the water ran deepest.

Three more Russians stumbled out of the tunnels, racing for them. But Raj's propeller was already churning the water. He shifted the boat into gear, picking up speed. The roar was deafening in the low stone tunnel. Addison watched the Collective recede into the darkening distance.

"You know," said Molly, "I'm getting pretty good at saving your life."

"Well," said Addison, "don't let it go to your head."

Chapter Sixteen

The City of Light

ADDISON'S ELATION AT THEIR escape was short-lived. As they sped underneath the great city, he could hear the whine of two powerboats pursuing. "Raj! Evasive maneuvers!"

Raj banked their craft into a larger culvert. He turned so sharply, Eddie was nearly flung overboard. Molly caught Eddie by his collar and hauled him back to a seated position.

Struggling to control the speeding boat, Raj cut too close to the stone walls of the tunnel. Rocks shredded wood paneling from the hull with a horrific screech. The boat fishtailed wildly, sewer water swamping the crew.

Addison cupped his palms together and began frantically bailing water from the now-leaking boat. "Raj, are you working for them or for us?"

Raj white-knuckled the steering wheel. "*You* try driving a boat for the first time—see how well *you* do!"

"Look out!" Molly shouted. A tunnel wall was fast approaching.

Raj spun the steering wheel, nearly swamping the craft as they swerved hard into a fresh culvert. Eddie was again nearly tipped out of the boat.

Molly snagged Eddie by his rumpled tie, tugging him back to safety. "Eddie, would it kill you to stay in the boat?"

"It might!" Eddie yelled. The edges of the wooden boat again splintered against the narrow walls of the tunnel.

Raj spotted city lights up ahead and punched it for the exit. For a split second, the speedboat was airborne. The giant tunnel spit them out, and they splashed into the River Seine.

Addison was relieved to be free of the catacombs and see the clouded night sky overhead. But his relief was soon punctured by the sight of two Collective speedboats spurting from the tunnel behind them.

"Hold on!" Raj shouted, opening up the throttle. The engine whined higher, the nose of the speedboat now rising in the air and slapping against the waves. Foam spraying off the river drenched the group. The famous

Notre Dame Cathedral flashed past their stolen boat, along with the town hall and several museums. Addison had always dreamed of seeing Paris, but not like this.

The River Seine was crowded with tourist boats that Raj barely managed to dodge. The Collective was catching up fast. Hunched over the wheel, eyes bugging, Raj knifed his way between two City of Light dinner cruises.

Addison knew he needed to think quickly. "Guys, remember when I had that bad idea to ride on top of the train? Well, I have a worse idea."

"Impossible," said Molly.

"Raj, crash the boat."

Raj did not see the wisdom of this plan. But before he could think of a better one, Addison spun the steering wheel and hurled Raj overboard.

The boat whizzed for the lip of the canal. Molly and Eddie, seeing a stone barrier rearing up before them, dove overboard as well.

Addison dove last. He held his breath underwater and swam for the far side of a large tourist cruise ship. He surfaced just in time to see their stolen speedboat collide with the edge of the canal, run straight up onto the quay, and smash into a flower stand. A flock of pigeons took wing, and a herd of accordion players scattered. There was a tremendous eruption of smoke and splintered wood. It was precisely what Addison was hoping for.

The enemy speedboats peeled around the side of the

cruise ship and slowed to examine the debris. The engine oil floating on the water burst into flames. The Collective backed off their boats, steering wide of the fire.

Molly, Eddie, and Raj bobbed in the frigid water near Addison, their teeth chattering. Addison held a finger to his lips for quiet. Together, they clung to the side of the largest tourist ship as it slid past the wreckage. On the top deck, several tourists snapped photos of the obliterated boat.

"The Collective will think we're dead," Molly whispered.

"Let's hope so," said Addison. Treading water, he turned to Raj and whispered, "I'm sorry I threw you off the boat."

"It's okay," said Raj. "I've been practicing free-diving techniques. I can hold my breath under water for almost a minute and a half."

Addison nodded. Raj was the one person he knew who was pleased to be hurled from a moving speedboat.

The group swam to the far shore and skulked up the embankment, sticking to the shadows. Addison watched a utility pole, damaged in the wreck, topple into the Seine like a falling tree. It sizzled and cracked when it met the water, the transformer blowing out in a shower of sparks. The nearest street plunged into darkness. Then, an entire city block. Then, the entire neighborhood. Addison realized with mounting horror that he had managed to shut off the City of Light.

Molly didn't say a word. She simply stared at Addison, her eyes boring a hole in his head.

"I know, and I'm sorry," he said. He clasped his hands together and turned to the group. "I recommend we get as far away from Paris as possible. All in favor?"

"How?" asked Eddie, miserable in his soaked clothes. "We don't have any money."

Addison grinned. "While Ivan the Terrible was rearranging my foot, I picked his pocket."

Eddie's face brightened. "Please tell me you snagged a credit card."

"I only got a stack of Métro cards." Addison shrugged. "But it'll have to do."

••••••

Outrunning a fresh downpour, Addison's team galloped down the subway steps and boarded the Métro to Charles de Gaulle Airport. They kept their heads down and tried to keep a low profile, but it was already quite late, and the train cars were sparsely populated. To his relief, Addison found that even though his group had spent the better part of two hours crawling around in the Paris sewers, they did not smell altogether much different from anyone else riding the Paris Métro at that hour.

Halfway down their train car, Addison discovered a

Belgian man selling fake watches out of a briefcase. The man spoke broken English, and after some bargaining and bickering, Addison traded his remaining Métro cards for three fake Rolexes. These he fastened all the way up his left forearm.

"What do you need with three fake Rolexes?" asked Molly, when Addison had returned to his seat.

"I don't know yet," said Addison with a wink. "I just know we don't need the Métro cards anymore."

••••••

Arriving at Charles de Gaulle Airport, Addison was still not sure how he was going to get his team out of the country. Without credit cards, he felt like a knight without his sword.

"You've talked our way onto airplanes before," said Molly.

"Yes, but only airplanes where the ticket agents spoke English." Addison was realizing just how much self-confidence he had lost in the five months since losing his aunt and uncle. The old Addison would have marched into Air France and attempted to buy the airline. But this new Addison . . . He sighed. If he was going to survive this dangerous journey, he needed to get his groove back.

Addison scanned the airport concourse, bustling with

travelers from every corner of the world. To his weary, wary eye, everyone looked suspicious: the young Italian man in sunglasses thumbing through a magazine in the bookshop; the Parisian businesswoman touching up her rouge in a makeup mirror by the water fountain; the old Belgian man casually eating an apple while watching the security line to the outbound gates. All of them seemed to be glancing at Addison.

"Back door?" asked Raj.

Addison nodded.

They retreated outside, shoulders hunched against the chill night air, and hustled around terminal two. Addison ducked a security gate and led the group onto the tarmac, dodging a melee of transporters, buses, container loaders, catering trucks, and forklifts.

"Where to?" asked Eddie.

Addison found the day's airport departure schedule lying on the passenger seat of an empty baggage tractor. He picked up the clipboard and flipped through the cities on the printouts. Manila . . . Marrakech . . . Mogadishu. Any of those sounded like safer options for them than Paris.

Yet Addison felt tired of running. Here he was, risking his life to protect a tablet, without having any idea what the tablet was even for. He shook his head. "We came to Paris for answers and all we got was more questions."

One single city on the manifest had caught Addison's undivided attention.

"All right," said Molly, catching the glint in Addison's eye. "So where are we going?"

Addison remembered one of the few clear things Grand Master Gaspard had told them about the tablet . . . Their only solid lead. He looked up at the group with a grim smile on his face. "Istanbul."

Chapter Seventeen

To Catch a Flight

ADDISON INSPECTED THE BAGGAGE tractor. He decided it was basically a glorified golf cart. He felt confident he could drive it since there weren't any gears to shift. There weren't even any doors. And if he had any trouble, he could always fall back on Raj. Addison took a seat behind the wheel.

The one thing the cart did have was keys in the ignition.

"Are you *trying* to get us caught?" asked Molly.

"On the contrary. We'll fit right in with one of these."

"Right," said Eddie. "Because when I don't want to look suspicious, the first thing I do is steal a car."

"Eddie, what looks more suspicious on a tarmac: four schoolkids or one baggage cart?"

It took Addison a minute to figure out the runway map and decipher the departure schedule. Checking his three Rolexes, he realized the red-eye flight to Istanbul was due to leave any minute from runway two. If there was any justice in the world, the flight would be delayed, like planes normally are. Surely this would not be the one plane that would actually leave on time. It was worth a shot. "All right, we've got a plane to catch. Terminal two, gate seven."

He gunned the cart across the airport, swerving around a giant, lumbering 767 cargo plane and zipping past a refueling truck.

Molly frowned. "How are we supposed to get on this plane, Addison?"

"Easy. We walk up the airstairs and Bob's your uncle." "Bob's your uncle" was a British expression Addison had picked up at Dimpleforth. Like many British expressions, he had no idea what it actually meant—he just loved saying it.

"What if there's a jetway?"

"One thing at a time, Molly. We don't have plane tickets and we don't have money. I'm doing the best I can, given the circumstances."

It wasn't until they rounded terminal three that Addison spotted their Turkish Airlines 747. Addison loved planes, and to him, the 747 was a triumph of engineering. Double the length of a blue whale, and it was going to fly six miles up in the sky at six hundred miles per hour. It staggered the mind.

The only trouble with this particular 747 was that it had left gate seven and was already taxiing to the runway.

"I think we're a little late," said Eddie.

Addison grimaced. He'd been on a bad luck streak for six solid months. He was beginning to wonder when the cards were going to be dealt in his favor.

"Um, Addison?" Molly pointed.

He swiveled his head around to follow Molly's sight line. Three black SUVs growled through the security gate and onto the tarmac, circling terminal two. They had black-tinted windows, twenty-four-inch tires, and steel bull bars mounted across their grilles.

Addison gaped. A few neurons pinged around in his head. One of them suggested running. Another suggested bursting into tears. A third neuron suggested turning into a pelican and flying off to Africa. A few neurons lit up, supporting this idea. But a fourth neuron, somewhere in the logic part of Addison's brain, piped up and reminded the other neurons that turning into a pelican was not possible because Addison's brain was currently awake and not dreaming. While all this debate was going on, the neuron in charge of making Addison's jaw gape fired continuously.

The black SUVs slowed to a stop in the center of the tarmac. For a moment, they simply paused there, three wolves eyeing the flock. From the hairs on the back of his neck, Addison felt he detected the precise moment the Collective spotted his team. The SUVs roared to life, speeding toward them on runway two.

This time, Addison did not hesitate. He floored the gas, or the electricity, or whatever it is that propels airport carts. The cart careened forward at a blistering pace of about six miles per hour. Mashing the accelerator and gnashing his teeth, Addison was able to will their speed up two miles per hour, about the pace of an elderly and asthmatic wiener dog. He wondered briefly if he should simply get out and push. The cart rolled serenely toward the Turkish Airlines 747.

Molly pointed frantically. "The plane's already on the runway, Addison. What are we supposed to do? Stick out our thumbs and hitchhike?"

Addison sized up the plane, idling, waiting its turn to take off. "Raj, options?"

"Well, there is one other way to board a plane," Raj said doubtfully. "But even Babatunde Okonjo says not to try it."

Addison peeked over his shoulder at the SUVs zipping between the wheels of parked airplanes, rapidly approaching. "Is it possible, Raj? Because I don't think we have a choice."

"Well, yeah. I mean, it's possible if the plane's not moving."

Eddie stuck his head forward from the back seat, his eyes darting back and forth between Addison and Raj. "I don't like the sound of this. Talk to me, guys."

"It's simple," said Raj. "We just need to climb up the nose wheel."

Addison hazarded another glance at the SUVs, closing in quickly. He gripped the steering wheel tightly and narrowed his eyes. The groaning cart caught up with the aircraft. The whine of the 747's engines grew terrifyingly loud as they passed under the shadow of the enormous tail fin.

With a lurch, the plane taxied ahead, moving into the on-deck position. There was only one plane ahead of it, waiting to be cleared for takeoff. As soon as Addison's cart entered the blast area of the 747's engines, he felt scalded by the gale-force winds.

Addison parked the cart near the front wheel of the plane. Jumping out, he was amazed to see that the wheel was almost as tall as he was.

Raj pointed to a ladder that led right up the back of the giant nose wheel, straight inside the neck of the 747. He and Molly shimmied right up.

Addison scrambled up the first few rungs and paused to scan the runway. The lead SUV jerked to a halt a good fifty feet away, outside the blast area of the plane's engines. Ivan stepped out, followed by three equally over-sized men. All of them drew small plastic canisters. As they stepped closer, Addison realized what the canisters were: pepper spray. He crinkled up his brow. "Why is everything about revenge with this guy?"

Eddie stood at the base of the ladder and seemed unable to climb it.

Addison watched Ivan's team marching closer. There was a hurricane blast of wind as the jet engines warmed up. Addison shouted over the deafening whine. "Eddie, hurry! Once this plane starts moving, our job will not get easier."

Eddie shook his head adamantly. "You've completely lost your mind! Sherlock Holmes, Nancy Drew, and the Hardy Boys could all put their heads together and be completely unable to find it!"

"If I ever lose my mind, Eddie, it will probably be your fault. Now show some hustle!"

Eddie looked back and forth from Ivan to the 747, unable to decide which option he liked worse.

The last plane ahead of the 747 took off down the runway with an earsplitting roar of its engines. The Turkish Airlines flight released its brakes, taxiing into takeoff position.

"Eddie, run!"

Eddie finally made his decision. He sprinted alongside the enormous rolling wheels, his peculiar loping gait like that of a dizzy antelope. The 747 reached the start of the runway and stopped, awaiting the all clear from the control tower. Eddie nearly crashed into the wheel he was chasing. He managed to bolt up the first few rungs of the ladder.

Ivan drew as close to the howling jet engine as he dared. He stared up at Addison's team and laughed.

"Why isn't he stopping us?" called Eddie.

"Because he knows this will kill us!" Molly shouted from above.

Addison climbed up the strut and into the wheel well. The engine whine rose to fever pitch. The brakes released and the plane blasted into motion. The acceleration mashed Addison against the rear wall of the bay. Below him, the asphalt whizzed by in a gray blur.

Eddie was still clinging to the ladder, fear plastered across his face. "This is *horrendous!*"

Raj and Molly seized Eddie's hands and pulled him up inside the wheel well. The well was sheet metal, covered with thick, snaking cables and wiring. Raj found a single door marked AVIONICS BAY. He shouted at the top of his lungs, "Quickly! When the wheel retracts, we'll all be squished!" His voice was drowned out by the screaming wind—he conveyed his meaning more through charades and bulging eyes.

Raj cranked open the avionics bay door and herded everyone through. The tiny room looked like a flying saucer—crowded with the plane's electrical equipment. Heaving with his shoulder, Raj sealed the door shut behind them.

So close to the wheels, the terrified team felt every bump and crack in the runway. With a maddening roar, their world tilted thirty degrees and their stomachs dropped out from under them.

They were airborne.

Chapter Eighteen

Stowaways

ADDISON STEADIED HIMSELF WITH his hands as the airplane packed on speed. The avionics bay was a dizzying tangle of wires and computers, lit only by buttons and switches that flashed like Christmas lights.

Raj found the hatch to the forward cargo bay, spun the wheel lock, and guided the team inside. The hold, illuminated by a single fluorescent bulb, was jammed full of shipping containers that shook with the roar of the engines.

"I liked our last plane ride better," said Eddie, blowing on his hands for warmth.

"It's not so bad." Addison rooted around the shipping containers until he found one marked MEALS. Inside, he discovered hundreds of frozen airplane dinners. He kept hunting until he found the special dinners reserved for first-class passengers—served on silver trays with their own little salt and pepper shakers. Addison grinned at Eddie. "Would you prefer chicken parmesan or beef stroganoff?" He picked up another stack of dinner trays. "There's even a vegetarian option."

Eddie couldn't decide, so he took one of each.

The group climbed over stacks of luggage to a secluded alcove at the back of the cargo hold. Molly built them a nest out of blue airplane pillows and blankets. Raj pulled a hot plate from his pack and set to work warming the frozen dinners. And although Addison did not find any Arnold Palmers, he did find some iced tea that was to his liking.

Addison felt bad taking meals from the airline without paying, so he had everyone leave their last remaining pocket money stacked neatly on top of the food storage container. That settled, they hungrily dug into their meals. Addison decided it was a good time to talk business. "Who's after us?"

Molly, chewing her beef stroganoff, called over the dull hum of the engines. "The Collective."

"And what do we know about them?"

"Ragar and Zubov were in it," said Molly. "They tried to kill us in Peru. Boris was in it—he tried to kill us in

Mongolia. And Ivan is in it—he just tried to kill us all over Paris. All these guys talk about is a prophecy and wanting to kill us."

"And who runs the Collective?" asked Addison.

Molly shrugged. "Ivan?"

Addison shook his head. "Ivan's just a big guy with a good gym membership and a bad barber. Whoever's behind Ivan owns a fleet of cars in London and a fleet in Paris. They can stake out a bank in London, get speedboats into the Paris Catacombs, and fill two different train stations with spies."

Raj piped up. "Did you notice how they drove right past the security gates at Heathrow Airport *and* Charles de Gaulle? They must be extremely well connected."

Eddie bobbed his head in agreement. "Whoever is after us, they are extremely well funded and extremely well organized. If guys like that ran Manhattan, there would be no more potholes and all the trains would run on time."

Molly shared a look with Addison. She knew what he was thinking. "The Shadow," she said quietly.

Addison nodded solemnly. "The Shadow."

The group ate in silence for a moment.

"Well, we're safe for the time being," said Addison, hoping to reassure everyone.

"Are we?" asked Molly. "Ivan saw what flight we boarded. He could be waiting for us when we land."

Addison knew she was right. "Well, he can't outrun a 747. We'll reach Istanbul first. Still, we'll have to be on the lookout."

Molly stopped eating and put down her fork.

"What is it?" asked Addison.

"I just realized," said Molly. "Tonight is Christmas Eve."

The group huddled over their dinners in the dark and freezing cargo bay.

"Happy holidays, guys," said Addison.

······

The sun was rising over the Asian continent when the plane touched down at the Sabiha Gökçen Airport outside Istanbul. Addison felt it was safest to deplane before they taxied to their gate, in case the Collective was waiting for them. So the group sneaked back into the avionics bay, into the wheel well, and crept carefully down the front wheel ladder. Eddie found this was much easier to do when the plane was not speeding down a runway for takeoff.

Addison felt a surge of gratitude when his feet touched the asphalt. He would have kissed the ground, but he didn't want the germs.

His bleary-eyed team had caught only a few hours' sleep on the flight. Addison knew he should feel exhausted. Maybe it was the adrenaline of running for his life, or maybe it was the excitement of finally escaping the Dimpleforth School, but something in him was returning to life. He did not feel tired at all. In fact, he felt as if his brain was finally revving into second gear after being jammed in first for months.

Addison scanned the tarmac for black SUVs and found none. He waved the group across the tarmac and raced up a flight of steps to an employee break room. There, Addison found private restrooms where he insisted everyone spruce themselves up.

"Why?" Eddie asked. "Shouldn't we be getting as far from this airport as possible?"

"Eddie, look at yourself," said Addison firmly. "You look like you spent the night in the cargo hold of a 747."

"I *did* spend the night in the—"

"That is exactly my point," said Addison. "We can't go traipsing around Istanbul looking like fugitives, or everyone will know we're fugitives."

Addison attempted to clean his blazer using wet paper towels from the dispenser. His jacket had been sweated in, rained on, and slept in, and was wrinkling up from all the hard travel. It was a tragedy. He thought about throwing the jacket away entirely, but just couldn't bring himself to do it.

After washing up, Addison's next order of business was to call his uncle Jasper. He found a pay phone in the main terminal, scrubbing it carefully for germs with a napkin from the break room. His uncle Jasper kept an 800 number for emergencies, which meant it was free to call from pay phones—even internationally. Uncle Jasper picked up on the second ring.

"Top of the morning, Uncle. It's me, your favorite Cooke." Addison turned to Molly and winked. "Everyone okay?"

"Addison, I'm thrilled you're alive," chirped Uncle Jasper. "Jennings and I are quite well, thank you."

Addison knew his uncle Jasper kept a safe house somewhere that was so safe, even Addison didn't know where it was. "And the Templar Grand Master?"

"The *gendarmes* took Gaspard to a hospital in Paris. When he stabilizes, T.D. will whisk him to a secure location."

"T.D. is alive?"

"By the skin of her teeth. Addison, I wish you had told me about the safe deposit key. This has put a lot of people in immense danger."

Addison went immediately on the defensive. "How could we have known the key was so important? We don't even know what it is! Maybe if people started telling us things, I wouldn't find myself on the run on the far side of Europe."

Uncle Jasper let out a long sigh. "I withheld information

to protect you. But perhaps it had the opposite effect. I apologize."

"I apologize, too," said Addison. He cupped the phone closer and plugged his free ear to block out the noise of the busy airport. "Right, then. You knew about the bronze tablet? You've seen it before?"

"Oh, yes," said Uncle Jasper.

"So what does the tablet say?"

"I have no idea, and I wouldn't tell you if I did."

"You've never tried to decipher it?" asked Addison, astonished.

"Why should I want to do a thing like that?" Uncle Jasper replied. "Think of all the times your aunt and uncle—rest in peace—were kidnapped. What would have happened if they had valuable information like that rattling around in their heads?"

Addison saw the sense in this.

"I say," said Uncle Jasper, "you aren't in Istanbul by any chance?"

Addison looked around the crowded airport. "As a matter of fact, we are. Why? Are you in the market for a rug?"

"Oh, jolly good. The Grand Master told T.D. you might be heading there. Something about visiting a mosque, of all places. I'm trying to arrange for your extraction. Listen, do you think you can all go a few hours without managing to get yourselves killed?"

Addison shrugged. "I give it even odds."

"There's a fish restaurant on the northwest corner of Sultanahmet Square," said Uncle Jasper. "Serves an amazing fish kebab. Be there by ten a.m. and one of my associates will whisk you home."

"Got it."

"Addison, listen to me. Do not *look* at the tablet, do not even *think* about the tablet. If you want to get out of Istanbul alive, be at that rendezvous no matter what."

The line went dead. Addison slithered out of the phone booth and nodded to his team. "We're going into Istanbul."

Eddie was sitting on the tiled floor of the terminal, his back against the wall, trying to nab a few winks of sleep. "Whatever is there, I'm not interested."

Addison had known Eddie for many years, and he knew all the levers that moved him. He knew, for instance, that Eddie had spent so much time hanging out in the kitchen of Restaurant Anatolia on West 86th Street that he had picked up Turkish. He cleared his throat. "Eddie, our rendezvous is a kebab restaurant."

Eddie was on his feet like he'd been electrocuted. "How soon can we get there?"

Chapter Nineteen

Istanbul

ISTANBUL WAS AN HOUR'S drive from the airport. The team had no cab money and no Métro cards, but they *did* have Eddie. And as luck would have it, Addison found Eddie a grand piano roped off in the main concourse. "Eddie, time to earn our bus fare," he declared.

Eddie sat down at the piano bench and regarded the throngs of travelers weaving past. "Are you sure we should be drawing attention to ourselves?"

"It's called hiding in plain sight," said Addison. He noticed Eddie's hands shaking and remembered Eddie's stage fright. He spoke gently. "The faster you play, the faster we can get out of here. Think of the kebabs, Eddie."

The thought of swallowing kebabs helped Eddie

swallow his stage fright. He began to play. Reluctantly at first, and then with growing confidence. A little Chopin, a little Mozart, and Eddie had earned enough Turkish *lira* to pay their bus fare to Istanbul. Soon, Eddie was reveling in the attention from the crowd. He wanted to get in a solid hour of piano practice, but Addison spotted two men in dark glasses across the concourse, whom Addison did not take to be Mozart lovers. Addison shut the piano lid, narrowly missing Eddie's fingers. The group skedaddled.

······

They took the public bus to Taksim Square and transferred to a tramway so crammed with people that Addison found himself longing wistfully for the 747 cargo hold. They swept past hundreds of fishermen lining the Galata Bridge spanning the Golden Horn of Istanbul. Raj checked the windows the whole way, eyeing the streets for SUVs. Soon, they passed the impregnable walls of Topkapi Palace, the opulent home of the Ottoman sultans, and deboarded the tram at Sultanahmet Square.

Turkish people bustled in all directions. Some wore dark robes with colorful turbans; some wore business suits and toted briefcases. To the west stood the fabled spice markets of the Grand Bazaar. To the north lay the horse racetracks built by the ancient Romans. And before them sat the Hagia Sophia—a magnificent domed mosque flanked by four towering spires of minarets.

Addison looked up from his *Fiddleton's Atlas* and gazed in admiration at the sparkling city. "Roland J. Fiddleton— explorer, chess master, big game tracker, and cheese connoisseur—says Istanbul is one of the cultural meccas of the world!"

"Great," said Molly. "Another famous city Addison can destroy. Are there any other towns still standing? How about Salzburg? Or Milan? How about Seville, in Spain? I love flamingo music."

"It's *flamenco* music, Mo. Flamingos don't make music."

Addison led the group to the northwest corner of the cobblestone square and found Uncle Jasper's rendez-vous. It was a small seafood restaurant and bar marked by a sign saying DRINK AND EAT FISH. Addison wondered if commas were optional in Istanbul.

They took seats facing the square where Raj could scan the crowds for any suspicious men in dark glasses. The proprietor was so impressed when Eddie ordered in fluent Turkish that he gave them their first plate of kebabs for free. Eddie was passionate about Turkish food with an ardor that bordered on criminal insanity. He had often stopped to get kebabs on his way to go get kebabs. Eddie shocked everyone by declaring the kebabs better than the kebabs at Restaurant Anatolia in Manhattan.

When the falafels arrived, Eddie was more discerning. He picked one out of his pita bread and held it aloft. "This," he declared, "is an awful falafel." Addison's group slowly nodded, but Eddie was not through. "It is so awful, it should be unlawful." He plunked it down on his plate with disgust. "It is an awful unlawful falafel."

They feasted on fish shish kebabs until they used up nearly all of Eddie's piano-busking money. For dessert, Addison thought about buying a persimmon, but felt too parsimonious.

Instead, he consulted one of the three fake Rolexes on his left wrist. "Our rendezvous isn't for another two hours." He drummed his fingers on the red-checkered tablecloth. The mystery of the bronze tablet was scratching away inside Addison's brain like a convict trying to escape. He desperately wanted to know what the tablet was and why the Collective needed it so badly. "This will never end," he declared. "If the Collective can track us to Blandfordshire Bank, they can track us home to my uncle's house. They can track us around the world forever. Besides, we can't just spend hours lounging around this kebab restaurant like sitting ducks."

"Speak for yourself," said Eddie, leaning back in his chair and rubbing his belly contentedly.

Addison folded his arms and creased his brow in thought. "The Templar Grand Master said he saw the tablet's runes inside the most beautiful mosque in Istanbul."

"How many mosques are in Istanbul?" asked Molly.

Addison already knew the answer. "According to Mr. Fiddleton, over three thousand." Addison knew that his brain was somehow connected to his feet—he did his best thinking while pacing. He stood and circled the table, lips pursed in concentration, hands clasped behind his back. "The thing I don't get is, the ancient Templars were Christian knights. So why would their runes be found in a Turkish mosque?" Addison frowned and took another lap. "I wish we had a clue, or even some sort of sign."

His thoughts were interrupted by a deafening roar from the Hagia Sophia across the square. Electronic speakers in its four minarets began blasting the Muslim call to prayer. It was a man's voice, singing an ancient and mournful melody. The beautiful song echoed across the alleys and courtyards of historic Istanbul. It rang up and down the crowded streets, overpowering the hacking motorbikes, honking horns, and hawking street venders.

Addison thumbed through *Fiddleton's Atlas* and smacked his face with his palm. "Hagia Sophia was a church for a thousand years before it was ever a mosque!"

Eddie tipped his chair back on two legs and frowned up at Addison. "So?"

"So in the time of the Knights Templar, the Hagia Sophia was a church. We have to investigate the runes!" Addison stared at the skeptical faces of his team. "Look, I know I'm going out on a limb here—"

"Addison," said Molly, "you've gone so far out on the limb, it's snapped."

"Molly, stick to me like suntan lotion. Stick to me like a vinyl car seat on a hot day—"

Molly was not interested in Addison's explanations. "Uncle Jasper gave us specific instructions to sit tight and not get into trouble."

Addison threw his hands up in exasperation. "We didn't fly all the way to Istanbul in a cargo hold so we could sit around in a restaurant eating fish kebabs!"

"I did," said Eddie.

"I'm going to the mosque to find the runes." Addison turned to leave the restaurant.

Molly called after him. "Addison, you're being reckless!"

"I am the opposite of reckless! I am reckful! These are calculated risks." Addison pointed to Molly's satchel, weighed down by the heavy bronze tablet. "If we're going to risk our lives protecting that thing from the Collective, we have a right to know what it is."

Addison marched confidently across the square toward the mosque, not even turning to see if his team would follow. He believed that like him, they would be unable to resist the lure of an ancient mystery. For the first time in months, he was beginning to feel like himself again.

······

Addison gazed up at the soaring arches of the Hagia Sophia and was pleased to hear the footfalls of his friends catching up behind him. The good news was that the Hagia Sophia was now a museum, so anyone could get inside. The bad news was that *everyone* wanted to get inside. A milling herd of tourists stood in line to buy tickets.

"This line must be an hour long," said Eddie.

"And we're supposed to keep a low profile," said Raj, his eyes scoping the crowd for dark-suited Russians.

"And each ticket is forty Turkish *lira*," said Molly, reading the sign by the entrance. "That's one hundred sixty *lira* for all of us."

Addison detested lines the way a claustrophobe detests a crowded elevator. He knew that cattle are made to wait in lines on their way into the slaughterhouse and lemmings form lines when they leap off of Norwegian cliffs. But Addison was neither cattle nor lemming, and he did not believe the precious gift of life should be wasted standing in lines. Particularly when one is the target of a manhunt. "We have neither one hour nor one hundred sixty *lira*," he declared.

"Back door?" asked Raj.

Addison nodded and was already on his way.

The group circled around to the back of the mosque and found the rear exit. Addison stooped to the pavement and collected four used ticket stubs that hadn't quite made their way into the nearest trash can. He dealt the ticket stubs out to his team and strode confidently up to the exit door. They were almost inside before a security guard flattened his hand against Addison's chest, stopping him in his tracks.

The guard grumbled something in Turkish.

"He says we can only enter through the front door," Eddie translated.

"It's okay," Addison said to the guard. "We have our ticket stubs."

Addison, Molly, Eddie, and Raj all held up their torn ticket stubs and smiled innocently.

The guard grunted something else in Turkish.

"He says this is not a movie theater," Eddie translated. "You can't go back through the exit after you've left."

"Front door," said the guard in accented English.

"We've already been through the front door," Addison explained. "We just left something inside and need to run back in for a sec."

The guard listened to Eddie's translation and firmly shook his head no.

The guard was a strong silent type, Addison could tell, with a mind unclouded by thoughts.

"Go!" the guard said, pointing away.

Eddie whispered to Addison, "Maybe we should just leave. Your uncle told us not to get into any trouble."

Addison stood his ground. Getting inside was now a matter of principle. "Eddie, we are going inside, and this guard is going to politely hold the door for us while we do it."

Eddie sighed. He knew there was no turning back now.

Addison smiled at the guard and spoke in his most let's-just-be-reasonable voice. "We promised our parents we would take a picture inside the Hagia Sophia, and we forgot. We just need to duck in for a minute." It was a bit thin, Addison thought. But what sort of monster would say no to such a request?

"No," said the guard.

"Five minutes," said Addison. "We promise we won't enjoy anything in your museum."

The man shook his head.

"The Hagia Sophia gets one million visitors a year," said Addison. "The world will keep spinning if you let four middle-schoolers inside for five minutes."

"Go!" said the guard again, gesturing east, perhaps toward Asia.

Addison was glad the guard was rude. It made him feel less guilty about what he had to do next. "All right. My parents would kill me if they knew I was doing this . . ." He rolled up his sleeve, revealing a glittering gold Rolex.

For the first time, Addison saw a flicker of life behind the guard's granite eyes. Addison unclasped the Rolex and handed it to the man. "My father's Rolex. If we're not back outside in five minutes, keep it."

The guard weighed the watch in his palm. He held it to his ear and listened to it tick. He looked around furtively for any witnesses. Then, without a word, he pulled open the rear door for Addison's team and waved them inside.

"Notice," said Addison, with an arm around Eddie's shoulder, "how he politely holds the door for us."

Chapter Twenty

The Secret Rune

ADDISON STOOD ON THE tiled floor of the spectacular structure. Light flooded in through dozens of windows, illuminating the massive dome that had stood for millennia. Addison wondered how many caliphs, Crusaders, and czars had stood on this floor gazing upward in wonder.

Molly reached out her hand and shut Addison's jaw. "I know staring at the ceiling is your idea of a good time, but remember, the guard wants us out in five minutes."

"The guard wants us to take longer than five minutes," said Addison, "so he can keep the Rolex."

"Fine," said Molly. "But our rendezvous is at ten o'clock and we can't stand here forever. The Collective knew enough to ambush us in London and ambush us in Paris, and they can ambush us here, too." She handed him her satchel. "But if you really want to sightsee, then *you* can lug around this heavy bronze block for a while."

Addison took the satchel from Molly, unbuttoned the flap, and carefully nudged the bronze tablet out a few inches. "This is the rune," he said excitedly, pointing to the image of a carved sword protecting a scroll. "Gaspard Gagnon said he's seen this rune in the most beautiful mosque in Istanbul. We'll just take a quick look around for it and then retreat. I promise."

Molly sighed. She scanned the atrium for any sign of the rune. Her eyes widened and she gasped, pointing.

"You found it already?" Addison asked.

"No!" Molly whispered fiercely. "It's Ivan!"

Addison spun to face the entrance. Ivan the Terrible, his terrible mop of hair, and his terrible gang of guards were sauntering into the mosque. With a signal from Ivan, the Collective members fanned out. Addison ducked low, hoping to blend into the crowd. "Guys, abort!"

He scurried toward the exit until he spotted men in dark suits and glasses covering the door. He wheeled toward an arched stairway leading down to the basement. "Hurry. Before they spot us."

"Look!" cried Raj. He pointed to the ancient capstone of the stairwell archway. There, worn and faded, was the faint figure of the carved rune.

Molly was already halfway down the staircase and pointing to a second archway below. "There's another one down here!"

"Follow them!" said Addison. "Quickly!"

The stairs reached a landing and took a hard right turn. Addison's team raced to the bottom and found the basement level sealed behind a heavy iron gate.

Eddie clutched the bars. "Why's it locked off?"

Addison drew his penlight and shone it through the bars. The basement area was dank, dark, and crumbling. "Probably isn't very safe. I mean, the masonry's fifteen hundred years old. They can't let tourists bumble around in there."

"Look," said Molly, who had the keenest eyes. She pointed through the bars to a basement pillar in the gloom. "Another rune."

Addison lit it up with his flashlight. "We have to get in there." He examined the thick padlock protecting the iron gate. "Eddie, you're up."

Eddie peered through bars into the menacing darkness and gritted his teeth. "Addison, just tell me right now. Are there graves in there?"

"What am I, a psychic? I've never been here before."

Eddie put his foot down. "I know rooting around in skeleton-infested basements is your great passion in life. But I would rather listen to polka music while pouring boiling hot Drano in my nostrils than subject myself to another one of your catacombs."

"Eddie, your voice is at a seven and I need you at a two. Also," Addison added, as gently as he could, "your personality is at an eleven and I need it at a three." He turned to the rest of his team. "Raj, Molly, you're our lookouts."

Raj retreated to the top of the stairway. Molly stayed at the nearest landing so she could relay his messages.

Eddie lay on his back underneath the heavy padlock, staring up at it. He mulled it over. Or, more accurately, he mulled it under. He mulled it under so long, he nearly molded over. After a period of time that Addison took to be several centuries, Eddie produced a lock pick from his pocket, made a few tentative pokes, and returned to mulling.

Addison's patience was fraying at the seams. "Eddie, could you do that a bit more slowly?"

Eddie glared at him. "When Michelangelo was painting the Sistine Chapel, did people stand around checking their Rolexes?"

Before Addison could reply, he heard the light hoot of a barn owl. He looked up the stairs in confusion.

Molly cupped her hands and whispered down from the landing. "It's Raj—he's seen something."

"Ask him what a live owl would be doing in a muscum," said Addison. "I mean, owls are nocturnal, right?"

Molly relayed this up the stairs to Raj. A few seconds later, she whispered back his answer. "He says it's not his fault we didn't come up with a prearranged signal and that you should be more concerned with the fact that Ivan's heading in this direction."

Addison fumed. "How is Ivan getting his information? How is he always right on our tail?"

Molly relayed these questions up to Raj, paused, and then turned back to Addison. "He wants to know if you're being rhetorical."

"Ask him what Ivan's doing!"

Molly communicated this and waited for Raj's answer. "Raj says Ivan's team is fanning across the entire main floor and zeroing in on this stairway."

"The Right Honorable Sir Alec Douglas-Home, First Lord of the Treasury!" Addison crushed his fist in his palm. He stared hard at Eddie, who was still fiddling with the lock. "Eddie, I don't mean to put more pressure on you . . ."

"This lock is old and Turkish, and I haven't got the right tools for it!" Eddie sputtered.

Addison heard the agitated calls of an extremely panicked barn owl.

Molly called from the stairway. "Addison, they're heading straight for us!"

Addison turned back to Eddie. "How's the painting going, Michelangelo?"

Eddie twisted and strained with his picks, his veins standing out in his temples. "I think it's rusted shut!"

Addison turned from the iron bars, searching for options in the dead-end hallway. He could see why a situation like this was called a dead end: he was about to be dead and meet his end.

Molly flew down the stairs, Raj at her heels. "They're coming, Addison!"

••••••

Addison looked left and right, desperate for options. Out of ideas, he even looked up and down. It was this last move that gave him an idea. He pointed to an iron drainage grate set in the flagstone floor. "Eddie, pick this open instead."

Eddie came up with a flathead and set to work on the screws.

Addison flicked out his butterfly knife. Raj pulled open his Swiss Army knife. Together they worked all four screws loose.

Footsteps echoed down the stone staircase above.

Molly hopped nervously from foot to foot. "Hurry!"

Straining together, they hoisted up the drainage grate, scraping it to one side.

"Addison, how many sewers are you going to put me in on this trip?" asked Eddie.

"As many as it takes. Now go!"

Molly crawled in first. One by one, they dropped down into the stone shaft after her. Inside, Raj and Addison managed to pull the grate over their heads just as Ivan's men rounded the staircase landing.

Addison's team retreated into the crosshatched shadows of the sewer as the Collective marched right over their heads. They listened breathlessly as men angrily rattled the locked iron gate. A few angry words were barked in Russian. Nearly all the men retreated back up the stone stairs with heavy, plodding footsteps. A shadow revealed a single guard left behind.

"They've gone to get keys," Addison whispered. "They'll be back."

"So are we stuck here?" asked Eddie, his voice quavering in the darkness.

Addison considered his options. He realized he could feel a slight draft wafting through the cramped passageway. He folded his body like origami and maneuvered past Molly. "Guys, this shaft keeps going! I think we can use it to get into the locked basement!"

"Quit pulling my leg," Molly whispered.

"I'm telling the truth!" Addison insisted.

"No, you're literally pulling my leg."

They crawled along the tiny shaft until they reached an open grate that fed them into the locked basement. Their only source of light was the iron gate, behind which they could still see the shadow of the patrolling Russian guard.

Molly pointed to another rune up ahead. It adorned a rotting stairway leading down into the belly of the earth. Addison cupped a hand over his pen flashlight to dull the beam. The group crept silently down the steps.

At the bottom stood a heavy wooden door, gray with the dust of the centuries. Addison tried the handle and was not surprised to find it locked tight.

"Should I pick it?" Eddie whispered.

Addison frowned. "I wish there was a faster way. The Collective could find their way in here any minute."

"I know how to break down a door!" Raj spoke excitedly, his eyes gleaming in the dark. "I read about it in *Mission: Survival III* by Babatunde Okonjo. The trick is to kick it exactly where the lock meets the doorjamb." He pointed to the exact spot on the ancient door.

"Well, here's the kicker," said Addison. He pointed to Molly.

She grinned, took a running start, and leveled a brutal sidekick at the ancient door. It splintered away from the door frame, gaping open like a broken jaw.

Addison grimaced at the loud noise. They needed to move fast now. He pushed open the crumpled door and stepped into darkness.

Chapter Twenty-One

The Hidden Headquarters

ADDISON ENTERED THE SECRET basement. It was quiet down here, the noises of the crowded mosque above fading down to silence. He ducked the low foundation stones and picked his way through the rubble of Roman bricks.

Raj cranked on his military-grade flashlight, the glare temporarily blinding. "Anyone see another rune?"

"I can't see anything," said Eddie, covering his eyes from the brightness.

Raj panned his light slowly over the cracked and gutted stones.

"There!" said Addison, his eyes glittering in the flashlight's aura. He dropped to his hands and knees to scramble through a crack in the rocks—a broken archway.

The group followed him into a lost part of the ancient church—a long-forgotten crypt. The ceiling here was only four feet high, the ground littered with stone tombs.

"I knew it!" said Eddie. "I knew you couldn't go one day without visiting graves. Addison, you're like a truffle-sniffing pig, except instead of finding mushrooms, you find dead people!"

"Eddie, it's not as if I wake up every morning and say to myself, 'Good morning, Addison! How can we spend today in an underground graveyard?' Underground grave-yards are just a thing that happens to me!"

"Underground graveyards don't just 'happen to you,' Addison. They're not like sneezes." Eddie shook his head. "I have plenty of friends who've managed to go their whole lives without ending up in an underground graveyard."

"Guys, take a look at this." Molly wiped dust from the lid of a granite tomb. Carved on the surface was a shield emblazoned with a crest. Below it was written two words: *Tutor Thesauri.* "Do you realize what this means?" said Molly.

Addison surveyed the surrounding tombs, all marked with the same two words. When he spoke, his voice was hushed with awe. "These men were all Templar Knights."

Raj was already poking around in a far corner of the room where the ceiling dropped down to a mere three feet. "Over here! I found the next rune."

The group rushed to join Raj. He pointed with his flashlight. The sword-and-scroll rune was carved on the top of a narrow coffin.

Addison nodded. Gravely. "We have to open it."

Eddie spread his arms in disbelief and let them collapse at his sides.

Raj gripped the lid of the coffin and hoisted it open. It yawned with spiderwebs as thick as yarn. Addison aimed his penlight into the tomb, preparing for whatever grim horror lay inside.

Instead, he saw a set of stairs leading down into the gloom. From the musty, dusty air, he knew this secret passage had not been explored for centuries.

"Ladies first," said Molly, taking the big flashlight from Raj and climbing into the coffin. She disappeared down into the earth.

•••••••

Addison and Eddie followed Molly down the steep, slippery steps. Raj went last, which he insisted on calling "rear guard."

The stairway led to a narrow shaft carved through the limestone bedrock. Addison ducked the rusted remains of a portcullis. Raj pointed out slots in the stone for hurling rocks down on intruders. At last the hallway opened into a circular room.

Raj swept the space with his high-powered flashlight. They quickly explored several small side rooms. Sleeping chambers with rotting oak planks for beds. A dining room with a single ash slab for a table. The group entered a larger room with the familiar words *"Tutor Thesauri"* etched in stone along one wall. Molly recognized the balance beam, the sword rack, and the practice dummies pricked full of stab wounds. "It's just like Uncle Jasper's training room!" she exclaimed.

Addison nodded with excitement. "This must have been a Templar headquarters."

The circular main room was decorated with colorful mosaics. Addison recognized images of famous castles and pyramids and even the lost city of Atlantis. Molly pointed to the Cooke family crest carved over a mosaic in the corner. The mosaic depicted a king on a throne with a crown and scepter and surrounded by piles of gold.

"Who is that?" asked Raj.

Addison had learned a smattering of ancient history at the Dimpleforth School. He recognized the king's noble bearing and his ivory throne adorned with golden lions. "King Solomon. He was the most powerful king of Israel and one of the richest people in history. But the ancient

Hebrews believed he lost his faith and was punished from above. His empire split apart. His son was defeated by Egyptians. Everything Solomon built was lost."

Eddie's ears had pricked up at the mention of wealth. "How'd he get so rich?"

Addison was pleased to realize he knew the answer. Perhaps his time at Dimpleforth hadn't been a total loss. "The fabled copper mines of Solomon in the deserts of southern Israel. Copper may not sound like much, but it makes bronze. And when you live in the Bronze Age, and all your tools and weapons are bronze, making bronze is a big deal." He rapped his knuckles against the bronze tablet in Molly's satchel for emphasis.

"Did Solomon leave a treasure?" asked Eddie hopefully.

"Did he ever. Solomon was so powerful, the kings of Arabia paid him a tribute of forty thousand pounds of gold every year. The spice merchants paid him with frankincense and myrrh. People believe Solomon's wealth exceeded all the kings of all the world. But the greatest part of his treasure was called the Ring of Destiny."

Addison stepped closer to the mosaic. He pointed to the dazzling ring on King Solomon's finger that glittered and danced in the rays of the flashlight. "The ancients believed it was forged in heaven. It was said to give King Solomon power over angels and demons. With this ring he worked wonders from his throne. He could make fire rain down from the heavens or waters surge up from the ground. The ring is one of the greatest missing treasures in history."

"Addison, there's a ring on our tablet, as well . . ." Molly pulled the bronze tablet from her satchel and held it up to Raj's flashlight. The group stared down at the strange circular symbol on the front of the tablet. A six-pointed star was inscribed inside.

Addison gazed up at the ancient mosaic and nodded. "I guess this bronze tablet is somehow connected"—he pointed from the strange bronze circle to the ring on Solomon's finger—"to the Ring of Destiny."

Addison's thoughts snapped into place like Lego pieces. He paced in a tight circle like an excited Labrador who knew he was getting a walk. "Maybe it's some sort of treasure map. King Solomon's Temple was destroyed by King Nebuchadnezzar the Second of Babylon. Solomon's treasure was hidden in the desert by his last remaining priests. It's been lost for ages."

"So how are we supposed to find it?" asked Raj eagerly. In his enthusiasm, he somehow managed to drop his military-grade flashlight on the floor. The impact emitted a metallic clang. Raj retrieved his flashlight and aimed it at the ground. "Um, guys? I think the floor is gold."

Addison knelt down and swept the dirty floor with his palm. "Not gold, bronze. Like the tablet." He took a deep breath and blew away a cloud of dust. "There's something written here!" The group scraped dirt from the bronze-tiled floor with their hands and shoes.

Addison took a few steps back and stared at the floor until all of its carved shapes and lines began to come together in his mind. "It's a map of the Crusades. These are the Holy Lands." He pointed excitedly. "This blob is ancient Syria. And these are the cedar forests of Lebanon! And this is where Richard the Lionheart fought Saladin at the Battle of Arsuf."

A few bronze tiles were missing from the map. Molly waved Addison over to a rectangular-shaped hole. "Addison, look! I think our tablet fits here!"

Addison squeezed the bronze tablet into the slot. It fit perfectly. Each squiggly line on its surface made sense now, joining up with the rivers and mountains of the map.

He pointed to the various mosaics adorning the room. "The treasure of Priam, the Valley of the Kings, the Hanging Gardens of Babylon. Guys, this room is a map of treasures the *Tutores Thesauri* found. Each of these missing tiles must point to a treasure. And each Templar family guards a different treasure."

"So, the Cookes' tablet shows the way to the Ring of Destiny . . ." Molly pointed to it on the floor. "And the ring is hidden in this square of the map."

Addison drew out his copy of *Fiddleton's Atlas* faster

than an Old West gunslinger. He flipped to a map of the Middle East and compared it with the bronze floor map. "If we're right, Solomon's ring is somewhere near Aqaba on the Red Sea."

"That's a big area," said Molly. "How do we narrow it down?"

Addison pulled the bronze tablet out of its slot and studied the ring-shaped pattern on its surface. "I don't know yet. There's more to this puzzle." He knew they couldn't lug the entire bronze floor with them, so he set to work copying the giant map into his notebook. He focused all his concentration on the page, sketching as quickly as possible.

That is how he completely missed hearing Ivan the Terrible step into the chamber . . .

Chapter Twenty-Two

Ivan the Absolute Worst

IVAN AND HIS MEN poured in quickly and silently. Raj barely managed half a barn owl hoot before they completely filled the room.

Once again, Addison was struck by Ivan's awful appearance. He looked like he had gotten his hair cut in an accident with a lawn mower. "You look like you got your hair cut in an accident with a lawn mower," said Addison.

Ivan surprised Addison by turning even uglier. The man's mouth wriggled into what could loosely be described as a smirk. "I'm going to kill you for what you did to my brother. And then I will have the tablet. And soon, the ring of Solomon."

"What do you need it for?" asked Molly. "I mean, why is Solomon's ring more important than his gold? Wouldn't you rather have the money?"

Ivan's oily eyes slithered over Molly. "We need it because of the prophecy."

"Okay, about this prophecy," Addison began. "We have a number of questions."

Ivan held up his hand. "All you do is talk, Addison Cooke. Talk, talk, talk. The Shadow is on his way. You can talk to him."

"*The* Shadow?" asked Addison, trying to keep the tremble out of his voice.

Ivan seemed to smell Addison's fear. His leer widened. Calling it a grin would be an insult to grins everywhere. His teeth looked like half-chewed Chiclets. "Vrolok Malazar wants to see you . . . personally."

Addison wondered why the room suddenly felt ten degrees colder. "I'm not sure I can squeeze him in on such short notice—I'm completely booked up." His eyes darted to the corners, searching for an escape. "Rain check?"

"You're not getting away. Malazar is a genius. He is a billionaire. He has operatives on every continent. And he runs the Collective. It will go easier for you if you just give up."

For a moment, Addison honestly considered it. His thoughts raced up and down the hallways of his mind for any hint of a plan; they came up empty.

Ivan pulled his hands from his pockets. They were gripping push daggers. Six-inch knives glittered from between the fingers of each of his clenched fists.

Addison blanched. Things just kept getting worse. "Are you as good with knives as your brother Zubov?"

"Who do you think taught him?" Ivan twirled the daggers in his hands with astonishing skill.

Addison swallowed hard. This would be like fighting a jaguar. He flicked out the butterfly knife he had taken from Ivan's brother in South America and assumed his fighting stance. He had learned a thing or two from Tony Chin, the Hong Kong triad whom Addison counted as a friend. And he had practiced knife drills regularly with Uncle Jasper. But when he raised his arms to square off with Ivan, he found he was suddenly drenched with nervous sweat. The shoulder pads in his blazer bunched up, and the tailored arms restricted his reach. It was too late to strip off the jacket. For the first time in his life, Addison found he was beginning to regret a fashion choice.

Ivan struck with an adder's speed.

Addison parried with his butterfly knife, sparks flaring in the dark room. He had been practicing for months, but Ivan had been practicing for years. Addison had learned a few tricks with his knife, but he knew that his best trick by far was running away. "Guys, a little help?"

Ivan advanced, backing Addison up against a wall.

"I have just the thing," said Raj excitedly. He grabbed a purple smoke ball from his pocket and held it high in the air. It was the size of a tennis ball and about half as intimidating. He turned to Ivan and laughed jauntily. "We'll be seeing you later, Ivan!"

Raj pulled the fuse and threw the purple smoke ball at the ground.

It lay there.

Other than that, nothing much happened.

Ivan looked up at Raj, confused.

A single bead of sweat broke out on Raj's forehead. He produced another purple smoke ball from the pocket of his army pants. "*Adios*, Ivan!" Raj yanked the fuse and hurled the new smoke ball at the ground. It lay there next to the first one, like two eggs in a robin's nest. They produced about as much smoke as two robin's eggs; that is to say, none.

Nothing continued to happen.

Ivan scratched his head with the point of one of his knives.

Raj found he was suddenly drenched in sweat like Addison. He decided to go for broke. He took a deep lungful of air and shouted his war cry, "*Bhandaaari!*" With both hands, Raj pulled all of the smoke balls from his pockets, yanked out the fuses with his teeth, and flung them on the ground.

They lay there. A few seconds ticked by. The earth blithely rotated on its axis. Other than that, exactly nothing happened.

Addison frowned. "Raj, I hope you saved the receipts for those. You may want your money back."

Before Raj could respond, the room exploded in a massive mushroom cloud of purple smoke.

•••••••

Addison's brain felt like a cracked egg. His ears popped and popped again. He coughed and gagged purple clouds of smoke in a purple sea. His entire world was purple. He couldn't see his purple hand in front of his purple face. It was like waking up inside of a grape.

Through the purple mist he could hear Ivan's men shouting and cursing in Russian.

Addison bent low and whispered in the direction he had last seen Molly, Eddie, and Raj. "Dining room! Quickly!"

He groped and fumbled his way through the purple veils until he crashed into the rotten remains of the dining table. He blinked purple smoke from his eyes and saw three purple shapes about the size of Molly, Eddie, and Raj.

"Where do we go?" croaked the gangly Eddie-shaped purple blob.

"Back door."

"How do you know there is a back door?"

"The Templars were soldiers," Addison whispered. "Nobody builds a fortress without a hidden rear exit. They wouldn't let themselves get trapped down here."

Addison—hands splayed before him like an avenging mummy—fumbled through the headquarters' kitchen and into a storage area, filled with decayed sacks and rotted shelves of broken clay jars. The purple smoke was clearer here. He frantically lifted jars and pressed on rocks in the mortared wall, searching for any kind of hidden lever or pulley.

Ivan's men screamed like maniacs, hunting for Cookes from room to room.

Raj shook Addison by the shoulder. "The smoke's drifting. There's fresh air this way!"

Everyone followed Raj into a bathroom. It was little more than a stone bench with a hole in it. Above the bench was a stone shaft, worn by centuries, feeding fresh air and a trickle of water into the bathroom. Addison peered up the shaft and spotted footholds carved in the slanted rock.

Molly was aghast. "The Templars' escape was by climbing on top of the toilet?"

Ivan's men crashed their way through the dining room and into the kitchen.

"Good enough for me," said Addison. He scrambled onto the toilet and up the narrow water shaft, his dress shoes sliding on the slick stone.

･･･････

The group climbed up the cramped chute. Russian voices echoing behind them sounded nightmarish in the tiny space.

"Addison, this is *horrendous!*" Eddie whispered. "If I wanted to be hunted by madmen in a haunted catacomb, I would have stayed in Paris."

"I don't know why you're so disgruntled," said Addison. "You should be happy to be alive. Imagine how annoyed you'd be if you were dead."

"For your information, I am not disgruntled—I am perfectly gruntled!" Eddie panted, huffing along on his hands and knees. "I am just pointing out that there are better ways to spend a winter vacation. That's my two cents."

"Eddie, your two cents is not even worth one cent. You've gotten to see London, Paris, and Istanbul—for *free.*"

Addison sensed a fresh breeze ahead. The shaft opened into a vast underground room the size of a football stadium. He climbed out of the narrow opening and splashed down into four feet of water. It was cold, but not as cold as the Paris sewer, and he was pleased to see the purple dye washing out of his clothes. He swam through the pool of water, his team crashing in behind him. They paddled past thick marble pillars and a dry wooden walkway.

"Where are we?" asked Raj.

"A Roman cistern," said Addison. "They're for storing water in case the city's under siege. The ancient Romans built hundreds underneath Istanbul."

"It's gigantic," said Molly.

It was one of the most beautiful places Addison had ever seen. A few torches reflected their flickering glow in the peaceful pools of water. The vast, shadowy room possessed the quiet, ageless calm of the inside of an Egyptian pyramid. The water went on for acres, supported by hundreds of massive marble columns.

Eddie split the silence with a yelp and splashed to catch up with the group.

"What's the matter?" Addison asked.

Eddie searched the water behind him. "I was just swimming over here and something came along and nudged me."

"Where?"

"On the *tuchas*."

"No, where in the water?"

"By that wooden walkway," said Eddie. "Scared me half to death. Then it happened a second time."

Molly frowned. "Eddie, if you were scared half to death twice, you'd be all-the-way dead." Before she could expand on this line of reasoning, she let out a yelp as well.

Addison shone his penlight at the water and tried to peer through the reflected glare. The shadow of an enormous fish wriggled past. "Giant koi," he said. "We'll live."

Russian voices sounded from the tunnel.

"Where do we hide?" Raj asked.

Addison took a calming breath. "They're going to fan out and search this whole place. There's only one spot they won't find us."

"Okay, I'll bite," said Eddie. "Where?"

"Under their feet."

Addison turned around and swam back toward the wooden walkway built in the pool of water. He guided the team underneath the wooden beams.

The Russian voices grew louder.

"Are you sure about this?" whispered Molly, treading water under the walkway.

"The trick to hiding in water," said Raj, "is holding your breath. I can hold my breath for nearly a minute and a half."

"We know, Raj," said Molly. "But that doesn't help the rest of us."

"I prefer to keep breathing," said Eddie, his voice rising. "It's a habit of mine."

"Eddie, could you keep it down?" Addison whispered. "Somewhere there are some construction workers trying to jackhammer concrete, and they can't hear themselves think."

Ivan and his team emerged from the shaft and splashed down into the water just a few feet away. Addison lowered himself into the water all the way up to his eyes and ears. He watched the men scramble up onto the wooden walkway and scan the cathedral-sized space. They spoke in hushed voices.

Addison whispered to Eddie. "I want to know what they're saying. Come with me—you have the best ears."

Eddie stared at him openmouthed. "Are you trying to kill me?"

"Not yet." Addison tugged Eddie by the shoulder, and they drifted soundlessly through the water. Stealth training was a key part of Addison's drills with Uncle Jasper. His uncle often tasked him with sneaking across the entire manor house undetected. This was easier said than done in a house as old and creaky as Runnymede. At first Addison had suspected that Uncle Jasper simply wanted more peace and quiet while he was in his study, but eventually, Addison saw the value in learning stealth. People are good at spotting movement, so the key to stealth is moving slowly and patiently.

He and Eddie lapped quietly through the water, gazing

up through the slats in the wooden walkway. Soon, Ivan was directly overhead, growling in Russian. Addison then heard a new voice that froze the breath in his lungs.

The man's voice was a harsh, raspy whisper, as if he had once spent a full night screaming and his throat had scarred and never recovered. Addison struggled to catch sight of the man's face through the floorboards, but could only glimpse the pale, burn-scarred skin on the back of his neck below a wide-brimmed hat. Still, Addison knew who the mysterious figure must be. It was the man called Malazar . . . *The Shadow*.

Addison listened intently to the Russian voices. It chilled him to know he was only three feet away from the man who had ordered the deaths of his aunt Delia and uncle Nigel. He quietly drew his notebook from his jacket pocket. It was soaked through, but he found a corner that was still dry. Pencil poised, he jotted down a word that Malazar mentioned repeatedly: *"Cantoo."*

Eddie listened carefully as well. He had a natural ear for languages. He took the pencil from Addison's grip and added a second repeated word to the margin of Addison's notebook. *"Politsiya."*

Addison suspected he knew what the second word meant. His fears were confirmed when the Turkish police arrived at the far entrance of the cistern, sealing off any escape.

Malazar waved to the police officers and strolled down the wooden walkway to greet them. Ivan and his men spread out across adjoining walkways, searching the dark reaches of the reservoir.

Addison listened to their overhead footfalls growing quieter, and beckoned to his team. Not even daring to whisper, he mouthed the words, *Now's our chance to escape.*

He knew the vast cistern must be fed by an aqueduct. He waded north, following the gently rippling current to its source. In the farthest corner of the reservoir, he scrambled up a slimy, moss-covered slope. Hip-deep in the rushing stream of water, he struggled against the rising rapids, his team behind him.

Raj pointed to a manhole cover immediately overhead. With all his strength, Addison shoved the round iron cover aside, revealing daylight. He breathed a sigh of relief and began to climb out of the cistern. Addison had no idea his situation was about to get much, much worse.

Chapter Twenty-Three

Shrimp Cocktail

ADDISON RAISED HIS HEAD through the manhole to peek outside, and immediately ducked to avoid the tire of a speeding truck. He was bewildered to discover himself in the middle of a busy Istanbul street. Roaring Vespa motorbikes zipped past, beeping their horns.

The driver of a delivery van spotted Addison's head poking out of the center lane of the road. The man mashed his brakes and swerved into a vender's passing fruit cart. This caused an explosion of twisted metal and juiced fruit, and set off a chain reaction of fender benders and vender benders across Sultanahmet Square.

Addison stared in guilty shock at the deafening chaos he had just unleashed on Istanbul. A single dented hubcap rolled up to Addison and scored a hole in one, falling into the open manhole.

Somewhere deep below him, Eddie yelped. "Ouch, my head!"

Addison spotted the Turkish police as they spotted him. The police blew their whistles, drew their batons, and sprinted for the open manhole. He called down the shaft. "Time to go!"

Addison squirmed out of the manhole and legged it south, Molly, Eddie, and Raj racing after him. The Turkish police seemed to be in excellent shape. Addison could see his team was not going to outrun them. He needed to get his group off the streets. Swerving hard around a street corner, he led them into the front entrance of the Grand Sultan Hotel.

The group stood for a minute on the red lobby carpet, dripping. There was gilt trim on the vaulted ceilings, and gold tassels on the starched uniforms of the hotel staff. Dazzling chandeliers illuminated the space in a warm, hazy glow. Addison raised his eyebrows—this was one classy establishment. He sized up his team: they were soaking wet, but at least they were no longer purple.

"Addison," said Molly. "What are we doing here?"

"We just need a spot to lie low for a sec."

"In a five-star hotel?"

"I wouldn't settle for less." Addison marched up to

the front desk clerk. "Addison Cooke, pleasure to meet you."

The prim hotel clerk looked like he parted his hair with a laser. His suit was finely tailored down to the molecular level. He looked doubtfully down at Addison's wet and bedraggled clothes. He swiveled his eyes over to Molly, Raj, and Eddie with even more concern. Still, these newcomers were clearly not Turks, and were therefore tourists. And tourists meant money. "How may I help you, sir?"

Addison was pleased so many Turks spoke excellent English. "I'm visiting my good friend Vrolok Malazar," he said breezily. "I forgot the old kook's room number. Could you ring the good fellow and tell him I'm in the lobby?"

"So, you are a friend of Mr. Malazar, no?"

"That is correct," said Addison. He was not a friend of Malazar's, but luckily the clerk had phrased the question in the negative.

"One moment, Mr. Cooke." The desk clerk picked up his phone. Addison cocked an elbow on the countertop and watched closely as the man dialed room 901. That was all the info he needed.

The clerk waited a few rings. "Mr. Malazar does not seem to be answering. Would you like me to leave a message for him?"

"No, thank you. I'm hoping to surprise him." Addison winked conspiratorially at the desk clerk. "I'll take it as a favor if you don't tell him I was here."

The clerk returned Addison's wink and nodded sharply. He figured there might be a tip in it for him down the road.

•••••

Addison made for the exit.

"How did you know this was Malazar's hotel?" Eddie whispered.

"It was logical," said Addison. "He's on the same quest we are, so he would grab the nicest hotel closest to the Hagia Sophia." Once Addison was out of sight of the desk clerk, he hooked a right and shepherded his team down the main hallway. He had spotted Turkish police patrolling just outside the hotel's revolving glass doors.

"Where are we going, Addison?" asked Eddie.

"Elevator bay."

"But we need to get to the fish shish kebab restaurant to meet Uncle Jasper's operative," said Molly.

Addison checked the two remaining Rolexes on his wrist. "It's too late. We can't be out on those streets with the police everywhere. We just need to hide out for a tick until the police realize they have bigger fish to fry."

"Fish kebabs," said Eddie longingly.

Speed walking, the group zipped past the hotel's main ballroom. A bedazzled sign advertised an international ballroom dance competition. Dancers of all ages in elegant tuxedos and elaborate gowns gave Addison's bedraggled team a wide berth.

Addison found the elevator and punched the button for the ninth floor. Glancing up at the brass floor indicator, he was pleased to see they'd be heading to the top of the hotel. "Malazar must have a nice room."

"Addison, what's your plan, exactly?" asked Molly.

"Remember how we evaded Malazar by hiding right under his nose?"

Molly cast her mind back eleven minutes. "I think I remember that."

The elevator doors parted. Addison rushed inside, accidentally bumping a maid pushing a cleaning cart. "My apologies, madam!" He held the elevator door for her, bowed, and ushered his team inside.

On the ninth floor, Addison found suite 901 right by the elevators. He casually leaned against the wall and crossed his feet at the ankles. "Top floor. The presidential suite."

Eddie examined the door lock. "Electronic card readers. I don't know how to pick these."

"Not a problem," said Addison. "I borrowed the all-access card from the maid." He held up a key card with two fingers and dipped it into the door lock. The light flickered green and the door opened.

"What if Malazar's in there?" asked Eddie uncertainly.

"He won't be—the desk clerk just checked for us." Addison held open the door.

Eddie hesitated. "Are you sure this is a good idea?

"It is not a good idea," said Addison. "It is a *great* idea. Look, Malazar will be searching all of Istanbul for us. What's the one place in Istanbul he won't look?"

Molly nodded. "His own room."

Addison grinned and beckoned them inside.

••••••

It had been a rough twenty-four hours, so Addison felt the team needed a morale boost. It took three room service waiters to wheel in the gargantuan amount of hotel food he ordered on Malazar's tab. Addison called it the United Nations special: five Spanish omelets, four French omelets, three French toasts, seven orders of French fries, six strips of Canadian bacon, an English muffin, nine Belgian waffles, eight Vienna sausages, seven Prague hams, a Swiss chocolate fondue, a Russian salad, ten Danishes, two dozen Swedish meatballs, one Greek yogurt for Molly, a Sicilian pizza, a plate of Louisiana shrimp cocktail, a dozen Maine lobsters, some Boston baked beans, a Denver omelet, two New York cheesecakes, and a teeth-gratingly sweet dessert called Turkish delight that Addison—to his surprise—did not find at all delightful.

After room service left the food piled in the living room of Malazar's presidential suite, Addison stripped off and examined his still-wet jacket. He was distressed to see it had wrinkled up like a beige prune. There was nothing for it but to cross his fingers and drape it on the radiator to dry. He flopped down in an easy chair and kicked up his feet on an ottoman. It felt good to use an ottoman in the former Ottoman Empire. "Molly, be a good sister for once and bolt the front door—we don't want any unexpected guests."

Molly locked the chain bolt and returned to the living room. "We should think about leaving."

"We've only just arrived." Addison picked up a platter of shrimp cocktail off the nearest dining cart. He had never met a shrimp cocktail he didn't like. For him, it seemed to be a food impossible to get wrong. He plucked up a shrimp and plunked it into his mouth. Perfection.

"What is it with you and shrimp cocktail, anyway?" Molly asked.

"I'm not sure," Addison mused. "Maybe it's because you only eat shrimp cocktail at fancy occasions, so it feels special. Nobody ever says, 'What's for dinner tonight? Shrimp cocktail, again?' " He dipped another shrimp in cocktail sauce, nibbled it down to the tail, and chased it with more shrimp and cocktail sauce. He sighed content-edly. "It tastes like adventure."

"Uncle Jasper says we have to keep a balanced diet."

"Molly, I am as balanced as a gyroscope," said Addison. "Besides, free food is one of the greatest gifts in life."

Eddie, tall and thin as a coat rack, was bent double over the dessert tray. He vigorously nodded in agreement. "This chocolate fondue is life changing." He mopped chocolate from his chin with the edge of the tablecloth. "Though it will do nothing for my figure."

Raj picked up an enormous lobster with both hands and set to work tearing it apart like a caveman.

"Unbelievable." Molly cocked her fists on her hips. "A little free room service and you guys completely forget we're being hunted by a deranged killer."

Addison dabbed the corner of his mouth with a napkin. "Molly makes a fair case. We are not in Malazar's hotel room just for the shrimp cocktail. We require informa-tion. Who is Malazar? What makes him tick? What are his hobbies, his interests? Does he have any credit cards we can borrow?" Addison folded his napkin and stood up. "I propose we make a thorough search of the place."

Addison, Molly, Eddie, and Raj each searched a differ-ent room of the palatial presidential suite. Raj checked all the pockets of the suits and trousers hanging in Malazar's walk-in closet. Addison felt under the mattress in the bedroom, hoping to find a passport or a money clip. Eddie successfully cracked the hotel safe, only to find it empty. It was Molly who, rooting through the bathroom garbage, found a stack of receipts.

She marched into the living room and fanned them out on the coffee table for everyone to see. The receipts were all Greek to Addison. But luckily, he could read a fair amount of Greek. Modern Greek writing was not all that different from the ancient Greek he studied at Dimpleforth.

"There are two receipts for a place called Kartal's Café. The rest are receipts for building materials. Concrete, lumber, and iron."

"Any addresses?" asked Raj.

Addison shook his head.

"Look at the times on the receipts," said Molly. "Malazar visited Kartal's Café first thing each morning until today, when he came to Istanbul. If we can figure out where this café is, that's where Malazar lives. I bet it's right down the street from his house," she declared.

Eddie, who had overeaten, did side bends to loosen up his belly. "Isn't that a stretch?" he asked. "Maybe Malazar was just vacationing near Kartal's Café."

"I doubt it." Molly picked up a receipt and waved it in the air. "Nobody goes on vacation and buys a thousand pounds of concrete. He's making home improvements."

Addison unfolded his jacket from the radiator, pulled out his pocket notebook, and tucked Molly's receipts carefully inside. "We have a mystery on our hands." He selected another shrimp from the platter, dipped it in sauce, and took a thoughtful lap around the dining carts to return to his seat at the ottoman.

Molly impatiently paced the carpet. "Addison, what if the Collective comes back? We have no escape route. We're on the ninth floor—we can't just climb out of the bathroom like a couple of Templars."

"Mo, they're out scouring Istanbul. What are the odds they'll return this quickly?" He answered his own question with the horseracing odds he had learned from Uncle Jasper. "I give it eighteen-to-one against."

That was the moment the door unlocked and creaked open.

Chapter Twenty-Four

Baby Bird and Dolphin

ADDISON AND HIS FRIENDS looked up in horror. The door swung a full three inches until the chain bolt stopped it tight. A giant Turkish man peered through the gap. His head was 80 percent chin and 20 percent stubble. Peeking above his suit collar were neck tattoos of knives, cards, and dice. This man, Addison decided, was unlikely to win Babysitter of the Year.

The man had thick fingers and a thick brow, and grunted with a thick voice. "Yunus, building security."

Addison rose to his feet. "Addison Cooke, *bon vivant*."

"What are you doing in this room?"

"Eating shrimp. How may I help you?" Addison took the man's measure. It was amazing the giant could see through his own eyebrows. From his brutish expression, Addison figured Yunus for a man who'd clearly cracked more bones than books.

The big man growled. "The police are in the lobby, looking for four children. The desk clerk saw four children asking for Mr. Malazar. A maid saw four children take the elevator to this floor after she lost her key card. Room service delivered seventeen pounds of lobster to four children in this room. I was sent here to find four children."

Addison raised his eyebrows. "That is excellent police work."

"You are four children," Yunus snarled. "I will take you to the police so they can throw you in jail for trespassing. Open this door."

"Fine, Yunus," said Addison, wiping his hands with his napkin and adjusting the lapels of his jacket. "But first I'm going to need to see some ID."

The man puffed up his chest, showing the metal security name tag on his hotel uniform.

Addison read it carefully. "Tell me, what does Yunus mean in Turkish?"

" 'Dolphin.' "

Addison frowned. It did not seem a fitting name for a man like this. Maybe "Gorilla" or "Wildebeest," but surely not "Dolphin." "Are there a lot of Turkish men named Dolphin?"

"Of course." Yunus puffed his chest up still further. "And I am Kurdish, not Turkish."

"But you live in Turkey, so you're Turkish."

Yunus's brow somehow seemed to grow even thicker. "Being a Kurd in Turkey makes me a Turkish Kurd, not a Kurdish Turk."

"Well, my Turkish Kurd, you have curdled my brain," said Addison.

"I can do more than that to your brain," said Yunus, and he smashed his shoulder against the door. It buckled. The slide bolt ripped off the door and dangled uselessly.

"I am not paying for that," said Addison.

As soon as Yunus muscled his way into the room, Addison could see there was not one but two of him. The second hotel security guard was nearly identical to Yunus in every way, except bigger.

"And what is your name?" Addison asked politely.

"Osman," growled the larger man in a rumbling voice that probably registered on Richter scales across the country. The man was a good six foot six, and altogether, Addison felt he could do with a bit less of him.

"Os-man," said Addison. "Now, there's a proper name for a security guard. What does Os-man mean in Turkish?"

"'Baby bird,'" said the enormous man.

Addison nodded. He clearly had a lot to learn about Turkish names, but that could wait for another day. He eyed his team. The only things separating them from freedom were three food trays and two Kurdish security guards. Perhaps one problem could take care of the other.

"A thought just occurred, my Kurds." Addison's brain clicked and whirred. "I have never before hurdled a Kurd. But I believe I can herd a Kurd."

Addison shoved the wheeled food carts. They smashed into the security guards with a satisfying crash that failed to budge either one. Still, Addison could sense the Kurds were stirred.

Yunus clawed his hands, bellowed in anger, and hustled around the food carts, spiraling in on Addison.

Addison knew he had incurred the Kurd's wrath. "Raj, mayhem!"

Raj swung into action. He picked up the closest thing to hand, which happened to be a two-pound lobster. He hurled it at Yunus.

The lobster bounced off the giant's head. Yunus immediately redirected his rage from Addison to Raj.

Molly scooped up trays of waffles and launched them at Yunus as well.

Eddie picked up the vat of chocolate fondue, and though it broke his heart to waste chocolate, he poured it all over Osman's head.

Osman was temporarily blind, but undeterred. The Kurd's fists swung so fast, they blurred.

"Addison," said Molly, "this is getting absurd."

Addison concurred. He ducked the flying fists and rolled for the exit. Molly, Eddie, and Raj barreled after him.

•••••••

The group raced down the hallway as if their lives depended on it, because, in fact, they did. The security guards charged after them like stampeding bulls.

Addison called over his shoulder, "Raj, more mayhem!"

Raj, finding no more purple smoke balls in his pockets, pulled the nearest hallway fire alarm instead. The alarm emitted two things: the first was a satisfyingly loud blast; the second was a jet of blue ink that splattered all over Raj. It continued to splutter ink like a frightened octopus. The ink was to deter pranksters from pulling the alarm without an emergency. Raj figured being chased by guards was enough of an emergency, but that did not change matters. Still, he felt that being dyed blue was an improvement over purple.

Raj tore down the hall, wiping blue ink from his face, desperate to catch up to his friends.

Dolphin and Baby Bird shoveled on speed, their long legs closing the distance.

Frightened hotel guests, already surprised by the fire

alarms, were more surprised when they streamed out of their rooms only to be plowed down by the two giant men at full sprint.

Addison felt bad for the innocent bystanders, scattering like bowling pins, but at least they were slowing down his pursuers.

Molly reached the elevators first and hit the call button. Addison's team jogged in place, frantically willing the elevator to arrive. When it finally did—with a merry chime—Addison's group packed in. Raj frantically pounded the Door Close button with his fist.

Yunus and Osman sprinted down the hall, picking up the unstoppable momentum of two freight trains. The metal elevator doors slid shut just in time for Dolphin and Baby Bird to crash into them with a satisfying thud.

•••••••

Soothing Muzak played as the elevator dropped. Addison's team panted for breath.

"That was cutting it a bit close," said Molly. She adjusted the heavy satchel on her shoulder, giving the bronze tablet a reassuring pat.

"Not to worry, young relative," said Addison. "We're almost out of this."

"Do you think Malazar will have to pay for all that lobster?" asked Eddie.

"He's a billionaire," said Addison. "And he killed my aunt and uncle. He can pay for the lobster."

The elevator doors opened onto the main floor of the Grand Sultan Hotel. Addison scanned the crowds of ballroom dance competitors and spectators. "I count zero police. With any luck, they're responding to the fire alarm on the ninth floor."

As soon as Addison marched into the carpeted lobby, he realized he had spoken too soon. A triangle formation of Turkish police blocked the main entrance. "Slight change of plans," he announced. Addison continued down the busy hallway, crowded with stalls of venders selling ballroom clothing and costume jewelry to the dance competitors.

A short salesman with a tall toupee attempted to pull Addison into his booth. "How are you enjoying Istanbul, my friend?"

"It's a killer city," said Addison.

Like all good salespeople, this man was a keen judge of character. He read Addison's troubled expression. "What's not to love about Istanbul? We have huge crowds, huge dance competitions, and huge deals."

"I like one of those things," said Addison flatly.

Molly waved her hand at Addison to hurry things along. Two policemen with walkie-talkies were striding directly toward them. Addison figured Yunus and Osman had probably spread word of their ninth-floor deeds. Escaping the hotel was going to prove a worthy challenge.

The salesman clung to Addison's sleeve. "Hadad is my name. And that is a fine jacket you are wearing. Sure, it is wrinkled up like a shar-pei's bottom. But, I can see that you clearly have exceptional taste. May I interest you in a ballroom dance suit?"

"I really don't have the time, Hadad."

"No one has time to look bad in a suit."

Addison had to hand it to Hadad. He made a decent point. Addison studied the racks of fine tailored suits. He pulled his team inside the vender's stall while the patrolling police paraded past. "What's the difference between a ballroom jacket and a regular jacket?"

Hadad beamed. He knew when he had a fish on the hook. He had been hawking ballroom suits all morning with hopes of clearing a decent profit by lunch. It was his granddaughter's birthday, and he wanted to buy her something nice. But all the hope Granddad Hadad had had had had no result. He turned to Addison and turned on the charm. "Why, a ballroom jacket will fit you like a glove, but you can still flap your arms around on the dance floor."

"So, you're saying, increased mobility?"

"Yes!" cried Hadad. "And look at these slits in the armpits—they vent heat. You can wear this suit in a hundred-yard dash and not break a sweat."

Addison was listening. "Do I have to iron it?"

"Of course not! It can't be wrinkled! You could crumple this suit into a wet ball, wear it on an airplane, and still arrive looking like you stepped out of a laundromat."

The salesman held Addison's interest.

"Here," Hadad continued. "I think I have something in your size. Let's try it on and have a look." He eased Addison out of his battered jacket and into a sleek new one, guiding his arms into the sleeves.

Addison examined himself in the full-length mirror. The suit suited him just fine. He swung his arms, as if lunging with a knife—he had complete range of motion. "You're telling me I can run, climb, and fight in this suit and still look like I'm walking a fashion runway?"

"Absolutely," said the salesman. "Are you interested?"

Addison studied his reflection. "Do you have anything in a glen plaid?"

Hadad smiled; he had his man. "And how will you be paying today?"

Bargaining was second nature to Addison. First nature, even. But today he simply did not have the time. "Charge it to my room," he said. "Room 901. Vrolok Malazar."

•••••••

Addison hustled his team out of the vender booth, checked both ways, and started for the main entrance.

"No dice," said Molly.

Ivan and his men were crossing the main lobby, pushing their way through the crowd of ballroom dancers and competition spectators.

Addison pivoted, herding his team in a new direction, keeping his head low. Turkish police blocked the hallway ahead. He saw only one choice. "Good news, guys. We're going to a ballroom dance competition."

He crossed to the entrance of the hotel ballroom. A guard stood behind a velvet rope. Addison did not have money for tickets, or time to haggle. He simply rolled up his sleeve, stripped off his second Rolex, and handed it to the guard.

The guard stared down at the watch, bewildered. "Sir, admission is free!"

"Keep it," said Addison. "I have plenty." He looked up to see Ivan hustling closer.

Addison leaned in closer to the guard. "You see that angry man who looks like he got his hair cut at a clown college?"

The door guard nodded.

"He's a kidnapper. He's armed and dangerous and chasing us. Please stop him."

The door guard squared his shoulders and nodded resolutely.

Addison and his friends slipped inside the grand ballroom.

Chapter Twenty-Five

The Competition

INSIDE WAS A GLAMOROUS affair. Hundreds of tables of elegantly dressed spectators filled the room. Before them, men in tail suits and women in ball gowns glided gaily across the gigantic dance floor. Judges peered down from their dais and marked their score sheets. It was behind the dais that Addison spotted what he was looking for: an emergency exit.

Addison, Molly, Eddie, and Raj feathered their way between spectator tables, trying to lose themselves in the crowd. Addison glanced over his shoulder to see Ivan violently shoving his way past the door guard. The Collective poured in after him, followed by a squad of mustachioed and officious-looking Turkish police. The two groups split up, searching the sea of spectators. Ivan's men spread across the left side of the massive room, and the police took the right.

"This is easy," Addison whispered to his team. "We'll just go back out the way we came."

That was a flawless plan all the way up until Yunus and Osman ducked into the ballroom. The two giants filled the entranceway, blocking any escape.

Addison gulped and returned his focus to the emergency exit on the far side of the dance floor. He huddled up with his team. "Molly has the tablet. She needs to get it through that exit door."

"Why me?" asked Molly, eyeing the prowling police.

"Because you're the only one of us who can really fight."

"So what do we do?" asked Raj, wringing his hands, which were still dyed completely blue.

"At all costs," said Addison, "we have to draw everyone's attention away from Molly. Eddie and Raj, you know what that means."

Eddie nodded solemnly. "Got it."

"Wait," said Raj. "What does it mean?"

Addison sighed, exasperated. "Raj, you beautiful blue-handed beast! You and Eddie are the diversion!"

"Ah," said Raj. "Excellent."

"Everybody meet up at that emergency exit door. Good luck."

Raj and Eddie split up, heading in opposite directions, looking for ways to create an epic distraction. Addison tugged Molly through the crowd, keeping one eye on Ivan's crew and one eye on Turkey's finest.

"How are we going to get behind the judges' dais?" asked Molly a little doubtfully. The dance competition was in full swing.

"I have an idea, Mo. One of my best."

"That is not a high bar," said Molly.

Addison sashayed between tables, working his way across the room. "There is only one way to that emergency exit door. And it's across the dance floor."

"Oh no," said Molly, fear beginning to register on her face.

"Oh yes," said Addison. "They won't be looking for us on the dance floor. Younger Cooke, we are going to dance our way out of here."

He goaded Molly behind a curtain to the on-deck area where competitors waited to be called onstage for the next heat.

Molly whispered frantically. "Addison, what if somebody asks us what we're doing back here?"

"We'll just play dumb!"

"Shouldn't be too hard for you," she grumbled.

The competitors filed onto the floor. Molly tucked her shirt into her cargo pants, shifted the satchel to her right shoulder, and took Addison's hand. He led her out onto the dance floor to thunderous applause.

As soon as Addison was under the lights, he felt that all was well in the world. He surveyed the other competitors. Sure, they looked professional in their snappy tuxedos, but Addison was feeling confident. The music kicked in, and to Addison's immense delight, it was a foxtrot. The tune was "Keep One Step Ahead" by Addison's favorite song-writer, Ira Frankfurt. "Molly," he whispered. "I want to win this."

Addison counted to eight in his head, led Molly in a feather step to a reverse turn, and they were off and running. He steered down the long side of the floor, maneu-vering past spinning couples. Already, he was nearly halfway to the emergency exit. With growing confidence, he realized he wasn't even going to need a distraction from Eddie and Raj.

Unfortunately, Eddie and Raj had no way of knowing that.

Raj was hard at work tipping over the stage light scaf-folding. It was a decent plan that would easily cause a considerable distraction, albeit with several thousand dol-lars' worth of property damage. He had rapidly removed two sandbags from a C-stand when Ivan spotted him. Raj found himself quickly surrounded by Russian gang mem-bers and had only one escape route: the dance floor.

Raj scuttled across the competition floor like a mouse surprised by the kitchen light. Two men in dark suits charged him, preparing to pounce. Raj did a head fake to the left and a shake-and-bake to the right. The flying Russian duo tackled couples number two and three to the ground, with the loud ripping sound of a ballroom gown. Raj turned to flee and steamrolled couple number seven in the process.

With couples suddenly dropping like cartoon anvils, Addison knew he had a decent chance at winning.

"Addison," Molly whispered, "let's just run for it!"

"Run for it?" Addison asked. "Molly, we're the best couple standing!"

Eddie spotted a fancy glass water dispenser in the on-deck area. Ice cubes and lemon slices floated on the surface. He hefted the ungainly jug with a vague hope of tossing it onto the electrical wiring of the floor lights and causing a short. But he only succeeded in dumping several gallons of water all over couple number five. Couples number eight and twelve slid in Eddie's ice cube puddle, banana-peel style. Eddie panicked, tried to run, and fell down, too.

Addison could see this was not going as well as some of his better plans. The crowd was in an uproar. The judges were on their feet, red-faced and shaking their fists. There were already more Turkish police on the floor than ballroom dancers. Things were moving a bit too fast for Addison's taste. He stopped dancing. "Molly, run for it!"

"But what about you guys? You'll all be caught!"

Addison surveyed the room as though it were a cricket pitch. If Molly was the bowler, the emergency exit was the batsman. The Turkish police were at short leg, fly slip, and gully. Addison saw there was only one way. "Molly, go now!"

For once, to Addison's amazement, Molly did exactly what he asked. She fled.

Addison turned to stare into the stony-eyed gaze of a Turkish policeman. The angry, rotund man looked like he'd gotten up on the wrong side of the bed seventeen years ago and not gotten a wink of sleep since.

He clamped a hand down on Addison's wrist. "Is this him?"

Ivan the Terrible appeared at the policeman's side. "That's the one."

Addison was pleased to see that Ivan was still tinged slightly purple from Raj's smoke balls. He also noticed that Ivan was shaking. The man was clearly upset. He looked like he could do a four-day spa treatment in the Alps with tea baths, hot stone massages, and New Age music and still be hopping mad. He looked like he could throttle Addison forty-six times and still be furious enough to throttle him a forty-seventh time.

Ivan brushed the greasy hair back from his face and glared down at Addison. "You have wasted my time today. I am going to make you regret it. Deeply."

"You should save your anger for whoever gave you that haircut," said Addison.

Veins pulsed in Ivan's neck.

Addison could see at a peek that Ivan was reaching the peak of his pique.

"Give me the tablet," Ivan growled.

Addison's thoughts flitted around like a moth in a lamp store. Eddie and Raj were zigzagging through the throngs of ballroom dancers abandoning the stage. Turkish police were holding the irate judges at bay. Addison was surrounded by Ivan's men and didn't have an abundance of options. All he could do was stall and hope that Molly—wherever she was—was making a brilliant escape.

He unbuttoned his suit jacket and turned in a slow circle for Ivan. "I don't have the tablet." Addison knew things were not looking wonderful for him at the moment. But he was buoyed by the fact that his new ballroom jacket looked sensational.

"Where is it?" Ivan's frenzied eyes searched the room.

Addison followed his manic gaze. He watched, horrified, as Malazar stepped from behind the judges' dais. The Shadow's white skin was shrouded by his black fedora and the upturned collar of his black trench coat. He held

Molly squirming in a chokehold, her feet bicycling inches off the ground. With his other arm, he pinned Molly's arms behind her back. Molly struggled, unable to fight or shout with an arm pythoned around her windpipe. No one in the panicked crowd seemed to notice her plight. Addison felt the hope wheezing out of him like air from a punctured tire.

Ivan's attention was split, and Addison knew he had to split, too. He jerked his wrist from the policeman's grip and bolted for the emergency exit. "Raj!" he cried. "Eddie! C'mon!"

The police tore after him. Addison saw Ivan's men rushing to help Malazar. They clutched Molly's hands and her kicking legs. Addison saw they were not just taking the tablet; they were taking her, too.

He hesitated at the door, paralyzed, unable to think of a plan to rescue Molly. Eddie and Raj joined him at his side.

Raj shoved open the emergency exit, sounding a fresh alarm. He yanked Addison out the door just as the police galloped up.

Addison struggled against Raj's grip. "We can't just leave her!"

"We're completely outnumbered," Raj shouted. "We can't help her right now. You know I'm right!"

Eddie grabbed Addison's other arm and helped drag

him down the service alley behind the hotel. "Addison, he's right! We have to help ourselves if we're going to be able to help Molly!"

Addison broke into a run alongside his friends. Turkish police clattered behind them, catching up quickly. Addison shouted in anguish, "Why do I keep losing family members?"

"C'mon, Addison!" Eddie pleaded. "We have to move!"

Raj hung a right at the end of the service alley. "There's a bazaar near the hotel. I spotted it from Malazar's suite. We'll lose the police in the alleyways." Raj took another right onto a cobbled lane with high walls that led to a dead end.

They were cornered. At this precise moment, Addison's mind had the emotional stability of a Jenga tower. "I try to be a glass-half-full kind of guy," he said, "but in this case, you two have smashed the glass entirely and stabbed us with its shards!"

"How is this our fault?" asked Eddie.

"You both managed to sabotage everyone on the dance floor *except* the people who were trying to kill us!"

The Turkish police halted at the end of the alley and grinned. They formed a line, blocking Addison's escape.

"I don't understand it," said Raj. "This alley should lead straight to the bazaar."

Addison pulled out his pocket edition of *Fiddleton's Atlas* and opened the local map. "We will see what Mr. Fiddleton has to say."

A stranger's voice called from the end of the alley. "You should take a shortcut."

Addison looked up to see a man in rags hunched in the shadowed doorway of a crumbling tenement. He hadn't noticed the man there a second earlier. Addison would have described the man as a poor beggar, but the beggar was so poor, he beggared description.

"You should get out of here," said Addison. "There's going to be trouble."

The Turkish police formed a military line, loosened their batons, and marched down the cobbled lane.

The beggar pursed his lips. "I can stand here if I choose!"

"I thought beggars can't be choosers," said Addison.

"Very funny, laddie," said the man, speaking with more than a bit of a Scottish accent. "I am not a beggar. This is just my disguise so I may travel unnoticed. Few people look too closely at a homeless person, I'm afraid."

Addison frowned. He was not trying to be drawn into a conversation right now. He consulted his atlas. "Fiddleton says we can climb the fence at the end of the alleyway, as long as we avoid the guard dog on the other side."

"Actually, there is an easier way to the bazaar," said the man. "But you must come with me."

The Turkish police drew closer and drew their batons.

"I only trust one person to tell me where to go," said

Addison, stabbing the atlas with his finger, "and that is Roland J. Fiddleton, Esquire."

"I quite agree. We share a similar taste in cartographers. And so, I advise you to trust me."

Addison wheeled on the strange little man. "And why should we trust you?"

The man straightened his mustaches with a flourish of his fingers and pulled back the hood from his head. "Because I," he said, stepping forward into the light, "am Roland J. Fiddleton."

Chapter Twenty-Six
Roland J. Fiddleton

ADDISON BLINKED A FEW times. It suddenly occurred to him to wonder why a beggar in Istanbul would speak in a thick Scottish accent. He looked down at the author's photo on the book jacket of *Fiddleton's Atlas*. He looked up at the mysterious man: same furry face of wiry white whiskers. The two pictures matched. There was no mistaking it: the man was Roland J. Fiddleton. "We're coming with you," Addison declared.

Roland J. Fiddleton, Esquire, beckoned the group through the rear doorway of an abandoned tenement. Once inside, he shut the door and locked it with a crossbar. Turkish police pounded on the door with their fists. Roland calmly guided Addison's team down a trash-cluttered hallway to the front of the building.

Addison's jaw hung open like a busted mailbox as he hustled to keep pace with his hero. "Mr. Fiddleton, sir. What are you doing in Istanbul?"

"I'm here for the annual cartographers convention, of course. But your uncle called and said you needed an extraction. I waited at that dreadful fish kebab restaurant for thirty-five minutes and sixteen seconds."

The front door was boarded up, so Roland simply climbed out the first-story window. Addison climbed down after him and found himself immediately in the heart of the bazaar. Colorful booths sold all manner of silver and gold trinkets. A group of street buskers strummed *ouds* and banged on *darbukas*. A juggler with a forked beard tossed scimitars into the air. A toothless man hawked jars of leeches from the basket of his bicycle.

Roland strolled into a merchant's tent filled with aromatic spices. "Your uncle warned me you might not show up. He said, 'Addison is so unpredictable, he never does the same thing once.'" Roland shed his costume of beggar's rags and tossed them in a trash can.

By the time they emerged from the far side of the spice tent, Roland was resplendent in a white three-piece suit, a white walking stick, and a white fedora with a black ribbon trim. His cheerful blue eyes, crumpled by the chubby cheeks of his smile, put Addison in mind of two blueberries in a well-buttered crumpet.

"I sat there," Roland continued, pinballing through vender stalls, "eating the most awful falafels and couldn't help but notice all the Turkish police running in the same direction . . . the ballroom competition at the Grand Sultan Hotel. Naturally, I became a wee bit curious. The Turkish police are not famous for their foxtrot. Speaking of which . . ."

Roland paused. A group of Turkish police froze at the end of the row of stalls. They spotted Addison, Eddie, and Raj, and yelped. They unhooked their batons and jogged along the aisle.

Roland watched them with mild amusement.

Addison shifted from foot to foot. "Shouldn't we be leaving?"

"Patience, laddie," was all Roland said.

A delivery boy with several cages of squalling chickens piled on his Vespa screeched to a stop in the aisle, completely blocking the advancing police. They collided with a spray of squawks and feathers.

Roland removed a pocket watch from his vest pocket. "Precisely on time." He tucked his walking stick under his arm like an umbrella and strolled ahead.

"How did you do that?" asked Raj, amazed.

Roland smiled. "I am a person who knows his way around." He crossed into a vender's stall and doffed his fedora to a carpet merchant in a red fez. The man immediately bowed, rolled back a floor rug, and swung open a trapdoor. Without missing a step, Roland proceeded to climb down the ladder.

Addison looked at his friends and shrugged. They climbed down as well, the merchant closing the trapdoor after them.

Roland flicked a Zippo lighter and held it aloft, guiding them across a storage basement stacked with marvelous handwoven Turkish carpets, until they reached a circular door with a wheel lock. Roland again pulled out his pocket watch and held up a flat hand signaling Addison, Eddie, and Raj to halt.

The cheerful old man waited three ticks of his stopwatch. "There. That should do it." He twisted the wheel like a submarine door. It swung open and he stepped through the portal.

Addison's group found themselves in an underground garage. An old-fashioned Yellow Cab squealed to a stop directly in front of them.

The driver saluted Roland with two fingers to the brim of his cap. Roland peeled open the rear door for Addison and his team. They piled on board. Roland slid in after them and tapped his cane on the roof. The driver took off with a squeal of tires and a cloud of rubber smoke.

Addison stared up at the man, utterly starstruck.

"Mr. Fiddleton, sir, it is a huge honor to meet you. I have read all of your books."

"He sleeps with your atlas by his bed," Raj put in.

Addison did not feel this was helpful information, but Roland seemed to take it in stride. "Mr. Fiddleton," he ventured to ask, "is it true you were once marooned on an island in the Seychelles and had to construct an escape raft out of rum kegs?"

Roland raised one furry white eyebrow.

Addison pressed on. "And what about the time you escaped a Somali prison by poisoning the jailer with a cobra?"

Roland raised the other eyebrow. "It was a black mamba in Djibouti," he said. "But yes."

"What about the time you were in Calcutta and were attacked by a man-eating tiger?"

Roland rolled up his trouser cuff to show a nasty scar on his calf. "That was a day I would sooner forget."

Addison gazed at the man with worship in his eyes. He had almost forgotten his sister was in the clutches of a dangerous lunatic.

The taxi whipped around the winding streets of Istanbul, bouncing in and out of potholes that had been deepening for centuries.

"Wait a second," said Addison. "Where exactly are you taking us?"

Roland smiled airily as if he could drift peacefully off to sleep at any moment. "To the most disgusting, disreputable, and dangerous tavern in all Istanbul."

"Why not take us to the second-most disgusting tavern?" asked Eddie. "Or the third?"

"Two reasons," said Roland. "One: the Turkish police are unlikely to set foot in this type of tavern—it's too dangerous for them. And two: the tavern is your extraction point. I am simply following your uncle's instructions."

Addison, Eddie, and Raj digested this information.

"They have my sister," said Addison. "And they have the tablet."

"I know, Addison," said Roland, his eyebrows crinkling up in concern. "I do not think the Shadow will hurt her right away. If I know the man, he will use her for bait."

The taxi gyrated down a cobbled street, heading toward the docks.

"How do you know my uncle?" asked Addison. "Are you a Templar Knight?"

"I am afraid not," said Roland J. Fiddleton. "But I do play tennis with a few of them. What few are left. Your uncle Jasper is a fellow member of the Explorers Club in London. I knew your parents as well."

The taxi rumbled to a stop where Istanbul's warren of alleyways grew too narrow for cars. Roland opened the door and stood on the running board, searching out the watchful eyes of the city. Satisfied the coast was clear, he beckoned Addison's team. They slunk out of the taxi and burrowed into the dark shadows of the dockside alleys.

"Mr. Fiddleton, I have questions about the Templars," said Addison. "And you're not bound by any Templar rules of secrecy."

"Fire away, laddie," said Roland.

Addison's mind was clogged with questions—they nearly formed a traffic jam on the way to his mouth. "Who are the Cookes? What are *Tutores Thesauri*? Why is my family crest carved into coffins from Paris to Istanbul? What are we after and what are we protecting?"

Roland maintained a surprisingly fast pace along the curving lane that led down to the water. At points, the stone buildings grew so close together, they were forced to inch sideways like crabs. "Do you wear a medallion?"

Addison pulled the bronze chain from under his shirt and handed it over to Roland.

Roland examined the chain, pausing to run a thumb over the Latin words *"Tutor Thesauri."* He turned, quickening his nimble gait. "Some Templar families are bankers, controlling what remains of the Templars' wealth. Some Templar families are soldiers, though I have never met one myself. And you, my wee Cooke, are a *Tutor Thesauri.*"

Addison nodded, wondering how many members of the secret society were still alive. Raj and Eddie, keeping pace behind, craned their necks to catch every word.

Roland checked his pocket watch and picked up his pace still further. "Turkish soldiers accidentally blew a hole in the Greek Acropolis. The Temple of Artemis—the Seventh Wonder of the World—was burned down by an arsonist who wanted to become famous. For all history, barbarians, vandals, fortune hunters, and fools have done everything in their power to ruin the marvels of mankind. Your family is part of an ancient lineage, with a sworn duty to find and safeguard the treasures of history."

"The Cookes are like the world's first archaeologists," Raj blurted out.

Roland nodded. "That is not far from the truth."

Addison furrowed his brow, considering. "That's how my parents died in Cambodia . . . how my aunt and uncle died in Mongolia . . ."

"Yes, Addison," said Roland. "Your family has been fighting to protect ancient relics for seven hundred years."

"What does it mean?" asked Eddie. "*Tutor Thesauri.*"

"It means 'guardian of treasure,'" said Roland. "Addison—you, your sister, your father, your aunt, your uncles, and all the Cookes . . ." He held the medallion aloft so that it glittered in the filtered light of the crooked alley. "You are the relic guardians."

······

Roland handed Addison his medallion and turned down a dark alley behind the ancient stockyards and loading docks of the Golden Horn of Istanbul.

"Mr. Fiddleton," called Eddie, out of breath from their march, "what does all this have to do with Raj and me? I can see why Addison has to risk his skin protecting artifacts—it's his family business. But my parents are lawyers—that's my family business. Maybe Raj and I should really be heading back to New York. I mean, no offense, Addison."

"None taken." Addison was happy Eddie and Raj had come to visit him in England, and it really wasn't his intention to lead them to their deaths in Istanbul. Good friends generally don't lure each other to their deaths. Addison would be very sorry to see Eddie and Raj go. But if the two wanted to go home, they really had every right to do so.

Roland peered over his shoulder at Eddie, his eyes glittering with merriment. "Your name is Eddie Chang, I believe?"

"How did you know that?"

Roland smiled. "In Chinese, Chang means 'archer.'

The Changs were Imperial Guards, protecting the Tang emperors. And if my Hindi is good, Bhandari means 'guardian of the treasury.' The Bhandaris formed the first police force to protect Bombay."

Raj and Eddie gaped.

Roland led the group through a breach in the ancient Roman wall that fortified Istanbul and hurried down a set of steps to an even darker passage. "Eddie, somewhere in the lower branches of your family trees, you and Raj are the descendants of guardians. Just like Addison and Molly."

"Well," said Eddie, "this could all just be a weird coincidence."

Roland cocked his head. "Eight million people in New York and you make friends with Cookes. Is it a coincidence? I don't know if I believe in those."

At last Roland slowed his pace. "We're here." He strode to an ancient wooden door cut in the stone façade of a tenement. "May I present the Rusted Dagger. Home to brigands, smugglers, thieves, and cutthroats since the Ottomans were ruled by Bayezid the Thunderbolt."

The crooked wooden door was not more than five feet tall. No sign marked the entrance, although Addison thought he saw dried bloodstains on the door frame. Roland took a deep breath and appeared to brace himself. "Keep one eye on the front door, one eye on the back door, and one eye on your wallet."

"That's three eyes," said Eddie.

"Well, there are more than two eyes in your group," said Roland. "Delegate." He pushed his way inside.

It took Addison a moment for his two eyes to adjust to the gloom. Kerosene lamps hung from the rafters. Ukrainian smugglers in fur caps hunched over playing cards at the bar. Greek sailors on shore leave reclined on satin pillows, curled over pewter hookahs. A belly dancer balanced on a table, jingling all the coins in her belt, hoping to add more coins to her collection.

Two Bulgarian men were locked in an arm-wrestling match near the fortune-teller's booth. The Bulgarians were so hairy, it took Addison a moment to realize they were shirtless. Over by the pool table, three Albanian longshoremen with wiry black beards like scouring pads took turns punching one another in the stomach.

One lone figure sat wreathed in shadow at a table near the back. Addison could see reflected lamplight gleaming in his eyes, but the rest of his face was darkened by the brim of his hat. The man was watching him.

Before Addison could react, Eddie let out a howl. A massive, slathering hound sprang from behind the bar and charged Addison, rearing up on its hind legs.

Addison did not have time to run. The enormous creature locked its bearlike paws on Addison's shoulders and proceeded to lick him from chin to ear. Addison sputtered and gagged, wiping slobber from his cheek.

The man at the back of the bar tilted the hat back on his head and lifted his face to the light. "Hello, kid."

Addison gasped, at a loss for words.

It was Dax Conroy.

Chapter Twenty-Seven

The Rusted Dagger

MR. JACOBSEN WAS A Great Dane with mediocre manners. Addison removed the paws from his shoulders and scratched the affectionate beast behind the ears. He drew a handkerchief from his pocket and patted dog slobber from his new jacket with as much composure as he could manage.

Dax rose from his seat. "Of all the dive bars in all the world . . ." He took the toothpick from his mouth and clasped Addison's hand. "It's good to see you, kid." Dax grinned broadly and shook hands with Raj, Eddie, and Roland, beckoning them to join him at his table. "Where's Molly?"

"The Shadow has her," said Addison gravely.

Dax returned the toothpick to his mouth, his expression darkening. "People sure like kidnapping Cookes."

Addison nodded. "We do have a knack for getting ourselves abducted."

"Do you have a plan?"

"It'll be a difficult rescue operation. Hard to pull off." Addison shook his head. "How are we supposed to rescue Molly without Molly's help?"

"It's true," Raj agreed. "She's really more useful than all of us."

A one-eyed barkeep with a leather-hilted dirk in his belt arrived carrying a round of Arnold Palmers.

"I took the liberty of ordering drinks," Dax said. "I hope you don't mind, the Rusted Dagger spikes their Arnold Palmers with curry powder and mint."

"It'll do," said Addison, who had never been more in need of a drink. He required fluids after so much dancing and running, but he also had a thirst for information. "Has anyone heard from T.D. or Grand Master Gaspard?" he asked when he came up for air.

"Tilda had her hands full in Paris," said Roland. "But she managed to get Gaspard to a safe location. She can't believe you're still alive. Between us, I didn't get the impression the lass holds a very high opinion of your survival skills. She says she's going to try to catch up with you if she can."

Dax sipped an inch off his drink. "I'll radio her coordinates when we know our next move."

Raj scooched his chair closer to Dax and stared up at his hero. "How did you get here, Dax? The last time we saw you, you were flying your Cessna Skyhawk to Tanzania to poach poachers."

"I had a run of bad luck." Dax took another slug of Arnold Palmer and squinted. "I got held up at gunpoint in a pool hall in Dar es Salaam. Had to fight my way out. One of the thieves turned out to be the mayor's son. Police tried to arrest me. I had to leave everything behind and flee the country."

Raj listened, wide-eyed. "Everything?"

"Besides my plane, I only have two things in this world: a Great Dane and a bad attitude."

Roland set his Arnold Palmer down on the knife-scarred tabletop. "Dax has returned to smuggling, and he helps out the Templars from time to time."

"But what about the rhinos?" Raj blurted out.

"There are fewer than fifty black rhinos left in Tanzania," said Dax, his voice more bitter than the Turkish tea in the Arnold Palmers. "It's the way of the world."

"Well, this has been a cheerful reunion," said Roland, in his lilting Scottish brogue. "But what we should be talking about is where the Shadow will be taking Molly. What's the Collective's next move?"

"I'm glad you asked." Addison pulled his notebook from his chest pocket and produced the receipts Molly had found in Malazar's hotel suite. "Eddie and I overheard Malazar saying one word. We think it might be the name of a place." He cleared his throat and read aloud from his notebook. "Cantoo."

Dax frowned.

Roland stared at him quizzically.

Addison realized he might be mispronouncing the word. Or he might be correctly pronouncing a word that Malazar mispronounced. Or he could be correctly pronouncing a word that was not an actual place-name. Addison's shoulders slumped.

Roland studied the receipts and held one aloft. "Kartal's Café . . ." He leaned back in his chair, and his eyes took on a dreamy, faraway look. "It was summertime. I was on leave from the merchant navy and bested the prince of Monaco in a fencing match. He took the loss poorly and sent the *gendarmes* to arrest me. I only escaped when a deep sea fisherman hid me belowdecks under some netting and ferried me out to the Mediterranean."

Addison listened, enraptured.

Eddie piped up. "What does this have to do with anything?"

"Well," said Roland, his blue eyes twinkling, "that fisherman's name was Kartal. And he later opened up a café that I have visited many times over the years. Come to think of it, it is near a town called Kantou."

"So what country is it in?" asked Addison.

"The island of Cyprus."

"Well, what are we waiting for?" said Addison, rising from his seat.

"Hold on," said Dax. "My instructions are to fly you to safety. Not fly you to Malazar's headquarters."

Addison turned to his old friend. "Dax, I can't lose any more family members. After Molly and Uncle Jasper, I'm fresh out. I don't want to get you in trouble. But I have to go after Molly. We owe it to her."

Dax looked Addison in the eye and slowly nodded. "I hear they have good casinos in Cyprus. When do we leave?"

"Now," Addison declared. "Or sooner, if possible."

The group stood up.

Addison held out his dog-eared copy of *Fiddleton's Atlas* for Roland to sign.

After penning his autograph with a flourish, Roland handed Addison a business card. "Addison, if you ever need me, just show this card at the London Explorers Club. They will know how to contact me."

"Where are you going now?" asked Addison eagerly. "A Saharan caravan to the gold markets of Mali? A canoe trip down the Ganges to climb the sacred Ghats? An elephant expedition to the fabled city of Bagan on the old Silk Road?"

"I am getting a haircut," said Roland. "It's been three months since I've had a proper trim and a shave."

"Just one more question, Mr. Fiddleton," said Addison, as they shuffled between the crowded tables on their way out of the tavern. "If each Templar family has a different specialty, what is T.D.'s expertise exactly?"

Roland shook his white mane. "That I do not know. She holds her cards close to the vest. If you find out her specialty, you will have to tell me."

"I will," Addison said, nodding thoughtfully. "When you come of age."

Chapter Twenty-Eight

The Crash

ADDISON HAD SAT ON couches that were longer than Dax's plane. The four-seat Cessna Skyhawk was a cramped ride even when you didn't have a 150-pound Great Dane named Mr. Jacobsen on your lap. The wings were mounted awkwardly on top of the plane, instead of sprouting from the sides. Addison wasn't sure if the plane was designed for flying or drying laundry. All in all, the Skyhawk had all the stylish sophistication of a garbage disposal, except with less pickup.

Still, after the harrowing taxi ride to Ataturk Airport, Addison thought Dax's airplane felt downright safe by comparison. Istanbul was already a pinprick in the distance when the plane reached cruising altitude, level with the clouds. The roaring engine seemed to lull Mr. Jacobsen right to sleep, along with Eddie and Raj. All three dozed in the back seat. Addison rode shotgun, watching Dax man the controls.

Dax eyed the back seat and seemed to sense that he finally had a moment of privacy with Addison. "Kid," he said, his voice only just loud enough to be heard over the beating propeller, "I went after your aunt and uncle."

"What are you talking about, Dax?"

"After I evacuated you and Molly from Mongolia in July. I went right back in."

Addison leaned forward in his seat. "You went back to the mountain?"

"Yes. I returned to the chasm where your aunt and uncle . . ." Dax's voice trailed off.

"That was dangerous," said Addison. "It was crawling with gang members—Chinese triads and Russian *vori*."

"They were cleared out by then," said Dax. "The Black Darkhad took care of the triads. And the Russians, well, I didn't see any sign of them."

"Did you do a fly-by or get out and explore?"

"I landed at the base of the mountain. I hiked until I reached the gorge. I combed the river where I figured your aunt and uncle might be. I hiked the banks on both sides for three miles."

Dax flew for a moment in silence.

Addison was afraid to ask his next question and afraid not to ask. "What did you find?"

Dax set his jaw and pursed his lips. "Nothing. Not a trace of them."

Addison puckered his eyebrows and frowned. It would be nice to have closure. It would make it easier to say good-bye. At last he spoke. "Thank you, Dax."

The plane soared over the sprawling and ancient land of Turkey. Where Achilles's Greeks once battled the Trojans. Where Antony cavorted with Cleopatra. Where Byzantines built underground cave cities to hide from Assyrian invaders. Where a half million men were cut down at the Battle of Gallipoli in World War One.

Dax broke the silence when at last the tiny plane chugged over the Mediterranean Sea. "The island of Cyprus is over thirty-five hundred square miles of territory. Addison, do you have any idea which square mile you're heading to?"

"Kartal's Café," said Addison.

"And where's that exactly?"

Addison realized he had no idea. He did what he always did in cases of emergency: he cracked open *Fiddleton's Atlas*, pausing briefly to admire the newly autographed title page. He quickly found Kartal's Café, near the town of Kantou. "The southern tip of the island."

Dax worked his toothpick across his mouth. "Why is

Malazar in Cyprus?" he mused. "And why there on the southern tip?"

Addison stared at his map and saw his answer staring right back. "Kolossi Castle."

Dax looked at him sidelong with a cocked eyebrow.

"The Knights Templar owned the entire island of Cyprus during the Crusades." Addison skimmed the description in *Fiddleton's Atlas*. "Kolossi Castle was their stronghold."

"What does Malazar want with that place?"

Addison shook his head. "I only know he's obsessed with Templars."

Dax leaned over to study Addison's map. "The international airport is way over on the east side of the island. Paphos Airport is way over on the west. Molly's in danger— we don't have that kind of time."

"So where do we land?" Addison asked.

Dax chewed his lip in concentration. He stabbed a finger at the map. "The southern tip of Cyprus is British territory. The Royal Air Force has a base just a few miles from the castle."

"Are you allowed to land this plane on an air force base?"

Dax tightened his grip on the throttle and edged the plane into a steep descent. "Better to ask forgiveness than permission."

"Dax," said Addison, suddenly nervous, "what are you planning?"

"What I do best," said Dax, one corner of his mouth lift-ing into a grin. "I'm going to crash-land."

••••••

Dax called a mayday in on his radio. He steered the plane into an ear-popping nosedive.

Eddie and Raj woke up in the back seat when Mr. Jacobsen fell off their laps.

"Are we there yet?" asked Eddie, rubbing his eyes.

"We're about to be," said Addison. "Tighten your seat belt—we're going to crash."

"Crash?" said Eddie.

"Relax, Eddie," said Dax. "We've crashed before."

"Why do I get in a plane with you?"

Dax didn't answer. He yanked a latch on the dashboard. The needle on a large gauge began spinning wildly.

Addison didn't like the look of it. "Dax, what are you doing?

"Dumping fuel." Dax winked at Addison. "Got to make it look convincing." He wobbled the steering, causing the plane to lurch.

Addison clung to the overhead grab bar.

The British Royal Air Force control tower crackled over the radio. Dax announced he was making an emergency landing.

Addison noticed he did not ask permission.

Chapter Twenty-Nine

Cyprus

BRITISH ROYAL AIR FORCE pilots, crewmen, mechanics, and technicians scrambled out of the path of Dax's speeding Cessna. He hammed it up, bouncing the wheels several times before skidding out at the very end of the runway.

As soon as the plane rolled to a stop, Dax leapt from the cabin and popped open the engine hood. "Got to break something quickly before they take a look," he explained to Addison.

Addison climbed out of the plane and kissed the ground, not even worrying about the germs. He looked up to see Dax unplugging engine circuitry.

Sparks shot from the hot engine, followed by a blast of smoke that looked like a nonpurple version of Raj's smoke balls.

Dax wiped soot from his face with the palms of his hands. "Oops."

"I thought you were trying to break it," said Addison.

"Well, I only wanted it to *look* broken," said Dax sheepishly. Smoke belched from the engine.

Raj, Eddie, and Mr. Jacobsen peeled themselves out of the Cessna and joined Addison, staring at the wounded plane. The engine heaved and gasped like a wounded creature.

"Dax, can you fix this?" asked Addison. "If we rescue Molly, we might need to make a fast exit."

"A rapid extraction," Raj agreed.

"Well, *I* can't fix it," said Dax. "But maybe they can."

A pair of British Royal Air Force officers jogged to the end of the runway, all polite handshakes and affable grins.

"Terribly good of you to drop in," said the first.

"And you're just in time for tea," said the second. "An awfully good landing," he added.

Addison had left England only a short while ago. But he realized with a smile just how much he had already missed the British.

•••••••

Addison, Eddie, and Raj left Dax in the capable hands of the Royal Air Force. Telling the RAF they just wanted a bit of exercise, they exited the air force base and hiked north along Queen Elizabeth Street in the dry and dusty afternoon heat.

They soon passed a vast salt lake that Addison was amazed to see was crowded with thousands of pink flamingos. The peculiar birds fished the shallows, balanced on their spindly chopstick legs. Listening to their warbles and chirps, Addison realized he owed Molly an apology. There really was such a thing as flamingo music.

The road overlooked the mild and mesmerizing Mediterranean. The trio followed it north, not far from the ruins of the ancient Roman city of Kourion, with its markets and theater and the houses of the gladiators. Addison was not at all surprised to see that Cyprus was dotted with more than a few cypress trees, like giant, dark green corncobs pointed at the sky. The surrounding fields were heaped with magnificent blue flowers.

"Raj," said Addison, "what do you call those perfect blue flowers? I can never remember the name."

"Forget-me-nots."

"Well, I'm in seventh heaven," Addison declared. He slapped a mosquito on his chin. "All right, maybe not *seventh* heaven on account of these mosquitoes. But at least fourth or fifth heaven."

"We should keep moving," said Raj.

"You're right," Addison sighed. "Molly's out there somewhere. And if she finds out we wasted time sightseeing instead of helping her, she'll kill us before the Collective has the chance."

At last the road wound its way over a hill, and Kolossi Castle inched into view. It was a square stone keep, crumbling around the edges. Out of nowhere, Raj yanked Addison and Eddie into the bushes and flattened them low to the ground. He held one finger to his lips and pointed his other hand at the castle.

Addison craned his neck until he saw that the castle was surrounded by black SUVs. Men in dark glasses were pouring concrete and hauling construction equipment up a network of scaffolding. "Malazar's rebuilding the castle."

"I wonder why," Raj whispered.

"Perhaps he's making it his stronghold. Like Grand Master Jacques de Molay before him." Addison looked at guards patrolling the forbidding castle. "Molly's locked in there. I'm sure of it."

He sat up in the grass and turned to his team. "All we need to do is unkidnap Molly and unsteal the tablet."

Raj smiled. "I've always wanted to rescue someone from a castle. That and break a Spartan shield wall."

"Raj, you have the strangest bucket list."

Addison scanned the landscape. Kolossi Castle was surrounded by open fields dotted with cattle. Any daytime approach to it would be spotted unless his team all grew four legs and udders. They were going to have to wait for nightfall. "Guys, I hope you don't have any overdue library books," said Addison. "We may be here a while."

"Good," said Raj, pulling out his binoculars. "That gives us time to come up with a plan."

Addison scratched the back of his head. "I'm guessing the castle door will be locked. So we need a way over that castle wall."

"We could use a grappling hook," Eddie offered.

"Great!" said Addison. "Raj, what do you think?"

"Sure. Where's the grappling hook?"

"It's in my father's satchel."

"Where's your father's satchel?" asked Eddie.

"Molly has it."

"Molly's in the castle," said Raj.

"Hmm." Addison frowned and crossed his arms. They were going to need something better. "We could light a bonfire," he said. "When they open the front gate to investigate, we rush inside."

"They'd see us," said Raj. "We'd have to be ready to fight."

"True," said Addison.

"Who's our best fighter?" asked Eddie.

"Molly is."

"Molly's in the castle," said Raj.

"Hmm." Addison furrowed his brow. "C'mon," he said,

growing impatient. "We must be capable of doing *something* without Molly. I want ideas. There are no bad ideas in brainstorming."

"We just need to take out the guards," said Eddie. "Knock them unconscious."

"Good. Raj?"

"We'd need some sort of long-range weapon."

"You mean like a sling?" asked Addison.

"Exactly."

"Who's our best slinger?" asked Eddie.

"Molly is," said Addison.

"Molly's in the castle," said Raj.

"Hmm."

All three were silent for a moment.

"All right," said Addison. "We need a great idea that doesn't involve Molly. There are no bad ideas in brainstorming, except for ideas that require Molly."

"What if," said Eddie, his eyes shut with concentration, "instead of lighting a bonfire *outside* the castle, we light a bonfire *inside* the castle."

"That's a pretty big distraction," said Addison. "I like what I'm hearing."

"All the guards run to put out the fire. So the castle gate is unguarded," Eddie continued. "I pick the lock, and one of us sprints inside while no one is looking."

"This assumes," said Addison, "that the gate is not shut

with a lock bar. And that we can find a way to light a fire inside the castle."

"Sure," said Eddie. "There are a few kinks to work out."

"Okay," said Addison. "Raj, what do you think?"

"It could work, but we'd need a fast runner to pull it off."

"Who's our fastest runner?" asked Eddie.

"Molly is."

"Molly's in the castle," said Raj.

"Hmm."

......

Dusk settled upon the land. The castle stood out black against the deepening blue of the evening sky. Addison, Raj, and Eddie grew hungry and divvied up a pile of pistachios Raj had pocketed during their feast in Malazar's hotel suite. Raj insisted the food was reserved for an emergency, but Eddie insisted that a missed dinnertime constituted an emergency, so they split open all the nuts with Addison's butterfly knife.

Addison felt bad that he had not thought ahead about bringing more food for dinner. But he explained to Eddie and Raj that he was in the business of rescuing sisters and stealing tablets, and not in the business of remembering meals.

A bone-chilling wind whipped in off the Mediterranean,

stinging their eyes with dust and tousling their hair. The wind howled across the desolate land, shaking the bent trees and scattering leaves across the dried rushes. Addison turned up the collar on his suit jacket and hugged his arms tightly around his knees.

It wasn't until they were on the last three pistachios that Eddie remembered what day it was. "Merry Christmas, Addison. Happy holidays, Raj."

"Happy holidays, guys," said Addison.

The winds blew colder, and the team settled in to wait for absolute dark. Once the night was as black as possible, they began their assault on the castle.

Chapter Thirty
The Break-In

FULL DARK ARRIVED BEFORE they had settled on a complete plan. Addison didn't love the plan, but he didn't love sitting around wasting time, either. This was a time for action, no matter how hastily planned or ill-advised.

The plan, in a nutshell, was to sneak into the castle and hope that Malazar and the Collective would have their collective guard down because it was Christmas.

Eddie found the plan preposterous. "What, do you think that Malazar and Ivan are going to be singing carols around a piano? Or maybe you're picturing them in their pajamas opening up presents around a Christmas tree?"

Raj was similarly skeptical. "More than half the people on earth don't even celebrate Christmas."

Addison sighed. "I'm not saying this is our best plan. I'm not even sure it can be called a plan. But we've had two hours to brainstorm, and we've barely managed a braindrizzle. Molly is in danger, and we can't wait any longer."

When clouds shrouded the luminous moon, Addison stole across the dry flats toward the castle. Raj and Eddie loped behind him. He had given them a few pointers from his stealth training with Uncle Jasper. Raj clearly had a talent for it. Eddie was more of a work in progress.

Addison froze when the moonlight broke through the moving clouds. He could see the dark silhouette of a guard in the high tower of Kolossi Castle. If the guard was watching the flats, he would have an easy time spotting their movement.

When passing clouds once more darkened the moon, Addison crept slowly forward. He crouched low, blending with the landscape, sticking close to clumps of stunted olive trees and a screen of waving reeds. When he closed within one hundred paces of the front gate, he slowed to a glacial pace, moving with the silence of a wraith.

Eddie moved with the silence of a rampaging moose. He somehow managed to walk smack into an oak branch, catching the brunt of it with his face. He clawed at the air and fell over backward into a thornbush.

Addison and Raj froze as if turned to stone. It was a

full five minutes before Addison allowed anyone to move. Very slowly, he and Raj freed Eddie from the thorns. Pulling Eddie out of a pricker bush proved to be almost as noisy as throwing him in would have been. At last, with sore thumbs and scratched arms, they worked him free.

Addison glared at Eddie in the half-light. "Eddie," he whispered fiercely. "Did you happen to bring your piano with you?"

Eddie shook his head.

"How about an accordion? Or a tambourine?"

Eddie shook his head again.

"Then how are you making so much noise?"

Eddie lifted his chin indignantly. "Do you want my help or not?"

Addison sighed. "Eddie, I apologize. Just move directly behind me and place your feet where I place mine."

Eddie nodded and they set off again.

Addison eased through the darkness so slowly that his motion was almost undetectable. Each step was an exercise in patience. He used each foot to clear a space on the ground of any crunching leaves or snapping twigs before placing his weight. It took fifteen minutes to cover the last fifty feet to the castle gate.

They stood protected under the shadow of the high castle wall. They were now invisible from the guard in the high tower. Lights were on inside the bailey, and a few snippets of Russian conversation carried on the wind. Addison knew there were plenty of Collective members collected inside the castle.

Raj began stretching his limbs and limbering up. He tied a length of rope around his waist. Raj's job was to use his rock-climbing skills to scale the castle wall.

Addison positioned Eddie a few feet away in the cover of a wind-bent cypress tree. From this vantage point, Eddie could spot anyone coming from the main road or attempting to cross the flats. "Eddie, what do you see?"

"Cows," said Eddie. "Lots of cows."

Raj stared up at the high wall looming over them. It seemed much taller up close.

Addison patted him on the shoulder. "Can you do it?"

"Maybe."

"Raj, Molly's in there."

Raj took a deep breath, steeling his courage. "Okay." He patted his hands in the chalky dirt to help his grip.

"The trick is to not get yourself killed," Addison added helpfully.

Raj found a toehold in the rock wall and began climbing. He wedged his fingers into the uneven stones, wind-worn by centuries, and gradually worked his way higher. Twelve feet up, he paused, searching for a foothold. His arms began shaking from the strain.

Far below, Addison held his breath.

At last, Raj stretched his leg wide and found purchase in a cleft of cracked mortar beneath a large stone. He got his breath back and scaled his way higher.

Addison managed to tear his nervous eyes from Raj and scan the dark horizon for any sign of an intruder. He didn't want Ivan to return home from a trip to the grocery store and surprise Raj halfway up the castle wall. He thought he spotted movement in the pasture to the south. "Eddie," he whispered, pointing past an olive grove. "What's over there?"

Eddie peered at distant shapes moving in the night. "Cows, cows, and more cows," he whispered, adding, "I'm having déjà moo."

Raj reached the crenellated bumps of the castle rampart. Against the dark sky, they looked like gapped teeth in a giant's jaw. He pulled himself over the lip and onto the high stone parapet.

Addison felt his heart start beating again. He wiped sweat from his brow and was thankful for his new sweat-proof ballroom dance jacket.

Raj untied the rope from around his waist and looped it around one of the stone merlons in the sawtoothed rampart. He rapidly tied a square knot, a bowline, and two half hitches, as only a Boy Scout can. He leaned over the parapet, gave a thumbs-up, and tossed the free end of the rope down to Addison's waiting hands.

This was the part Addison dreaded most: the climbing. He didn't love being chased through London by gun-toting Russian mobsters. He wasn't thrilled about speedboat races through Paris sewers. But he would take either one in a heartbeat over having to climb a massive stone wall. He reminded himself that he had somehow succeeded in climbing one castle wall already, back at the Fortress in Paris. Castles walls should be old hat to him now. But Raj's rope did not have foothold knots like Molly's, and the entire experience seemed altogether less pleasant.

Halfway up, Addison looped the trailing end of the rope around his waist so that if he fell, he wouldn't fall quite so far. He chanced a glance down at the drop, which, if it didn't kill him, would not improve his health. He clamped his eyes shut and continued climbing.

Addison felt he had aged ten years by the time Raj grabbed his trembling arms and pulled him over the battlement. He lay down on the parapet, gasping until the world stopped spinning, or at least, stopped spinning in the wrong direction.

By the time Addison felt ready to attempt the long climb to his own feet, Eddie had scaled the wall as well. Addison admired Raj's square knot and half hitches, tied to textbook perfection. Those knots had held his life in the balance. He shook Raj's hand. "Thank you, Raj."

Raj looked down shyly at the stone floor and shucked his feet.

Addison gripped Raj's hand more firmly. "I'm serious. Pulling you out of Boy Scouts is like pulling da Vinci out of art class. It's a crime."

Raj sighed. "Thanks, Addison."

Eddie dusted himself off. "Should we take the rope with us?"

"No, leave it," whispered Addison. "We may need a quick escape." He made a mental note of the location of the rope: the fifth stone merlon to the left of the main gate. He peered over the inside parapet into the castle courtyard below. It swarmed with activity. Outdoor lights were powered by a generator. Men dug trenches, filling wheelbarrows with dirt. Others sifted the dirt through screens. To Addison's surprise, he realized he was looking at a full-blown archaeological dig.

He recognized members of the Collective swinging hammers and pulling saws. Addison figured they were building living quarters to house the crew. There was a stacked pyramid of paint cans by the well, where some men were painting the freshly built barracks. The new buildings were black with blood-red trim, giving the castle a sinister air. Addison counted seventeen men in all, but no sign of Ivan or Malazar.

"What are they digging for?" Raj whispered.

Addison shrugged and shook his head. He scanned the castle for any sign of a dungeon or steps leading down to a basement. "If you were keeping Molly prisoner, where would you put her?"

Without a word, Raj pointed to the high tower looming over them, casting them in its ominous shadow.

"You're not suggesting we go up there," Eddie said, his whispered voice tremulous in the thin night air.

Addison nodded solemnly. The crooked tower narrowed at the top like a witch's hat. The group hunched low and followed the parapet to the tower's grim, crumbling entrance. It was time to find Molly.

Chapter Thirty-One

The Castle Tower

ADDISON LED THE TEAM through a low stone arch-way and onto a catwalk over the main gate. Raj pointed excitedly. From their high vantage point, they could see the defensive works of the castle. Loop holes for raining arrows down on anyone attacking the gate. Murder holes for pouring boiling hot oil onto any intruders who survived the arrows.

They inched along the jagged wooden planks. The catwalk took a dogleg and ducked below a turret. Addison followed it and reached the far side of the gate. Eddie clomped after him, with Raj bringing up the rear. Addison would have preferred if Eddie were just a few hundred decibels quieter. But since there was a gas generator running outside, powering the courtyard lights, Addison felt they could get away with a little extra noise.

The catwalk fed to a winding stone staircase, leading up to the next level.

At the top of the steps, they reached a landing. Before them were two heavy oak doors. Before continuing farther upstairs, Addison motioned that they should check them out.

Eddie drew out his lock-picking set and dropped to one knee. He wiggled a pick into the first lock, pressing his ear to the door, his tongue out in concentration. Addison and Raj stood by as lookouts on the stairs.

Within seconds, Raj's eyes bulged and he began waving his arms in silent alarm. Footsteps were plodding downstairs, closer and closer.

Addison saw a man's shadow coming into view against the stairway wall. The shadow had a massive, tangled bird's nest of hair . . . Ivan.

Eddie just barely managed to pop the first door open in time so he, Addison, and Raj could scramble inside. The three huddled in the dark until Ivan's heavy boot steps trudged past.

Raj lit a strike-anywhere match, revealing they were inside a storeroom. It was packed with building supplies and digging equipment. "What are they up to?" Raj whispered.

Addison shook his head. "Doesn't matter to us right now. We just need to find Molly and jet out of here."

Carefully, they filed back out onto the landing. Eddie picked the second door lock faster, now that he had the hang of it. When the last tumbler clicked into place, he pushed against the door, but it did not budge.

Eddie shoved hard with his shoulder, straining against the heavy oak. "A little help?" he whispered. "I think it's stuck."

Addison leaned his weight against it.

It was Raj who got a running start and made a flying leap at the door. It slammed open, crashing against the inside wall.

All three friends fell into the room in a jumbled heap. They looked like a game of Twister that had gone horribly wrong. Addison switched on his pen flashlight, scrambled to his feet, and gasped. There, chained against the rocky wall, sat Molly.

......

"It's about time," said Molly.

"Merry Christmas, Mo," said Addison. He had been planning to say this when he rescued Molly, and he meant it to sound suavely heroic.

"Merry Christmas yourself," she retorted. "Do you have any idea how much noise you just made? You'll alert half the castle!" Molly stood up, but the chain around her ankle kept her tethered to the wall.

"Listen, we're here to rescue you. The least you could do is show a little gratitude!" Addison crossed to the rusted chains and gave them a stiff jerk, attempting to wrench them free of the ancient, crumbling mortar.

"Ouch." Molly grimaced. "Addison, you're yanking my chain."

"No, this is our real rescue attempt!"

Molly just sighed.

"Look, if you don't want to be rescued, just say so." Addison made a show of leaving the room.

"Of course I want to be rescued," said Molly. "But you can't tear these chains out of the wall. I've been trying that for hours. And thank you, by the way."

"You're welcome." Addison bowed. "It was really Raj who got us inside the castle."

Raj blushed.

Eddie set to work on the lock around Molly's ankle. Raj held his flashlight for him.

Molly patted Eddie on the shoulder and turned to give Raj a quick hug. "Thank you, Raj."

Raj blushed even deeper. "Molly, weren't you afraid? You don't seem like you were scared at all."

"Of course I was scared," said Molly. "But I knew you would all come for me."

With a snap of metal, Eddie unlocked Molly from her leg chain.

She rolled down her sock and rubbed circulation back into her ankle.

Addison knelt down and, on an impulse, decided to do something very unusual. He gave her a hug as well. "Molly, my favorite sister, I'm glad you're alive and all that. Now quickly: where is the tablet? We can't leave without it."

Molly pushed the hair back from her forehead and looked grim. "I have an idea where it is. But you're not going to like it."

••••••

"Malazar's room?" Eddie exclaimed. "You want us to go in there?"

"Where else would he hide the tablet?" asked Molly.

"Okay, sure," said Eddie. "But how many times are we going to have to break into this guy's rooms?"

"If we're lucky, there will be more shrimp cocktail," said Addison. "Molly, lead the way." He felt a growing sense of foreboding. He was not a superstitious type, but he couldn't help but notice that getting into the castle and finding Molly had gone exceptionally smoothly. Therefore, by the laws of the universe that seemed to govern his life, Addison knew that getting out of the castle would prove extremely difficult.

They sealed the door to Molly's former cell and crept farther up the spiraling stone staircase. Molly cautioned them with a hand to keep their voices low. "I don't know where the guards are. I haven't been up these stairs before."

"Then how do you know Malazar's room is up here?" Eddie asked.

"Because I keep hearing him climb these steps."

Addison crept silently forward. It made sense. They were in the most protected part of the castle. He stared upward into the gloom and shut off his flashlight—no sense advertising their presence. So far, they hadn't spotted Malazar, so they could be marching right toward him. Addison craned his ears for any sound, his senses on their highest alert.

"There's one other thing," Molly whispered as they rounded the curving steps. "I'm not the only prisoner here."

"What are you talking about?" asked Raj.

"The whole time I was locked up, I kept thinking I heard voices. A man or a woman, somewhere up these stairs."

Addison frowned, processing this new information. "Stay sharp, everyone. We could have more people to rescue."

The staircase ended at the next floor. Before them was a locked cell. Raj peered through the iron bars. "Whoever was here, they're not here anymore."

Addison scanned the empty cell. "We need to know their identity. Eddie, can you work your magic?"

"Sure." Eddie swung open the cell door, which was unlocked.

The group crept inside. Addison panned the walls with his flashlight. Scores of hash marks were scratched into the walls, marking days and weeks. "Whoever it was," said Addison, "they were here for months."

"Blood!" cried Raj, trembling with excitement. He held up a roll of used bandage from the floor.

"Gross," said Eddie. "Why would you touch that?"

Raj, embarrassed, dropped the bandage back on the stone floor. He wiped his hand off on his camouflage pants.

"So who was Malazar keeping here?" asked Eddie.

"I'm sure he has lots of enemies," said Molly.

Addison narrowed his eyes. A thought was circling the edges of his mind like a hunting shark. "There's something I keep wondering. How did the Collective know to watch the Blandfordshire Bank? How did they know the bronze tablet was in there? How did they know we'd get a key to the safe deposit box once Aunt D and Uncle N were buried? The only people who would know that information are . . ."

Molly answered for him. She spoke quietly, her eyes wide in the darkness. ". . . Aunt Delia and Uncle Nigel."

Addison knelt down before the bloody rag. "Supposing they were here. Supposing they were tortured for that information . . ."

"Hold on," said Raj. "You're saying they're still alive?"

"They were alive at some point," said Addison slowly. "I don't see any other way for the Collective to stake out Blandfordshire Bank the same week as the funeral."

"Or for them to know the Templar safe house in Paris," Molly piped in.

"Or for them to know the tablet would lead us to the Hagia Sophia in Istanbul," Addison added. "These guys have predicted our every move. If they've been torturing Aunt Delia and Uncle Nigel, that explains everything."

"But how could they have survived that fall in Mongolia?" asked Eddie.

"I don't know," said Addison, shaking his head. "It's just a theory."

The team fell silent.

Addison felt his legs growing weak, like he might faint. He knelt down to the ground and covered his face with his hands.

"Are you all right?" asked Molly.

A tight lump grew in Addison's throat, and for a minute he could not speak. Ever since he had lost his aunt and uncle, everything in his life had gone wrong. It wasn't just losing the two people who had been parents to him, and raised him and Molly as their own. It wasn't just leaving his home in New York and moving three thousand miles away from his two best friends. It was doubting himself. Doubting his every decision. He was convinced

---

that his aunt's and uncle's deaths were his fault and his fault alone. That if he had somehow done things differently, they would still be alive. And now, for the first time in months, he felt a remote glimmer of hope. Maybe, just maybe, they were alive after all. And if that were true, then their deaths weren't on his shoulders. Maybe, somehow, everything wasn't his fault.

He drew the Templar medallion from under his shirt and read the five ancient words emblazoned on its golden skin. He translated the Latin in his mind: "teamwork," "knowledge," "faith," "perseverance," and "courage." He focused on the word "faith," tracing each letter with his thumb.

Addison wiped his eyes and rose to his feet. He felt as if there was a fire in him that for months had slowly simmered down to cold embers. And now, that fire was roaring back to life. "So," he said, when he knew his voice was firm enough to speak. "Where is the tablet?"

Molly spoke up. "Malazar's room will be at the very top of the tower."

"Well, no time like the present." Addison confidently led his team out of the cell.

•••••••

Addison circled back to the staircase and found a wooden ladder that fed up through a hole in the stone ceiling, leading to the top of the tower. He set a finger to his lips for absolute quiet. Then, in a rare display of self-control, he shimmied up the ladder without any of his usual dizziness or fear.

The team followed Addison up the ladder, and even Eddie managed the feat without a sound.

In the high tower stood a single door. Addison could see there was no need for Eddie to pick it. It was already open a crack. Gently, very gently, as though petting a sleeping tiger, he edged the door open.

On the far side of the room, bent over a writing table, sat a tall, thin, pale man.

Malazar.

Chapter Thirty-Two

The Theft

MALAZAR'S BACK WAS TO the door. Addison again counted his luck. He'd been getting lucky chances ever since entering Kolossi Castle, and he knew it might run out any second. Best to work quickly.

Addison and his team peered into the room. Malazar, working by candlelight, was scribbling something into a notebook. The walls were covered with pages torn from ancient texts—architectural drawings and ancient schematics on frayed parchment. Addison had no idea what Malazar was working on, but it was clearly more than a passing hobby.

Whistling wind whipped through the open arrow loops. For a man who owned fleets of SUVs, commanded Mafia armies across Europe, and could pay off entire police departments, Malazar's room was surprisingly barren of any sign of wealth. The room was small and sparsely furnished. This, Addison felt, would make it easier to search. Besides the writing tablet, there was only a simple cot. And beneath the cot, to Addison's delight, was a single chest.

The chest was the only spot in which Addison could imagine hiding the bronze tablet. Solid oak, it appeared to be too big to drag without making a racket. There was nothing for it: Eddie was going to have to sneak in and pick the lock.

Addison turned to Eddie, who was already wearing a look of mortal dread. He made a lock-picking motion with his hands and then pointed at the chest.

Eddie shook his head no.

Addison pointed again. This time, he made his charades even clearer.

Eddie shook his head vigorously, like his brains were ice cream and he badly needed to make a milkshake.

Addison knitted his hands in a gesture of pleading.

Eddie still shook his head.

Molly glared hard at Eddie and crushed a fist in her palm.

Eddie swallowed hard. He reluctantly looked back inside the little room. Malazar was seated a mere ten feet from the chest. Eddie crawled slowly inside.

......

Addison held his breath. He was terrified to look and terrified to look away. All he could do was hope that a little bit of his stealth training had somehow rubbed off on Eddie.

Eddie flattened so low to the ground, he was practically slithering on his belly. He inched his way across the room until he reached the locked chest.

Malazar shifted in his seat and looked up.

Addison's heart stopped beating, packed its bags, and fled to Mexico. His eyes, however, kept working overtime. He could see that Eddie was sweating profusely and his hands were shaking—all signs of Eddie's stage fright. If Eddie's teeth started chattering, Malazar would surely hear, and then they'd really be done for. He noticed that Eddie was clenching his jaws together tightly.

Malazar crossed to the narrow window and closed the sash against the chill night air. He returned to his seat and continued writing.

Addison's heart returned from Mexico, deeply tanned, relaxed, and ready to get back to work. For a long moment, Eddie did not move. Addison wondered if perhaps Eddie's brain had blown a gasket with all the nervous tension. Finally, he saw Eddie's back rising and falling as he drew deep, calming breaths.

With steadier hands, Eddie inserted his pick into the

lock of the chest and began working the tumblers. In under a minute, he sprang the lock and silently eased the chest open. Feeling around inside, he removed Molly's leather satchel.

Molly's eyes lit up and she quietly pumped her fist.

Malazar shifted in his chair, scratching his chin with the tip of his pen.

Eddie groped around inside the chest again. This time he pulled out a pile of socks. He frowned, dug a hand back into the chest, and came up with a neatly folded stack of pajamas.

Addison watched impatiently. Soon, he saw Eddie straining to lift something heavy out of the bottom of the chest. At last, the bronze tablet came into view, glittering when it reached the light.

Slowly, ever so slowly, Eddie retreated backward on his elbows and knees, clutching the heavy slab of metal. When Eddie's ankles were within grabbing distance, Molly and Raj simply latched on to him and slid him out of Malazar's room.

Addison gave Eddie two silent thumbs-up. He took the tablet from Eddie and cradled it in his arms like a new-born baby. Raj gently slid the door shut as they left. Molly took her satchel from Eddie and shouldered it. Together, they eased themselves quietly down the ladder and the spiraling stone steps.

Raj had never been in the military, but he had seen enough TV to be familiar with the hand signals used for sneaking around. He held a fist in the air to pause the group when they reached the storage room where Molly had been imprisoned.

The group strained their ears, listening to the sounds of activity around the castle. Sure enough, they heard the sound of heavy boot steps. Ivan was making his rounds, strolling the perimeter of the castle wall like the minute hand around a clock.

Addison waved everyone into the storage room that Eddie had unlocked earlier. Inside, he whispered to the group. "Ivan's heading this way. We'll have to wait for the coast to clear."

Raj sat with his ear pressed to the door.

"Can you hear him?" asked Molly. "Is he past yet?"

"I'm not sure," said Raj, frowning in concentration. "I can't hear the footsteps anymore."

"Let's give Ivan another minute."

They sat in silence. Addison could hear his fake Rolex ticking.

Eddie spoke up. "Anyone know any good jokes?"

"Just another minute, Eddie," said Addison. "Raj, anything?"

Raj listened hard and shook his head.

Addison turned the tablet over in his hands. He studied it closely with his pen flashlight. There was a thin seam running around the edge. Addison figured there must be a way to open it up. Perhaps the tablet was designed to open only for a Templar Knight. Maybe there was some secret code the Templars knew that had been lost to the centuries. When he examined the ring carved into the back of the tablet, it tickled something in the back of his mind.

He traced the ring with his finger, lost in thought. He studied the strange glyph carved into the center of the circle. It was no language he knew or had ever seen. And yet it seemed mind-bendingly familiar. He ran his thumb over the letters and felt the hairs rise on the back of his neck. "Only a Templar Knight can open this," he said aloud. "A *Tutor Thesauri*. A relic guardian."

Eddie looked at him quizzically. "Are you okay, Addison?"

Addison's eyes spread wide like rings in a pond. "I know where I've seen this word before."

Molly, Raj, and Eddie crowded close, staring at the tablet glowing gold in the beam of Addison's flashlight.

"This indecipherable word is in Latin. Only backward." Addison drew the Templar medallion from around his neck. The five familiar words were written in Latin. But only the word for "faith" was raised: *fides*.

He fit the medallion into the circular depression on the bronze tablet. It clicked perfectly into place.

"Now what?" asked Eddie.

"It's a key," said Addison. "We turn it." He pressed his medallion firmly into the circle and rotated it to the left. He felt the bronze ring turning and heard springs winding deep inside the tablet. Finally, he heard the snap of a latch.

And the bronze tablet folded open.

Chapter Thirty-Three

The Secret
of the Tablet

ADDISON OPENED THE TABLET like a book. Molly,
Eddie, and Raj huddled around him, their faces illuminated by the flashlight reflecting off the gleaming bronze.
It took a few seconds for the random squiggles and wavy
lines before them to congeal into a pattern. Addison
gasped. There was no mistaking: it was a treasure map.

The relief map was etched into the bronze; slight swells
in the metal indicated hills and cliffs. A deep jagged line
described the path of a riverbed. And in the center of the
tablet, by a sharp bend in the river, was a six-pointed star
set inside a ring.

"X marks the spot," said Molly.

Addison flipped open his notebook and found the map of the bronze floor he had sketched inside the Templar hideout. The notebook pages were creased and wrinkled from being dunked in the cistern, but the map was still readable. He studied the missing tile in the bronze floor, and compared it with the bronze tablet before him. All of the squiggles and bumps lined up perfectly. "It fits," said Addison excitedly. "This completes the treasure map!"

"Well, what are we waiting for?" said Raj, his eyes glowing. "Let's escape this castle and find Solomon's treasure!"

"Well," said Addison, grinning, "I don't see why not."

Unfortunately for Addison, this was the exact moment that Ivan kicked in the door.

••••••

The heavy oak door slammed into Raj. The impact sent him sprawling into Molly, who knocked over Addison and Eddie like a trick shot on a pool table. For a second, all four were on their backs, legs in the air like upturned beetles.

Molly pulled her trusted sling from her father's satchel. She loaded a heavy lead slug into the pouch and started it swinging. Raj and Addison dove for cover. In the tiny room, she barely had any room to maneuver. She tried to whip the sling up to speed, but Ivan was already on her, slashing with the push daggers that sprouted between his fingers. The lead slug dropped out of Molly's sling as she twisted and dodged.

Addison and Eddie, both running from Ivan in the tiny room, managed to knock heads. Addison dropped his flashlight. It skittered across the floor, casting a carousel of spinning shadows. This was it, Addison realized—his supply of luck was beginning to run dry.

Molly discovered that the only problem with fighting a highly skilled knifeman in the dark with nothing more than a leather sling was that it was impossible. She tried whipping her sling again and succeeded only in thwacking Raj's leg. She realized Uncle Jasper was right: a sling wouldn't work in close quarters.

"A sling won't work in close quarters," said Ivan, wearing his best approximation of a human grin.

"Thank you," said Molly, between gritted teeth, "for pointing that out."

Ivan gripped his daggers and dove for her.

Molly rolled out of his way. She, Addison, Eddie, and Raj dashed out of the tiny storeroom.

Addison took the liberty of slamming the door shut. He heard the lock click into place.

A split second later, Ivan began screaming and pounding against the wooden door.

"We should probably go," Addison suggested. He hoofed it down the spiraling stairs, leading by example. He bolted over the wobbling wooden catwalks spanning the gatehouse, his arms spread wide for balance. Reaching the parapet on the far side, he floored the gas, sprinting at top speed along the battlements.

Below him in the courtyard he could see Russian gang members pointing at him and shouting. He didn't know what they were saying, but he imagined it was not complimentary. He called over his shoulder to his friends. "We just need to make it to the rope! Remember: the fifth stone left of the gate!"

His feet flying along the stone rampart, Addison reflected on how lucky they'd been. Rarely had one of his plans been pulled off without a single hitch. And yet look at them: they'd managed to break into the castle, rescue Molly, and steal the tablet, and they were now making a brilliant escape. All they had to do was hop over the wall, wriggle down a rope, and be on their merry way. Addison knew their castle raid had been an excellent plan, flawlessly executed. But when he reached the fifth stone left of the gate, his heart sank. Their escape rope was gone.

......

Eddie, Raj, and Molly skidded to a stop behind Addison. They all gaped at the stone wall where the rope should have been. It was appalling how much the rope was clearly not there.

A gang of Russian construction workers grabbed sledgehammers and began climbing a ladder to reach the parapet.

Addison's mind was clinging to sanity by its fingertips. He double-checked his math. This was clearly the fifth stone merlon left of the main gate. He double-checked the wall. This was definitely the wall where he had left the rope. He double-checked Raj, who shook his head, bewildered. Addison triple-checked everything. This was, in fact, the same Kolossi Castle in which he had left the rope. He was quite sure he hadn't left the rope at some other Kolossi Castle.

It was funny how life flipped things around on you, Addison reflected. A half hour ago, he was desperate to break into the castle. Now he was desperate to break out.

Still, here he was. Leaping over the castle wall was not an option, or at least, not a very good one. The thirty-foot drop was about twenty feet more than was really advisable. Addison could think of only one other option. "Run!"

Ivan, freshly escaped from the storage room, galloped up from behind.

Addison realized his day was not about to get any easier. Peeking over his shoulder, he noticed for the first time that Ivan was wearing a new brown fedora. He wondered if all his taunts about Ivan's hair had gotten under the poor man's skin. Running for his life, Addison now regretted not finding a few positive things to say to Ivan.

Raj led the sprint around the castle parapet. Ivan was quickly closing the gap from behind, nipping at Eddie's heels. Russian gang members were racing around the rampart from the other direction, bearing down on Raj.

Addison could see: they were about to be the filling inside a Russian sandwich. Or, as he paused to think about it, a kid sandwich with Russian bread.

Raj saw the Russians rushing toward him and reacted first. "Guys, follow me!" Raj took a flying leap off the rampart and onto the roof of a newly built courtyard barracks. It was either an act of inspired bravery or reckless self-endangerment. Either way, the barracks were not well built, because Raj plummeted right through the roof, leaving a gaping Raj-sized hole.

The Russians kept barreling toward Addison's group.

Addison was terrified by Raj's jump, but on the other hand, he didn't have any better ideas. He took a running leap off the parapet, too.

He crashed through the roof, creating a new hole to match Raj's. The roof was plywood, and clearly not built to last. Still, the building must have been far more temporary than the builders intended, because Addison created more damage than a cannonball. Plywood and scaffolding collapsed around him, slowing his fall. He landed painfully on a heap of painting tarps and barely managed to roll out of the way as Molly and Eddie came flying in after him.

Addison had the wind knocked out of him from the fall, but it was better than having the guts knocked out of him by Ivan. He struggled to his feet and helped Eddie struggle to his.

Raj was already beckoning them down a stairway to the first floor of the barracks. The group chased Raj down the steps, out the front door, and into the courtyard of the castle.

The good news, Addison could see, was that they were no longer trapped up on the rampart. The bad news, he realized, was that they were now trapped in the courtyard. On the whole, their situation was not much improved. A dozen Russians raced toward the group. Or, more specifically, toward Addison. He knew what they wanted: the bronze tablet. So he tossed it to Molly.

The crowd of Russians instantly veered, like a spooked school of fish. They zeroed in on Molly.

Molly carried the tablet a good ten yards across the courtyard, with the front gate as her end zone. When the Russians encircled her, she hurled the tablet to Eddie.

This was a slick move except that Eddie was not

looking. His eyes were locked on the exit as if by tractor beam.

The bronze tablet missed him entirely. It sailed wide, bounced off a pile of two-by-fours, and splattered into a fresh vat of red paint.

Raj plunged armpit-deep into the red paint vat and snatched out the tablet. To his pleasure, he saw that he was no longer dyed blue or purple. Bright red, he decided, was an improvement. Seeing Russians closing in fast, he heaved the dripping tablet to Eddie, who—as it happened—still wasn't looking.

The wet tablet smacked Eddie full in the back, drenching his blazer with red paint. Eddie yowled and collapsed like a felled oak.

Raj stood there, aghast. He was not in the habit of knocking over his friends with heavy bronze objects and he did not want to be.

By the time Addison scooped up the tablet from the dusty ground, Ivan had materialized in the courtyard. He wrenched Eddie's wrists behind his back.

Eddie struggled and writhed.

Ivan favored Addison with his signature smirk. "The tablet, or I kill your friend."

Addison, Molly, and Raj circled up, standing back to back to back. A ring of Russians surrounded them. Large men, vicious men. Men without conscience.

Addison could see he was wholly surrounded. General Custer could not have been more surrounded when he made his famous last stand. Even if Addison could break Eddie free, the castle gate was still shut tight.

He tossed the bronze tablet at Ivan's feet, defeated. "Happy holidays, Ivan."

Chapter Thirty-Four
The Firing Squad

IVAN'S GARGOYLE FACE TWISTED into a sneer that Addison knew was his best version of a smile. "Our trap worked. You took the bait. Malazar knew you would try to rescue your sister."

Addison followed Ivan's gaze across the courtyard and spotted Malazar, in his funereal black suit, watching from the shadows of the arched doorway to the tower. As ever, his features were cloaked in darkness. Every time Addison looked at the man, he felt a cold shudder down his spine.

Addison turned back to Ivan, hoping to come up with a clever barb, but he was still completely out of breath. His body ached from crashing through the roof of the barracks. He bent over and braced his hands on his knees, trying to recover.

Ivan took a step closer to Addison. "Not only were you lured into our trap, but you opened the tablet for us." He picked up the bronze tablet, dripping with paint, and admired the map before handing it off to a lackey to wash it clean. "You've brought us one step closer to the Ring of Destiny."

"Why do you care so much about this ring, anyway?" Addison was eager to keep Ivan talking. Not only did he want answers, he wanted to buy time to think up an escape. "Do you believe the ancient legends? That the ring is magic? That it can control angels and demons? That Solomon conjured fire from his throne?"

If it were possible, Addison would have said that Ivan's sneer grew even wider. The Russian chuckled and shook his head. "Malazar does not believe in hocus-pocus."

"So it's the treasure you're after. Solomon was one of the richest kings in history. Malazar wants to beef up his bank account."

Ivan again shook his head. "No. Malazar needs the tablet for only one reason."

Addison sighed. "The prophecy."

This time, Ivan nodded yes. "He needs the ring, the golden whip, and the other treasures to come. Malazar is going to win the prize. And we will fulfill the prophecy by killing you, your sister, and the last of the Templars."

Ivan gestured to his men with a jerk of his chin. The gang members grabbed Addison, Molly, Eddie, and Raj and hustled them up against the castle wall. Molly struggled and kicked, but it was no use. Two gang members kept her elbows tightly pinned.

Addison could see they were being lined up, firing-squad-style. He had lost all control of the situation. He turned back to Ivan. "Are my aunt and uncle alive?"

Ivan did not answer. He hefted a coil of rope from the construction area and began to unwind it, his expression unreadable.

Addison raised his voice and called to Malazar across the courtyard. "Did you rescue my aunt and uncle from Mongolia? Are you keeping them alive to help you solve the clues to reach the Ring of Destiny?"

Malazar stood shrouded in the gloom, the black of his suit blending into the darkness of the tower. Addison could see why they called him the Shadow—the man was downright difficult to see. Still, he could feel the man's eyes on him. It gave Addison a cold feeling in his chest, as if icy hands were reaching out to stifle his very heartbeat. And then Malazar stepped forward into the light.

Addison stopped breathing.

Horrific burn scars had mangled Malazar's face. One ear was a rounded nub. One eyebrow was entirely gone.

The nose was a twisted bump, like melted candle wax.

Addison felt a twinge of pity and a bolt of fear. Something terrible had clearly happened to the man. Addison was immediately reminded of Professor Vladimir Ragar, who had kidnapped Aunt Delia and Uncle Nigel in pursuit of the lost treasure of the Incas. It couldn't be a coincidence that both Ragar and Malazar had suffered some awful accident with fire. He wondered what tragedy had happened. He wondered if somehow the Cookes were involved. He wondered if this drove Malazar and Ragar's madness, and their obsession with killing Cookes. But all of those questions would have to wait.

Malazar was staring at Addison with cold fury. He pointed one gloved finger at Addison and then drew the finger across his own neck.

Addison understood. He was going to die.

•••••

Addison thought that firing squads usually had the decency to hand out blindfolds, but Ivan didn't appear to be troubling himself with such details. Ivan was, however, troubling himself to tie everyone's wrists together. Given how much Molly was squirming, this was probably going to take a while.

Eddie sighed, waiting his turn for Ivan to bind his wrists. "I could be in New York right now. I could be ice-skating in Rockefeller Center."

"Oh please," said Molly. "You hate ice-skating."

"That's true," Eddie admitted. "But not as much as I hate being executed."

Addison was at his wits' end trying to think of a plan. He was in no mood for Eddie's pessimism. "Eddie, don't be dramatic. You're acting like this is our first time being sentenced to death."

Ivan finished tying Molly's hands and moved on to Raj.

Addison cleared his throat and spoke to his sister. He had to talk across Eddie to do so. "Molly, there's something I need to tell you," he began.

Eddie groaned. "Addison, if you're going to get all sentimental, someone just kill me right now."

Addison ignored Eddie and pressed on. "Mo, our family have been relic hunters and relic guardians for seven hundred years. It's our destiny. The *Tutores Thesauri* were a group that—"

"I know," said Molly, interrupting him.

"What? How?"

"Malazar told me."

Eddie cut in. "You spoke to Malazar?"

"Sure. When he kidnapped me. He's really not such a bad guy once you get to know him."

Eddie raised his eyebrows. "Really?"

"No, of course not! He's horrible! He's . . ." Molly

searched for the right word, a word that Eddie could understand. "He's *horrendous.*"

Ivan finished cinching Raj's knots. Raj had been tempted to give Ivan a few pointers on tying a proper square knot, but thought better of it. When Ivan set to work on binding Eddie, Raj took a deep breath and plucked up his courage. "Molly, there's something I need to say, too."

"What is going on?" asked Eddie. "Why does everyone need to start telling things to Molly all of a sudden?"

"Molly," Raj began, his cheeks a little flushed. "Well, I just wanted to say I think you're absolutely—"

"Hold that thought, Raj," Addison interjected. "I just need to concentrate for a second." He needed a plan, and he wasn't going to hatch one with all this chitter-chatter going on.

Raj blushed and fell silent.

Addison closed his eyes and took a deep meditative breath. He had read that it was important to clear the mind when you needed to think of a solution. He wasn't sure how deep breaths could help with anything, but he didn't have anything better to do at the moment. He took a second deep breath and was about to take a third when he thought he smelled something in the breeze. A strange and powerful scent. A smell that instantly filled him with hope . . . *It worked,* he thought. *Deep breaths really can solve problems.*

Before Ivan could begin tying his wrists, Addison took a confident step forward. "Ivan, how dumb do you think we are?"

Ivan crinkled his brow at Addison, unsure how to answer.

Raj spoke up. "Addison, are you being rhetorical?"

Addison shook his head and pressed his point. "Ivan, you really think you've got our backs up against the wall, don't you?"

Ivan looked from Addison, to Eddie, to Molly, to Raj, and to the castle wall. He nodded.

Addison chuckled and shook his head with genuine pity. "Ivan, Ivan, Ivan. Do you really think we're stupid enough to waltz in here without any protection? How staggeringly dense would we need to be to shimmy into a Collective stronghold with nothing but three seventh graders and a sixth grader with a leather sling?"

Ivan pouched his lip in thought, his brow creased like a juiced lemon. He clearly had no idea what Addison was driving at.

Addison paced in a circle in the way he'd seen courtroom lawyers do on TV. "No, Ivan. We have protection. You can't lay a finger on us."

Ivan growled. "What are you babbling about?"

"Take off your hat," said Addison.

"Are you going to make fun of my hair?" asked Ivan.

"Would you like me to?" asked Addison.

Ivan frowned. He wasn't sure where Addison was going, but he saw no harm in playing along. He slowly took off his brown fedora.

"Good," said Addison. "Now hold your hat high in the air."

"Why?"

"You'll see," said Addison.

Ivan held his hat in the air.

"Higher," said Addison.

Ivan lifted his arm higher.

"Perfect," said Addison. He made an imaginary gun with his fingers and held it up for all the Russians to see. Then, with his pretend gun he carefully aimed and pointed at Ivan's hat. Addison pulled his imaginary trigger.

A deafening rifle shot split the air. Russians covered their ears and ducked. The hat was blasted from Ivan's hand.

Molly, Eddie, and Raj stared in slack-jawed amazement.

Ivan turned white like he'd been soaked in Clorox.

The courtyard erupted in pandemonium, with Russian gang members diving for cover.

Addison smiled and blew smoke from his imaginary gun. It had been a perfect shot. The kind of shot that could be made only by an incredible sharpshooter. A sharpshooter who used Pizzazz shampoo.

He sniffed the breeze and smelled it again. Somewhere up on the ramparts was the deadly aim of Tilda d'Anger.

Addison heard more shots ring out and saw more men ducking and running. He watched the chaos of the court-yard with satisfaction and turned to his team. "If you're all in favor," he said, "I think we should be leaving now."

Chapter Thirty-Five

The Hidden Map

ADDISON DARTED UP A flight of stone steps and onto the parapet. Molly, Eddie, and Raj scurried after him, their rope-bound hands clasped in front of them like penitent monks.

They sprinted along the high walkway until they rounded a corner and nearly ran smack into T.D.

"I knew you could not survive without me," she said in her flowery French accent.

"We had everything under control!" said Addison. "Why did you take our rope?"

"I did not want anyone to know you were in the castle. What if a patrol guard had noticed it? You should never leave a trail."

"Well, what about you with your Pizzazz shampoo? Isn't that leaving a trail?"

"Ah, so that is how you knew I was up here," said T.D. "Well, if I had not used Pizzazz, you would not have known I was covering you."

Addison was pretty sure T.D. was contradicting herself somehow, but he didn't want to argue with the person who had just saved his life.

She beckoned them to a rope slung over the castle wall.

"That's my rope!" shouted Raj.

"Yes, thank you," said T.D. "It helped me climb in here. Now hurry up."

Molly swung a leg over the parapet and began climbing down the rope. Her, Eddie's, and Raj's wrists were tied, but at least they were tied in front. They could still grip the line.

T.D. kept a sharp eye on the courtyard below. Anytime a Russian gang member showed his face from behind a barrel or crate, she fired off another shot from her rifle. "A pity," she said wistfully as Addison climbed over the parapet. "The Shadow never shows his face."

"I saw his face," said Addison. "You're not missing much."

......

The group raced across the cow pastures in the darkness. They ran until they were out of breath, and then they ran some more. T.D. insisted they build as big a lead as possible, because Ivan would be herding his men into trucks and coming for them soon.

At last T.D. agreed to allow them a one-minute break. Eddie bent double, sucking air.

Addison paced in a circle, his hands massaging a cramp in his side. He fished out his butterfly knife and began sawing the ropes from Molly's wrists. Her hands free, she took the knife and set to work cutting the ties from Eddie and Raj.

"So," said T.D., "Malazar has the tablet?"

Addison was annoyed to realize that T.D. was not even the slightest bit out of breath.

"Yes," he admitted. "He has the tablet. And we opened it for him. Now he knows the treasure map and we don't. We've lost." Addison sat down on the ground, exhausted. He felt completely and utterly defeated. He let his chin sink onto his chest.

There were many things about the English language that Addison did not understand. Why, for instance, were "know," "knot," and "knock" all spelled with a "k"? There seemed to be knothing to explain it. Why, for that matter, was "people" spelled with a silent "o"? The term "double jeopardy" should be punished for committing this same offense twice. Why, Addison wondered, did a "fat chance" and a "slim chance" mean the same thing? But of all the things he didn't understand about English, Addison was most perplexed by Molly's next sentence.

"Well," Molly said, cocking a fist on her hip, "we have the treasure map, too."

Addison's eyebrows crinkled up like well-chewed bubble gum. He turned to look at Molly.

Raj turned to look at Molly.

Eddie turned to look at Molly.

T.D. turned to look at Molly.

Several nearby cows lifted their heads from chomping grass, and turned to look at Molly.

"I noticed it earlier," she said.

"Well, where is it?" asked Addison.

"Eddie has it."

"Me?" Eddie pointed a finger at his chest and stared at her in bewilderment.

Molly took Eddie by the shoulder and spun him around. The back of his Public School 141 jacket was splattered with red paint where Raj had clobbered him with the bronze tablet. And there, for all the world to see, was a perfect mirror impression of the tablet stamped on his back. The squiggles of cliffs, the big wavy line of a river, and the six-pointed star marking a spot in the center. There was no mistaking it . . .

. . . It was the Templar map pointing the way to the Ring of Destiny.

III

THE
RING OF
DESTINY

Chapter Thirty-Six

The Chase

ADDISON HAD BUT ONE goal in life: to jot down the paint-splatter map on Eddie's back as fast as he possibly could. But before he could open a fresh page in his notebook and put pen to paper, he heard an ominous sound. A sound that was becoming all too familiar to him. The sound of a fleet of SUVs.

Their headlights appeared over the ridge, along with the sound of their gunning engines.

Eddie, who had been faint with exhaustion only a minute earlier, was already rocketing south like a startled pheasant.

Addison chased after him. "Eddie, be careful! You have the map to a billion dollars painted on your back!"

His biggest fear was that Eddie would somehow stumble into a pond in the dark, and their map would be washed away.

The dark SUVs raged across the pastures, bumping and jostling on the uneven ground.

Addison's group hurdled waist-high tufts of grass and dodged dozing cattle. Yet Addison could see that his team was slowing down. The trouble, he saw, was twofold: the first problem was that the SUVs were running on full tanks of gas, whereas his group was running on a quarter tank at best. The second problem was that even if they each had a square meal and a full night's sleep, they still couldn't hope to outrun a fleet of six-cylinder SUVs.

"Just a little farther!" Addison gasped, avoiding a crowd of brown-spotted calves. "We've got to reach Dax's plane!" He was so sapped of energy, he had the dreamlike feeling of running in slow motion.

"Let's hope Dax got his plane working," Eddie panted. "Otherwise, we're going to have a very long swim to get off this island."

The SUVs were eating up the distance. Addison realized there was no way to outrun them.

It was Raj who drew to a halt.

"Raj, don't give up!" Molly called.

"It's okay!" Raj cried excitedly. "Babatunde Okonjo!"

"What about him?"

"His second book! It explains how to stampede cattle!"

The pack of SUVs tore up mud and grass, raging across the hillocks.

Raj began whooping and hollering at the herds of Cyprus cows. He smacked the giant beasts on their rear ends. He pushed on them with his hands. The cows regarded him with puzzled curiosity.

Addison decided it was worth a shot. "Guys, pitch in!" he cried. He flapped his arms at the cows and shouted. Eddie and Molly joined in as well.

A few of the cows stopped chewing their cud and gazed at them with mild interest, slowly blinking their enormous eyes.

T.D. shook her head. "Let me handle this." She unshouldered her rifle, racked the bolt, and fired a shot in the air.

The cattle launched into flight as if lit by a fuse.

Addison figured it was even odds whether the cattle would run in the right direction. They might stampede the SUVs, or they might simply flatten Raj and then head down to the beach for a dip. Luckily, Addison's friends had already annoyed the cattle enough to set the herd running in more or less the correct path. The cows took off away from Addison's group and bore down on the SUVs.

The ground soon shook with the thunder of a thousand hooves. A massive dust cloud enveloped the plain. Addison could just make out the headlights of the SUVs as the vehicles slammed on their brakes and reversed course, fleeing the galloping herd of cattle.

Addison's group managed to limp another quarter mile before they again heard the revving engines of the SUVs closing in. The ground was more even here, and the vehicles chewed up the distance fast.

Addison was so worn out that he found he could muster little more than a slight jog.

"What now?" Eddie shouted as the engines grew louder. "We don't have any more cows!"

"But we do have friends," Addison called.

"Who are you talking about?" asked Eddie.

"Whom," said Addison.

"Whom!" Eddie hollered.

Addison pointed just over the next ridge to where Dax was standing with a convoy of military jeeps. "The Royal Air Force."

Chapter Thirty-Seven

The Road to Aqaba

ADDISON'S GROUP CROSSED INTO British territory like they were crossing the finish line of an ultramarathon.

Eddie collapsed on the ground. He was covered in dust from the cattle stampede. He looked like he'd combed his hair with the lint trap of a Maytag dryer.

Addison patted dirt and brambles from Eddie's back. The paint-splatter map was still intact. He breathed a sigh of relief.

The SUVs halted fifty feet from the border fence of the military base and sat there, engines idling, headlights gleaming. The British Air Force stared them down. Finally, after a tense minute, the SUVs reversed in three-point turns and sped away into the night.

Addison plucked prickers from his new ballroom jacket. The magnificent cloth seemed to repel dirt. It had been an excellent investment. Next time he saw Malazar, he was going to have to thank him for picking up the bill.

He turned north to watch the last red glimmer of the Collective's taillights disappearing over the pastures. "Well, I hope none of you were planning on visiting Cyprus again anytime soon."

Molly joined him at his side. "This is a first," she said. "We've been chased out of cities before. But never an entire country."

"It's good to always set higher goals," said Addison.

•••••••

Within minutes, the Royal Air Force was waving Addison's group goodbye as Dax taxied down the runway. Mr. Jacobsen had been well fed and watered by the British airmen, and Dax's Skyhawk was working better than ever. The plane bolted along the runway, straight toward the Mediterranean Sea, and lifted into the sky at the last possible second. Dax was a former navy pilot, and Addison suspected he was just showing off.

"Any idea where we're going?" asked Dax, once they were airborne.

"Not yet," Addison admitted. "Just travel east while we figure it out."

Dax shook his head. "One of these days you're going to know where we're flying *before* we take off."

Eddie shuffled off his school blazer in the back seat and handed it up to Addison, who was riding shotgun with Molly. T.D. was wedged in the back seat between a paint-soaked Raj and a drooling Mr. Jacobsen. She did not look ecstatic about the lack of seating options.

Addison copied Eddie's map into his notebook as best he could. The tricky part was that he needed to draw everything backward, because the paint splatter was a mirror image of the bronze tablet itself. Still, he could see how the rivers and cliffs of the tablet fit cleanly into the empty square of the Templar map.

He compared the completed map with *Fiddleton's Atlas* and smiled in satisfaction. "The Arabah Desert," Addison announced. "In southern Jordan."

"The Arabah is about three hundred miles from here," said Dax. "You guys can get in a good two hours' sleep before we land."

"Dax, you spoil us."

"Not that much," said Dax. "See, the thing about deserts is they're full of sand. If I land you in the Arabah, we might never be able to take off again. Besides, if Malazar gets there first, my engine will sort of take away our element of surprise."

"So what's your plan?" asked Molly.

"I can fly you as far as the Gulf of Aqaba," said Dax. "From there we need to take local transport."

"You mean like a taxi?" asked Eddie.

Dax worked his toothpick to the corner of his mouth. "Yeah. Something like that."

······

They touched down in the city of Aqaba as the enormous desert sun erupted over the rim of the world. Dax insisted that they steer clear of major roads, lest they run into the Collective, so he rented camels from a group of Bedouin traders. The camels, he explained, would do better in the rocky desert than any SUV.

The Bedouins sold them long black robes to protect them from the sun. The robes covered their bodies from head to toe and would help to disguise them should they run into any Russian *vori*. Eddie, who was ravenous, bought a day's supply of flatbread, rice, dates, and yogurt from the Bedouins. The nomads even agreed to take care of Mr. Jacobsen for a few days, since the Great Dane was not partial to deserts and heat.

Their provisions secured, Dax and T.D. were leading the caravan into the Arabah by the time the sun had cleared the horizon. Their path meandered north and west, heading toward the land of Israel.

Addison, poring over his copy of *Fiddleton's Atlas* from

the swaying saddle of his lumbering camel, learned that "Arabah" is the Arabic word for "desert." That, he reasoned, was why Dax had not called it the Arabah Desert. Calling it the Arabah Desert would be like calling it the Desert Desert, which would be repetitive repetitive.

Because he was immersed in *Fiddleton's Atlas*, the first few miles of the trek passed quickly for Addison. He learned they were crossing the Great Rift Valley, a depression in the earth's continental plates that runs the whole length of the Jordan River, through the Sinai Peninsula, and all the way to sub-Saharan Africa. The desert around him had once been a part of Solomon's kingdom. It was as parched and desolate a place as Addison had ever seen.

The sands were an endless tapestry of reds, yellows, oranges, browns, grays, and even blacks. Near the empty pits of long-abandoned copper mines, dotting the earth like termite holes, the sands appeared light green or even blue. Ancient cliffs, hewn by centuries of wind and water, were sculpted into towering pillars and broken arches— like the last fallen ruins of a lost city of giants.

•••••••

It was midday when Addison began to struggle with the heat. The sun battered his head like a jackhammer, and the windblown sand stung his eyes. Already, everyone's water canteens were dry. It was a great relief when Dax finally discovered the riverbed, or *wadi*, indicated on the Templar map. The group rested, refilled their canteens, and followed the winding river north, trudging ever closer to the circular mark in the center of the Templar map— the hiding place of the ring of Solomon.

Addison urged his camel into line between T.D. and Molly. He still had many questions for T.D., and he figured it would be difficult for her to dodge his questions in the middle of an open desert.

"Tilda, how much do you know about Malazar?" he began.

"More than I'd like to," she replied. Only her eyes were visible behind the black turban and robe that covered her hair and was wrapped around her face.

"How is Malazar so rich? Why does he hate the Templars? How many treasures are there? And what happens if he gets them all?"

T.D. shook her head. "I can only tell you—"

"—when we come of age," Molly finished.

"All right," said Addison. "Are you allowed to answer questions about yourself? How did you become a Templar Knight?"

T.D. was silent for a while. Just when Addison was sure she was ignoring his question altogether, she spoke up. "D'Anger is not my real last name."

Addison and Molly shared a look.

After a few more lumbering steps of her camel, T.D. continued. "The d'Angers were an ancient Templar family, like the Cookes. But they were driven to extinction. My grandmother was a driver for the last d'Anger. Monsieur d'Anger had no heirs, so he trained my grandmother instead. He taught her the Templar secrets. She took the family name to carry on the tradition."

"How many Templars are left?" asked Addison.

T.D. squinted out at the endless sands and sighed. "Once, there were Templars all over Europe, North Africa, and the Middle East. Some even traveled to the Americas and even to Asia. But they have been hunted for centuries."

"How many?" asked Addison again.

T.D. shook her head. "Many have vanished, many have gone into hiding."

"Well, what about our branch?" asked Molly. "How many *Tutores Thesauri* are there?"

T.D. looked at Molly and then at Addison. "Your parents arc dead. Your aunt and uncle are dead. The other families are gone. If neither of you live long enough to take the Templar vows, that leaves just your uncle Jasper. After seven hundred years, he is the last of your line."

"And he's no spring chicken," said Molly.

Addison tried to find a silver lining in all this. "Well,

if Molly and I live long enough to be allowed to take the oath, it will triple our membership numbers."

"If," was all T.D. said in response.

"T.D., do you believe in the prophecy?" asked Molly. "All the Templars must be killed. And then there will be some sort of prize?"

"I don't know anymore," said T.D. "Maybe I do."

"It's all superstitious claptrap," said Addison. "Like how the Ring of Destiny gave King Solomon power over angels and demons. It's nonsense. I don't believe in prophecies."

"That's funny you say that," said Molly.

"Why?"

Molly shrugged. "I keep thinking about the fortune-teller we met in the Khentii Mountains in Mongolia. The blind shaman with the deerskin drum. Don't you remember what he said?"

Addison did not answer. He remembered the fortune-teller vividly, but he had spent months trying to forget the man's words.

Molly recited aloud. Addison found that her memory of the man's strange speech was nearly identical to his own. "I see a catacombs under a great city. I see your sister held prisoner on an island. I see a perilous journey through a hostile desert. I see a prophecy. You will feel alone in the world, but you have powerful allies you do not yet realize."

Addison rode in silence for a long while as the little caravan plodded across the desert. Treacherous, jagged cliffs loomed overhead. The stream they were following tapered to a trickle and vanished altogether. It was nearly sunset before the dry riverbed forked and they spotted the Collective.

Chapter Thirty-Eight

The Arabah

ADDISON RECOGNIZED THE FORK in the riverbed from Eddie's map. Immediately north was the valley they were heading to. The map marked it like a bull's-eye with the symbol of Solomon's ring. The valley was encircled with cliffs, and it seemed the only way in was directly through the Collective's encampment.

Dax drew the camels to a halt, and the group shielded their eyes from the setting sun to survey the scene below.

Addison watched Collective gang members scurrying to and fro in the valley, lighting cook fires and setting up tents. He saw a massive military helicopter parked on the sand. This explained how Malazar had beaten them to the location. Squinting, Addison could make out Ivan's distinctive mop of hair; he was directing the men unloading crates of equipment from the chopper.

T.D. shook her head. "They're blocking us from entering the valley. See how they're using those crates to form a defensive wall?"

Addison followed her gaze and saw she was right. Guards were pointing in their direction, and Ivan appeared to be staring directly at them.

T.D. covered her face with the end of her turban and motioned to the others to do the same. "Bunch up the camels so they can't count our numbers."

Addison clicked his tongue and urged his camel to double up behind Molly's.

"Let's keep moving," said Dax quietly. "And don't look in their direction. With any luck, they'll take us for Bedouins."

Addison knew that the Collective would be on high alert and doubted they would be so easily duped. But it was worth a shot. Three hundred yards away, Ivan was now training binoculars on them, the setting sun glinting off the lenses. Addison hunched over his camel and drew his hood low over his face.

They led their camels along a dry, crumbling sandstone ridge, making as if to pass the valley entirely. Addison spoke just loud enough for the group to hear him. "The way I see it, we have two choices. One: we let Malazar find the Ring of Destiny first and then attack his entire gang, hoping to win it back . . ."

There were a few grunts and murmurs. Nobody seemed to favor that option.

"And the other choice?" asked Molly.

"The other choice," said Addison, "is we wait for full darkness. We sneak past their camp into the valley and find Solomon's ring ourselves. Then we escape in the night before Malazar even knows we were here."

"We cannot beat Malazar in a fight," said T.D. "The second choice is our least bad option. Find the ring and steal it before Malazar has the chance."

"All in favor?" asked Addison.

One by one, everyone nodded.

The camel train was approaching a rocky crag that could shield them from the watchful eyes of the Collective encampment below. Dax twisted in his saddle to call to the group. "Jump down off your camels when you pass behind this rock."

"What's your plan, Dax?" asked Addison.

"I'll keep the caravan heading toward the horizon. They'll see the dust rising and the shapes of the camels and assume we're Bedouin nomads heading into the Negev Desert."

"How do we find you again?" asked Molly.

"I'll double back with the camels under full dark.

Sometime after two a.m., I'll meet you back here at this rock and cover your escape."

Addison saluted Dax with two fingers to his forehead and slithered down off his camel. Molly, Eddie, Raj, and T.D. jumped down as well. They watched Dax grow smaller down the trail, his shadow enormous in the dying sun.

Addison clapped dust off his hands and turned to face the group. "Well, that leaves five of us to find Solomon's ring."

"Four," said T.D., stepping forward. "I am not going with you."

"What?" asked Molly, spreading her hands wide in disbelief. "We could use you! Whose side are you on, anyway?"

Addison squinted at T.D., backlit by the sun. "Are you running away?"

"Running away?" Anger flashed in T.D.'s eyes, but she kept her voice calm and even. "The Templars never retreat. They are the first onto the battlefield and the last to leave. The Templars fought the Mongol horde in Hungary, when they were outnumbered by tens of thousands. Five hundred Templar Knights took on Saladin's army of twenty-six thousand at the Battle of Montgisard. Saladin fled, escaping to Egypt on a camel, his army wiped out of existence. No. A Templar Knight never runs away."

"Well, then what are you doing?" asked Molly, her fists clenched. "Because it sure looks like you're running away."

T.D. straightened to her full height, towering over Molly. "'Tilda' means 'warrior.' The d'Anger family are the descendants of Norsemen, living in Normandy for a thousand years. Our family motto is Strength. I have saved your lives twice. You will need to have faith in me."

Addison took a step closer to T.D. "The Cooke family are relic guardians. Every Templar family has a purpose. What exactly does the d'Anger family do?"

T.D. looked at him, her expression cold and determined. "I cannot answer that question, Addison. All I can tell you is . . . I am the last of my kind." She shouldered her rifle and wrapped the loose end of her turban across her face to guard against the wind. She climbed down the rocky escarpment until she reached a narrow trail. And she strode away without a backward glance.

Addison watched her go until she disappeared into the blowing sands.

••••••

With the older people gone, Addison suddenly felt alone. The utter isolation of the desert didn't help. What would help was getting some rest. Addison realized they had slept only a few hours in the cargo hold of the 747 the night before. And they'd slept only two hours on Dax's flight to Aqaba. That, coupled with a twelve-hour camel journey through the Arabah, and Addison's crew was sorely in need of any sleep they could manage.

The group assigned watches and succeeded in grabbing a few hours of rest. It was Raj who woke everyone around ten p.m., tying his red bandana around his head and declaring it was "go-time."

The moon was high in the sky as Addison's group began working their way along the ridge, heading toward the valley marked on the Templar map. The sheer line of the cliffs was broken only by the small gap occupied by the Collective's encampment. There was no way into the valley except to crawl right under the Collective's collective noses.

It took the better part of a half hour for Addison's group to reach the edge of the camp, and the worst part of an hour to crawl past it without making a sound. They stole past the soft red glow of the dying cook fires and scrambled up onto a rocky ledge. Before them, Addison could see a tall Russian guard patrolling the pass that led into the hidden valley.

Eddie rubbed his tired legs and stretched his aching back. He grimaced. "Remind me how big this treasure is again?"

Addison shushed him with a hand and consulted his

fake Rolex. After waiting a long beat, he determined that the guard was patrolling the path in a loop every three to four minutes. The next time the guard disappeared around the rocky bend below, they would need to bolt through the pass.

Addison's shoes were noisier than he preferred, crunching grains of sand against the gritty rock face of the ridge. Remembering his stealth training, he slid off his shoes and socks. His feet were about to get incredibly sandy, and he was miles away from anything resembling a bathtub. He paused, taking a fortifying breath. This, he felt, was a character-building moment.

When the guard strutted around the bend below, Addison waved his team into action. They scrambled down from their hiding place among the boulders and dashed through the pass between the cliffs. It seemed to Addison they were making an astonishing amount of noise. He did not dare stop sprinting until he had climbed high up a hill on the far side of the pass. Molly, Eddie, and Raj crouched beside him, keeping low to the ground. When they looked back at the pass, they saw no sign of the Russian guard.

Addison counted time on his Rolex, waiting a few minutes to make sure they had not been spotted. He took in his new surroundings. Towers of red sandstone loomed overhead. Below, the eerie silence of the desert.

No buzz of insects. No rustling of leaves. Just sand, rock, and emptiness. Every tiny sound they made seemed amplified, as if it would carry for miles. Addison cringed when Eddie spoke up.

"So which way is the treasure?"

Addison cracked open his notebook and consulted his copy of the Templar map. He could see the forked riverbank before him, precisely as it was carved into the bronze tablet. Solomon's ring, emblazoned with its six-pointed star, was drawn above the forked river. The trouble was, the ring was drawn so large, it seemed to cover at least two square miles of land in the basin below. Addison had no idea where they were supposed to start looking. Checking his Rolex, he saw that it was already pushing midnight.

Molly scanned the desert basin, a grimace etched on her face. She seemed to be having similar thoughts. "Do we know what exactly we're looking for?"

Addison puckered his brow. "Solomon's Temple was sacked in 587 B.C. His priests took his treasure to protect it from pillaging Babylonians. The treasure will be well hidden in some sort of chamber."

"So where will this well-hidden chamber be?"

"Some place the Israelites would know well but the Babylonians wouldn't." Addison cast a line into the dark waters of his cerebellum. He could feel an idea nibbling at the line. If he waited patiently, and didn't yank the hook, he might be able to reel it in.

He paced in a circle on the sandy bluff, tapping a thoughtful finger against his chin. Lost in his reverie, his bare foot scuffed against a heavy lump of rock. Addison bent down to examine it. It was a clump of shiny metal, like a piggy bank's worth of pennies. Eyeing the rocky pass, he could see similar bits of metal glimmering in the moonlight. "Copper," he said aloud.

The idea that had been quietly tickling his brain chomped down on the hook. Addison's eyes lit up. "I bet I know what we're looking for: King Solomon's mines! That was the source of his wealth. That's why the map took us out here in the middle of nowhere. What better place to hide a treasure from Babylonians than a deep hole in the middle of a desert!"

Addison turned and hurried up the ridge, scrambling over rocks and between boulders. It was a minute before Molly, Raj, and a panting Eddie caught up with him at the summit of the hill.

From their high vantage point, they eyed the vast valley below that hid the treasure of King Solomon. "There," said Addison, extending a finger.

Visible in the glimmering moonlight was the open pit of an ancient copper mine. Addison smiled in triumph.

"What about there?" asked Molly. She pointed to a

different gaping hole. "Or there?" She pointed to another.

Clouds parted, and the moon brilliantly lit up the valley. Addison's eyes adjusted and his heart plummeted. The valley was swiss-cheesed with open pits. There were not dozens of copper mines. There were not hundreds of copper mines. There were thousands.

Addison panned his head from left to right, taking them all in. There seemed to be a circular pit, the size of a well, every ten or fifteen feet. The valley was more hole than desert.

"So which mine is it?" asked Molly.

Addison mutely shook his head. He had no idea.

Chapter Thirty-Nine

King Solomon's Mines

ADDISON RETURNED TO PACING. "There's some clue we're missing. There must be a way to pin down the location of the ring. Eddie, let me look at your back again."

Eddie obliged, turning around and spreading his arms, revealing the paint stain on his blazer. Addison, Molly, and Raj gathered closely, studying the splatters on Eddie's back like three witches over a crystal ball.

Addison ping-ponged his head between Eddie's jacket and the valley below. He could make out all the features of the map: the forked riverbed, the hairpin turn in the river, the cliffs surrounding the valley. He narrowed his eyes at the six-pointed star symbol inside Solomon's ring on the Templar map. And that is when a solution snuck up behind him and smacked him on the back of the head. "No. Way," he said quietly.

"What is it?" asked Eddie. "What's on my back? Have you found something?"

Addison swiveled Eddie around. He knelt to the ground and used his finger to draw a ring in the sand. Inside the ring, he traced the six-pointed star. The points of the star touched the circle in six exact places. "Do you see?"

Eddie shook his head blankly. Molly and Raj shrugged.

"Look!" Addison pointed to the circular valley below. It was surrounded with cliffs, roughly forming the shape of a ring. Six large mines dotted the outer rim of the valley, exactly as in Addison's drawing. "The symbol on the map is exactly where it should be. If you connect those dots, you form a star. This entire valley is an image of the Ring of Destiny!"

Raj's mouth hung open, also forming a perfect ring. "Radical," he whispered.

"There are six caves," said Eddie. "Which one holds the treasure?"

"None of them," said Addison, smiling. He spun Eddie around, pointing again at his blazer map. Inside the Ring of Solomon, at the exact center of the star, was a tiny speck of paint. "I didn't see it before. It's almost too small to notice. But there is a dot in the middle of the star." He pointed down to the valley below. "If you trace lines from all six points, they intersect in the middle. Do you see it?"

Molly, Eddie, and Raj nodded. Of all the thousands of abandoned mines dotting the landscape, only one mine sat in the geometric center.

"That mine." Eddie shook his head in awe. "I mean, the mine isn't mine. It's ours. But it's a mine. It's our mine." Eddie stopped talking.

Addison patted the sand from his hands. "Malazar's men weren't able to see the pattern because they're down in the valley. Only we can see it because we had to climb the ridge to get past them." He nodded with satisfaction. "We have the advantage."

••••••

It took only a few minutes for the group to scramble down off the ridge. They raced across the floor of the desert, chasing their long shadows in the moonlight. Addison zigged around the endless pits of copper mines that cratered the earth as if from a long-ago missile bombardment. The valley air was filled with a pungent oily smell like the stink of a gas station. Addison spotted black puddles of desert oil, shiny in the starlight, oozing through cracks in the rocky ground. He kept running, wrinkling up his nose and breathing through his mouth instead.

"Our footprints," said Raj, pointing back at their sandy trail. "We should cover our tracks."

"There's no time," Addison called. "Besides, by the time Malazar's men wake up in the morning, we'll be long gone."

Molly was first to reach the mine at the exact center of the valley. The rest of the group loped up behind and paused for breath. Addison took a moment to wipe off his feet and put his dress shoes back on.

Before them was a circular hole in the ground no more than five feet wide. Raj clamped his flashlight in his teeth and eased himself down into the pit. He disappeared under a lip of stone.

Addison heard the scuffling sound of feet scraping on rock. He cupped his hands around his mouth and whispered into the darkness below. "Raj, you okay?"

Raj's excited voice floated right back up. "I'm fine! It's not too deep and not too hard to climb! Maybe ten feet, tops."

"What's down there?"

"A tunnel!" said Raj. "It winds around too far for my flashlight to see."

Addison felt confidence stirring in him once again. They were on the right track.

Molly tightened the laces on her shoes and lowered herself into the hole.

Eddie loosened his shoulders and stretched his legs, limbering himself up for the climb. He turned to Addison. "Real quick," he said. "King Solomon might be buried down here, right?"

Addison shrugged.

"So, once again, Addison, you've got us going into a catacomb."

"Eddie, there's a reason ancient treasure gets buried underground instead of, say, hidden in a tree. A tree might only last thirty years, but a pit in the ground can last forever. So it's really not my fault we always find ourselves mucking around underground."

Eddie swung his legs so that his feet dangled over the pit. "So I'm supposed to just climb down there like some grave robber?"

Addison blew a speck of dust from the sleeve of his ballroom jacket and shook his head. "Grave robber sounds so . . . déclassé."

"What else can you call it?"

"You heard Mr. Fiddleton. We're not grave robbers . . . We're *relic guardians.*"

"Whatever helps you sleep at night," Eddie grumbled. He eased himself down into the hole in the earth.

Addison gazed up at the twinkling stars and smiled.

He planted his palms on the ground and lowered himself in after Eddie.

•••••••

Addison climbed down to the floor of the mine and turned in a circle, taking his bearings. The open pit had dropped them into the middle of a tunnel that led off in either direction, vanishing around a bend. The tunnel was low enough to cause Eddie to stoop, and it was almost perfectly round.

"Which way?" asked Raj. "Right or left?"

Addison looked both ways, peering into the gloom. He could see no difference. He shrugged. "Right," he declared.

They set off down the tunnel, Raj leading the way with his high-powered flashlight. The walls of the mine were smooth and chalky, eroded by time. Addison was surprised by how light the sandstone was in the glare of the flashlight—almost the color and texture of marshmallow. The tunnel constantly bent to the right, but its shape remained a perfect cylindrical tube. Addison imagined they were inside the ossified blood vessel of some massive and long-dead creature. He tried to picture the copper miners laboring with picks and trowels, thousands of years in the past.

The path forever wound to the right. The walk became a hike. After a few minutes Addison's excitement began to fade. And after a few more minutes, Raj let out a startled cry. "We're right back where we started!"

Addison stared up at the night sky through the open hole in the mineshaft. They had just walked in a complete circle. "It's another ring." Addison scratched the back of his neck. "Solomon's priests were hiding the treasure from Babylonians. If it's stayed hidden for nearly three thousand years, they must have done a decent job. We've missed something. Let's take another lap. Look for anything unusual!"

The team took a second lap around the tunnel, this time more slowly. Raj halted to play his flashlight over every stray rock and pebble they crossed. He even knelt down to examine the sand beneath their feet.

"What is it, Raj?" asked Molly, joining him at his side.

Raj let a handful of sand filter through his fingers. "Some of this sand is green. Does that mean something?"

"It means we're in a copper mine," said Addison. "The Statue of Liberty is copper, and when it was built, it gleamed like a shiny new penny. But copper turns green when it mixes with air. So now the Statue of Liberty is as green as this sand."

Raj looked at the sandy green splotches staining the floor of the cave. "So everywhere we see green, there's copper?"

Addison nodded. "If treasure hunting doesn't work out for us, we can always become copper miners."

They kept moving. Addison pulled out his pen flashlight to study the walls as they passed. They were exactly halfway around the loop when Addison made a discovery. "Raj, over here!"

Raj backtracked to where Addison was standing and lit up the cave wall with his flashlight. "What is it?"

Addison scraped dirt from the wall with his hand. "Solomon's priests seem to be using rings as a theme." He backed away from the wall. There in the sandstone stood the faint outline of a large circle, shaded in with green.

Raj scratched at it with a finger, fascinated. "That's a lot of copper. Why is it in the shape of a circle?"

"Because it's a hatchway," said Addison. He removed one of his dress shoes and used the hard heel to scratch away the sand that had melded with the copper. Raj, Molly, and Eddie joined in. Soon they revealed a circular copper door molded into the rock.

Addison pushed hard against it. Eddie and Raj threw in their shoulder weight. Metal screeched as it tore against stone. The entire copper disk popped inward, like a cork being pushed into a bottle. The copper door clanged as it struck the stony ground.

Before them was a tiny tunnel winding deep into the earth.

Chapter Forty

The Dark Spring

MOLLY TOOK THE FLASHLIGHT from Raj and led the way inside. The tunnel was small enough now that everyone needed to stoop. The air smelled coppery, like blood, and was so stuffy that Addison felt quite sure this tunnel had been sealed for centuries. The atmosphere grew more cold and damp as they descended, the tunnel winding in tight coils like a spiral staircase. Addison's shoes squelched when he stepped through puddles of oozing oil and tar that seeped from the rock.

In a few minutes the shaft leveled off and widened into a chamber no bigger than Addison's old New York apartment. It was an abrupt dead end. Before them was a deep pool of water, twenty feet across. It appeared black as ink in the flickering halo of Raj's flashlight.

Raj dropped to one knee. "It must bubble up from an underground spring." He dipped a finger in the water and sampled it. "Tastes fine to me." Raj filled his canteen.

Water was not what Addison was thirsting for. He played his penlight over the cavern walls. "Look for more green sand. There must be another door here somewhere."

They spread out, scouring the room. Addison pushed on rocks, hoping for a secret switch or panel. Eddie studied the ceiling. Molly scraped at the floor with her heel. No one found anything worth reporting.

At last, Addison set his hands on his hips and turned to the pool of water. "There's only one place we haven't searched."

"There's no telling how deep it is," Molly mused.

The still water was impenetrably dark. When Addison ran his light across the surface, it only reflected back at him. But the pool was circular, like a ring, and that fueled Addison's curiosity.

Raj stepped forward, beaming with pleasure. "I'll search the water. I can hold my breath for—"

" over a minute and a half," said Addison, Molly, and Eddie in unison.

Raj began sucking deep breaths through his nose and blowing them out through his mouth. His chest heaved like accordion bellows.

"Guys," said Eddie, "Raj is going into labor!"

Raj shook his head vehemently. "I'm oxygenating my lungs!"

After a minute of this, Raj gulped one last breath of air, clasped his palms together, and swan dived into the water. He steered for the opposite wall of the cavern and vanished into the gloomy depths.

The water eventually grew still. The team waited for any sign of Raj to emerge.

Addison checked his fake Rolex. "Thirty seconds," he declared.

Soon, a minute had passed. "It's no problem," said Addison a little nervously. "He can hold his breath for nearly a minute and a half."

Molly and Eddie nodded.

Addison watched the second hand of his watch orbit past the two-minute mark. He peered intently at the dark water, willing Raj to appear.

Nothing.

"Okay, I'm worried," said Molly.

Addison paced in a circle. He ran his hands through his hair. Once again, someone he cared for was in trouble and it was probably his own fault. He knew he could not handle losing anyone else close to him. His watch slithered past three minutes.

Still no Raj.

"We have to do something!" said Molly, wringing her hands.

"Okay," said Addison. "What do we do?"

"We should go in after him!"

Eddie shook his head. "If Raj got lost down there, we could get lost, too!"

Addison held his flashlight close to the water. If Raj was somehow lost down there, he hoped Raj would see the beacon and find his way to the surface.

"I'll go in," Molly volunteered.

Addison shook his head. "Eddie's right. If Raj got trapped, you could get trapped as well."

"Well, we have to do something!"

Addison turned to his sister. "Molly, I can't lose you twice in two days."

Molly folded her arms.

Together, they watched the water in silence.

At last, Molly spoke. "How long has it been?"

Addison checked his watch one last time. "Four minutes," he said. He took a few steps and sat down by the pool. He buried his head in his hands.

That is how Addison got thoroughly soaked when Raj burst out of the water.

●●●●●●

Raj climbed out of the pool and shook himself off like a golden retriever.

"We thought you were dead!" cried Molly. She threw her arms around his shoulders. Raj did not appear to be any worse for wear. He did not even appear to be out of breath. He did, however, seem to be enjoying the new-found attention.

Addison pointed to his watch. "Raj, it's been nearly five minutes! You broke your record!"

"I wish," said Raj. "This tunnel continues on the other side of the rock wall. The pool of water is just clever cam-ouflage. It only takes about ten seconds to swim under the wall and reach the other side."

Addison tried to remain calm. "If you were only under water for ten seconds, why did you wait five minutes to come back?"

Molly was trembling with anger. "We were worried sick about you!"

Raj shrugged helplessly. "Well, first I wanted to look around. And then I needed to do my free-diving breath exercises. You know that takes at least a minute."

"Let me get this straight," said Molly, staring daggers at Raj. "You needed to do your free-diving breath exer-cises in order to swim for ten seconds?"

"Well," said Raj, looking sheepishly at his dripping combat boots. "It's good practice."

"Okay," said Addison. "The good news is Raj is alive. I mean, I guess that's good news." He turned to Raj. "How do we swim under the rock? Is it a tunnel?"

"You can't miss it," said Raj. "Just aim straight and keep kicking."

Addison did not love getting wet, but at least he knew his ballroom blazer was wrinkle-free. "Let's keep moving. We have a treasure to find."

He dove into the freezing water.

Chapter Forty-One
The Pendulum

ADDISON SWAM BREASTSTROKE, FORCING himself deeper and deeper. He was not sure if his flashlight was waterproof, so he switched it off just in case that helped prevent a short circuit. In pitch dark, he felt the edge of the rocky wall ahead of him with his hands. Feeling his way along, he passed underneath the stony ledge, and then allowed his buoyancy to pull him back up to the surface. He breathed clean air. He was on the far side.

He shook the water from his flashlight and switched it on. To his relief, it was still working. One by one, his friends burst through the surface of the water. Raj appeared last, presumably because he needed to perform his breathing exercises.

Addison surveyed the new chamber. It was a mirror image of the room they had just left. He hoisted himself, dripping, out of the pool and skimmed water from his hair with the blade of his hand.

Before them, the tunnel continued into the darkness. They didn't have to follow it for very long before the ceiling rose and the passage opened up into a larger cavern. Ahead of them, a treacherously steep flight of stone steps led up to a circular copper door. It was covered with a series of small copper disks.

Addison turned to Eddie. "What do you make of it?"

Eddie stared thoughtfully up at the distant door. "It looks like a very, very ancient combination lock."

Addison was thinking the same thing. "A safe."

"So we've made it," said Molly. "This is the door to the treasure vault."

Addison guided Eddie to the base of the stone steps. "This is all you, Eddie. This is your moment."

Eddie glanced nervously up the stairs at the gleaming copper door. "Do I go up alone?"

"Yes," said Addison. "The stairs are too narrow and there's only room for one person to stand at the top."

Sweat broke out on Eddie's brow. His hands began trembling. "Is the safe safe?"

Addison could see that stage fright was already wreaking havoc on his friend. He tried to buck up Eddie's confidence. "Of course the safe's safe. Solomon's priests were more concerned with keeping the treasure hidden from Babylonians. They weren't interested in hurting anyone. We haven't seen any booby traps so far."

"So far," said Eddie.

"This treasure was hidden nearly three thousand years ago," said Addison. "There simply wasn't enough technology for elaborate booby traps. All the priests could do was bury their treasure in a cave and hope for the best. Eddie, you've got this."

Eddie wiped the sweat from his palms on the front of his slacks. He sighed and nodded. He turned and mounted the narrow staircase with the eagerness of a prisoner heading for the gallows. There were no railings to keep him from plummeting over the side. Soon Addison, Molly, and Raj were far, far below him.

Nevertheless, Eddie plodded onward, climbing the steep flight of steps. And it wasn't until he reached the tiny platform at the top that he triggered the booby trap.

•••••••

Addison had to hand it to Eddie. If there was a booby trap within a hundred-mile radius, Eddie would find a way to trip it. Still, it wasn't entirely Eddie's fault. The whole platform at the top of the stairs seemed to be the trigger.

With a creak and a groan, a massive copper pendulum

swung from a crevice in the cave wall. Suspended from a heavy brass chain, the copper wrecking ball sizzled past Eddie, missing him by inches. Eddie shrieked. Within seconds, the pendulum reached the end of its arc and swung back toward Eddie, picking up speed.

"What do I do?" Eddie shouted.

Addison could see that if the pendulum struck Eddie, it would blast him off the steps, sending him plummeting fifty feet down to the jagged, rocky floor of the cavern— not a good way to end the evening. But he also knew that if Eddie retreated, he would never get Eddie back up those steps.

"The safe!" Addison cried. "Open the safe!"

Eddie wheeled to face the round copper door. The pendulum sliced past him, grazing the back of his blazer. The door was covered with dozens of copper disks the size of teacups. On each disk was carved either a curving line or a straight line. He tried to make sense of the dizzying array.

The pendulum whooshed past. He could feel the wind on the back of his neck.

Eddie took a deep breath. He picked one of the copper disks and swiveled it. It rotated like the dial on a master lock. He spun it, straining his ears to hear it click into place.

The giant copper wrecking ball swept past again.

Eddie shook his head. Even if he swiveled this one copper plate into position, there were still dozens to go. "Addison, this is the mother of all locks!"

Far below, Addison realized that the pendulum was rigged to gradually swing closer and closer to Eddie. "You've got to hurry!" he called.

Eddie twisted another copper disk, trying to feel if there were any tumblers clicking home inside. It was hard to concentrate. He couldn't detect anything. He wiped sweat from his eyes. Panic was rising in his gut.

Addison raced halfway up the steps, trying to get a closer look at the pattern of curving lines on the disks. Maybe they spelled something in ancient Hebrew. That would make sense—Solomon's priests wouldn't want Babylonians opening the treasure vault, and the Babylonians wouldn't know Hebrew. The only trouble was, Addison didn't know Hebrew either. He turned to Molly and Raj, who had joined him on the stairs. "Any ideas?"

Raj shook his head.

Molly pointed to the pendulum. "It's getting closer to Eddie. Pretty soon, he won't have any room left on the platform. He could die, Addison!"

Addison gritted his teeth. "Think, you guys! As hard as you can!" He shut his eyes and took a deep breath to summon his thoughts. He pictured the curving lines and the straight lines in his mind's eye. "Scratch that—stop thinking so hard." His eyes flickered open. "We're way overthinking this."

"Which is it?" asked Molly. "Do you want us to think or not?"

"It's a ring," said Addison. He cupped his hands and shouted up to Eddie. "Spin the copper plates to form a ring!"

Eddie stood pressed close to the door, the pendulum swinging ever nearer. "Are you sure?" he called. He didn't want to turn the disks the wrong way and risk an even worse booby trap.

"It's got to be!" called Addison. "Every other clue they've left has been a ring. The curved lines form the ring; the straight lines form the six-pointed star. Eddie, hurry!"

Eddie didn't have any better ideas, and he was nearly out of time. It was the only shot he could take. He frantically swiveled disk after disk. The curving lines on the outer disks connected to form a circle. He turned the straight lines on the inner disks to form two interlocking triangles—a six-pointed star.

Somewhere, deep inside the earth, Eddie felt a lock spring.

The next thing he felt was the pendulum smacking him on the back.

At that precise moment, the circular copper door swung open, and Eddie fell forward into the dark.

Chapter Forty-Two

The Treasure Chamber

ADDISON, MOLLY, AND RAJ hustled up the staircase, ducked the swinging pendulum, and stepped cautiously through the doorway.

"Are you okay, Eddie?" Addison called into the dark.

"Define 'okay.'"

Addison's flashlight beam found Eddie sprawled on the ground. He was rubbing the small of his back and grimacing.

"You did it," said Addison. "This must be the biggest safe you've ever cracked."

"I think it's my back that got cracked," said Eddie bitterly. He struggled to his feet.

The tangy smell of copper and the pungent smell of oil were much stronger in this room. Addison's flashlight beam was not powerful enough to reach more than a dozen feet into the pitch-black.

Raj found an ancient torch hanging in a wall sconce. He pulled out his box of strike-anywhere matches and selected the driest one. He sparked it on his boot and lit the torch.

Molly grabbed a second torch. Together, they lit more torches in the wall sconces as they moved deeper into the chamber. The walls of the colossal space were lined with beaten copper that reflected the flickering torchlight in a thousand directions. For the first time in millennia, the room came into view.

The ceiling rose high overhead. Near the tops of the pillared walls were carved stone gargoyles—hideous and demonic beasts—their faces formed into fanged screams. Higher still were carved stone angels, wings sprouting from their shoulders, their lips parted as if in song.

Addison plucked a freshly lit torch from the wall, held it aloft, and crossed into the center of the chamber. His feet drifted to a halt, and he nearly tripped over his own jaw.

"Eddie," he said, his voice tremulous, "will this cheer you up?"

Eddie limped to join Addison at his side.

Before them were thousands of bars of solid gold. They were stacked like bricks, forming endless rows like bookshelves in a library.

Addison saw that Eddie's lip was quivering, his expression transfixed with joy.

"I can't feel my face," said Eddie.

"Take deep breaths," said Addison.

Molly and Raj joined them in the center of the chamber. The gold twinkled in the torchlight.

"It must be worth a fortune," said Molly.

"It's worth more than that," said Addison, taking in his surroundings. "The priests re-created Solomon's entire throne room. His palace was destroyed thousands of years ago, but now we can catch a glimpse of what it looked like. Guys, we are standing in one of the most important archaeological finds in the world."

Addison found a solid gold scepter, inlaid with rubies, casually laid on top of a pile of gold bars. He hefted it in his hands, feeling the weight. He tried to wrap his mind around the fact that the scepter had once been held by the fabled king of Israel over three thousand years ago, but his brain could barely stretch that far.

Eddie, his eyes on the rows of gold bars, tripped over a giant golden chalice, sending it clanging across the stone floor. Emeralds and rubies scattered everywhere.

"Watch it, Eddie!" Molly hissed. "This is an archaeological site. We shouldn't even be here without gloves on."

"Sorry!" Eddie struggled to pick up all the jewels and return them to the chalice.

In the center of the chamber stood Solomon's throne. Addison gazed up at it reverently and mounted the six steps, each one flanked by golden statues of animals.

The golden throne was centered at the top. And there, resting on the arm of the high-backed chair, sat a ring. The ring was not covered in jewels. It was not even gold. It was a simple ring of iron and brass. On its face was carved a six-pointed star. Addison picked it up and turned it over in his hand. He felt tempted to slip it on his finger, but he hesitated. He stared up at the stone faces of the gargoyles leering down from above and shuddered. Hairs prickled on the back of his neck and stood up straight on his forearms. He held the ring carefully in his palm, afraid to put it on.

Raj let out a warning whistle. Men's voices echoed from the stairway outside.

"C'mon," said Addison. "We're about to get trapped in here!"

The group started for the entrance of the chamber but quickly skidded to a halt. Men's voices called from just outside the doorway. Addison only had time to whisper a single word. "Hide!" But before anyone could even begin searching for a hiding spot, a tall man stepped through the doorway at the front of the chamber, firelight reflected in his eyes.

Malazar.

......

"Wow," Addison began, taking a step back. "What are the odds we would both visit the same treasure chamber on the same night? Crazy, right?"

Malazar's fiery gaze took in Addison, took in Molly, and then took in the splendor of the throne room. Ivan filed in behind, followed by his men. Addison noted that Ivan's hair was even more swampy and disheveled than usual, and then realized it was because Ivan was dripping wet. All of the men would have needed to swim under the reservoir to make it to the chamber.

Ivan's men fanned out, surrounding Addison's group.

Malazar inched closer to Addison. "Addison Cooke," he began, his burn-scarred mouth twisted with sneering disdain. His voice was a rasping, reedy whisper, as if his vocal cords had been filed with sandpaper. "Thank you for finding the treasure vault. And thank you for opening it for us."

Addison wanted to appear courageous in front of his team. But the sight of Malazar had him rattled to his core. Confidence was fleeing him like steam from a hot kettle. He knew there was no way out of the chamber. He struggled to steady his voice. "How did you find us?"

"It was simple," said Malazar. A smile wafted across his face like a curl of smoke. "Ivan followed your footprints in the sand."

Addison clenched his jaw. He had handed Malazar the golden treasure on a silver platter.

"You killed my associate Vladimir Ragar in Peru," Malazar continued. "And thanks to you, his brother Boris met his end in Mongolia."

"Strictly speaking," Addison replied, his voice sounding small and weak in the vast chamber, "that wasn't entirely my fault."

Malazar ignored this. "Now at last, I am going to kill you. And your sister. And your friends." He spread his skeletal arms, gesturing to the heaping piles of gold lining the chamber. "This will fund the Collective, making us even more powerful. Now, give me the ring, Addison."

"What ring?" asked Addison.

"The one you are holding in your right hand."

"Oh, that ring." Addison tried to think of a way to stall, but found his brain stalled instead. He looked down at the iron ring resting on the flat of his palm. He glanced up at Malazar's burn-scarred face. "You know, they say the ring is magic—that it gives command over demons."

"It doesn't," Malazar growled. He took a step closer and snatched the ring from Addison's palm with his gnarled fingers. "I don't need it for magic tricks, I need it for the prize." Malazar held the ring in the air, admiring it with gleaming eyes.

Addison felt completely defeated. He had lost the ring,

he had lost his aunt and uncle. Now he was going to lose Molly, Eddie, Raj, and even himself. And it was all his fault. He could have planned better. He could have acted faster. He could have listened to Raj and covered their tracks in the sand. He could have, he could have, he could have.

"Addison," Eddie whispered. "What do we do? Please tell me you have a plan!"

Addison stared at the ground, shoulders slack. "We're done," he said simply.

Molly looked to Addison. "King Solomon lost everything because he lost his faith. If we don't believe we can get out of this, we've already lost."

"You can't get out of this," said Ivan, his lopsided grin leaking across his face. He closed in on Molly.

Molly was not ready to give up. She brandished her flaming torch at Ivan.

And then the scales fell from Addison's eyes. For an instant, he was no longer in the chamber. He was on a cricket pitch. Eddie was at cow corner. Raj was at deep midwicket. Molly was the batsman. Malazar was the wicket keeper. And suddenly, for the first time ever, Addison felt he understood the game of cricket. Taking the ring from Malazar was as easy as bowling a yorker off a back-footed biffer. He knew what to do.

"Molly!" he cried. "You're the striker!" He pointed to Malazar's hand. "Bat me that ring!"

Addison started for the far side of the chamber.

Molly, unlike Addison, had a knack for sports. She was already one of the best strikers on the Wyckingham Swithy School for Girls' cricket team. Gripping her wooden torch like a bat, she spun away from Ivan to face Malazar. He cringed at the sight of the snapping flames. Molly wound up her torch and cracked Malazar hard in the hand. The ring flew into the air.

Even as Addison sprinted across the glittering copper floor, he could see Molly's hit was a sizzling slog, right in the sweet spot, sure to be a sixer.

It was a sitter, hit so high it seemed to hang in the air. Addison bolted down the narrow walkway between the heaps of gold. Stretching his arm nearly out of its socket, he caught the ring on the run, one-handed. It was easily the greatest athletic achievement of Addison's life, though that was not saying a tremendous amount.

"Guys! This way!" Addison kept running, straight up the six steps to Solomon's throne. Molly, Eddie, and Raj raced toward him.

Ivan and his men gave chase.

Addison reached Solomon's throne and spun to face the rushing Russians. "Stop!" he shouted, holding the Ring of Destiny high in the air like a live grenade.

Ivan's men slowed uncertainly to a halt.

Addison's friends joined him at his side. He felt the

power of the ring in his hand. In his mind it seemed to sizzle with electricity. In this moment, he needed power over demons—his own demons. And he realized now that his demons were fear and doubt. He needed to regain his old confidence. He needed to find his faith.

"Get them!" shouted Ivan.

But Addison held one hand aloft and spread his fingers wide. He slid on the Ring of Destiny.

Chapter Forty-Three

Demons and Angels

IVAN'S MEN PAUSED. THEY stared up at Addison uncertainly as he waved Solomon's ring.

At first, nothing much seemed to happen. And then, absolutely nothing happened. Addison's mouth went dry. He swallowed hard.

A sadistic grin spread across Ivan's face and spread to the rest of his men like a contagious virus. They slowly closed in on Solomon's throne.

Addison realized he and his friends were cornered. They needed options. He thought of the legends of the magical feats Solomon performed from the seat of his throne. His brain burned through all its gears until he worried that exhaust fumes would pour out of his ears.

Ivan climbed the first step to the throne. He mounted the second step and the third as well. He flexed his push daggers and clicked them together menacingly. He was thoroughly enjoying this.

It was when Ivan reached the fourth step that Addison saw it: the mystical seal of Solomon emblazoned on the right arm of the throne—its six-pointed star carved into the gold. It was the exact shape and size as the seal on the ring. *Maybe, just maybe*, Addison thought . . . *maybe the ring does have powers*.

Ivan mounted the fifth step, his eyes gleaming as brightly as the edges of his blades.

Molly drew her sling from her satchel and started it swinging.

Raj raised his fists.

Eddie cowered behind Raj.

Addison called to them. "Guys, get as close to the throne as possible . . ."

He sat in the throne of Solomon and pressed his ring to the six-pointed star on the right arm of the chair. It fit, locking into place. It reminded him of the way his Templar pendant clicked perfectly into the bronze tablet. Now he knew where the Templars got the idea for such a design.

Ivan climbed the final step, raising his push daggers for a lethal slash.

Addison twisted the Ring of Destiny in the socket of the throne.

Ancient machinery whirred behind the bronze-covered walls of the chamber. The stone gargoyles lining the ceiling opened their demonic mouths. Their razor-sharp fangs ground together, striking like flints and shooting sparks. Geysers of oil sprouted from their stone throats.

And the room was engulfed in flame.

••••••

Malazar shrieked, shielding his face from the torrents of fire. He ran in a blind panic, hurling himself behind a row of gold bars.

Ivan and his men flattened themselves to the ground, covering their heads from the searing flames.

Addison watched the mayhem. He heard the screams and felt the room grow fiercely hot. The stone demons were doing their work. But Addison was not a demon himself. When he saw Ivan's coat burst into flames and heard Ivan's terrified shriek, he wondered if he could gain power over angels as well.

He unscrewed the signet ring from the right arm of the throne. The jets of fire slaked and petered out. Addison turned to the left arm of the throne and inserted

Solomon's ring into an identical six-pointed star on that side.

He twisted the ring, and the stone angels mounted around the edge of the ceiling spit plumes of water, squelching the fire from the clothing of the burning Russian *vori*. The angels belched tens of thousands of gallons of water. Gang members lost their footing. The room became a treasure chamber–shaped toilet, flushing the Collective out the door and down the fifty steep steps.

Through the hissing, misting spray, Addison heard something that made his heart do a double back flip in his chest. His aunt and uncle. It was just two words, shouted from a distance, over the pounding roar of the deluge. "Addison! Molly!"

Addison shook his head, unsure whether to believe his ears. He decided it must be some trick of the gushing water. He twisted the Ring of Destiny out of the throne socket and watched the water trickle to a stop. He listened for the sound of his aunt and uncle and heard nothing.

Molly marched down the steps of the throne, looking for a Russian chin or shin in need of a swift kick. The flood had swept all of the gang members clear out of the room. All except one.

Ivan had somehow managed to cling to the edges of the doorway to avoid being plunged down the stairs. With his long hair soaked, he looked like a drenched sheepdog.

He rose to his feet, dripping and mad and gasping and sputtering for breath. He clenched his fists, gripping his daggers.

Molly drew her sling, loaded it with a lead slug, and marched up to Ivan.

Raj watched her, his face draining of color. "Molly, are you sure you want to fight him?"

Molly set her sling spinning until it was nothing but a whirring blur. "Positive."

Ivan grinned and beckoned her closer.

Molly attacked, attempting to clock Ivan across his hairy head.

Ivan deflected the sling's blow with his push daggers, and took a swipe at Molly's face. "You need a real weapon."

Molly kept the sling spinning, whipping it toward Ivan's head again and again.

He struggled to parry the raining blows. Molly herded him, backing him up. Ivan retreated two steps, and then a third. Overwhelmed, he stepped backward out of the treasure chamber and onto the outside platform. That was where the giant copper wrecking ball clobbered him, sending him flying off the high ledge.

Molly watched him tumble and fall. "How's that for a real weapon?"

Addison and Eddie cheered.

Raj rushed to her side and shook her hand enthusi-astically, pumping it like he was tolling a church bell. "Molly, there's something I've always wanted to tell you." He beamed a smile at her.

Molly looked at him expectantly. "Well?"

"Well, it's just that . . ." Raj stammered a bit and looked at the ground. "Molly, you're amazing."

"Um, thanks, Raj."

"No, I mean, you're just . . . You're really . . . You're incredible."

Addison took off the ring and cupped it in his hand.

Molly scanned the drenched room. "Wait, where's Malazar?"

Addison looked left and right. "I thought he was behind the gold."

"Did anyone see him pushed out by the flood?" asked Molly.

Addison sensed movement from the heaps of golden treasure behind him. Before he could even begin to turn, something hard and metal walloped him on the side of the head. Addison collapsed to the ground, rolling in pain. The ring rolled away as well. Addison found him-self on his back staring up at the demented face of Vrolok Malazar.

Malazar's newly burnt features were twisted in rage as he raised King Solomon's golden scepter high over his head. Addison saw the manic fury in Malazar's eyes. The man brought the scepter crashing down at Addison.

Addison swiveled his head. The scepter missed him by an inch, denting the copper floor and sending precious rubies skittering in all directions.

Addison's ears rang. He couldn't seem to find his feet.

Malazar reared up for a lethal blow.

Addison looked for any sign of help. Molly was running toward him, but she was still too far away. The same was true for Raj. It was Eddie—of all people—who smashed into Malazar. This time the heavy scepter dented the floor millimeters from Addison's neck. He rolled out of the way.

Malazar tossed Eddie against a stack of gold bricks with a sickening crack. He snatched the Ring of Destiny off the ground. Clutching the fresh fire burns on his arms and face, he barreled for the exit. Unlike Ivan, he paused for the pendulum before disappearing out the door.

Addison was woozy from the blow to his head. Raj helped him to his feet. Eddie, clutching his lower back, could only move in a limping gait.

The group hobbled after Malazar as quickly as they could manage. They dragged themselves through the pendulum door and down the steep steps. At the bottom they could see that all of the Russians had fled.

"Don't they want the treasure?" asked Molly.

"Malazar's burned—he needs a hospital," said Addison. "Ivan can't be in great shape, either. Besides, they got what they came for: they have the ring."

Addison loped along as quickly as he could, hoping to catch up with the Collective, but each step jarred his aching head. They reached the reservoir and swam below the rocky wall. Raj, sensing the urgency, even skipped his breathing exercises. The group limped and shuffled all the way back to the mine entrance. But when they reached the mouth of the cave, all they found was a blinding sandstorm.

Malazar, Ivan, and the Russians were gone.

Chapter Forty-Four

The Assassin

ADDISON KNEW FROM HIS experience in the Gobi Desert that they had no choice but to wait out the sandstorm. Blundering blindly in the blustering storm could mean getting hopelessly lost in the desert and facing certain death. He, Molly, Eddie, and Raj sat in the hollow of the mine entrance nursing their bruises and waiting for dawn.

When at last the howling winds began to subside, Raj poked his head from their hole like a groundhog scenting for the first sign of spring. He searched the sands for any Collective footprints to follow, but the gale-force winds had long since blown away any trace.

Molly clambered out of the mine and sat down

dejectedly on the desert floor. "Malazar got away with the ring."

"But we know he can be beaten." Addison stood beside her, his hair tousled by the stiff wind. After a moment, he spoke again. "Molly, inside when the flood poured in . . . did you hear something?"

Molly looked up at him. "I thought I heard Aunt Delia and Uncle Nigel. Like they were calling for us. Did you hear it, too?"

Addison held her gaze for a long moment. He slowly nodded.

Like a mirage, T.D. emerged from the billowing clouds of the sandstorm. She looked exhausted and dirty. A filthy handkerchief protected her face, and her dreadlocks were dusted beige from the sands. She unslung the rifle from her shoulder and dropped to one knee to rest. Nodding to Addison in greeting, she unscrewed her canteen and drank for a long time.

Addison waited for her to finish drinking before he spoke. "Each Templar family has a specialty. And now I know what the d'Anger family does. I know why you're good with a rifle. I know why you have access to planes and getaway cars. I know why you won't tell us what you do . . ."

T.D. looked at him steadily.

" . . . You're an assassin." Addison watched T.D.'s eyes

for any sign of reaction, but she was as cool as the underside of a pillow. She took another pull from her canteen and said nothing.

Addison continued. "That's why you only came with us as far as the Collective's encampment last night. You let us go to Solomon's mines as bait. You wanted a shot at Malazar. I'm guessing the sandstorm spoiled your plans and he got away."

T.D. squinted into the wind. "The Cookes guard the relics," she said at last. "The d'Angers . . . we guard the guardians."

T.D. stood up. She capped her canteen and reached into her pack. "I searched Malazar's encampment and found something that belongs to you." She handed Addison the bronze tablet.

Addison wiped the sand from its surface and passed it to Molly to stow in her satchel. He nodded his thanks to T.D. "Without the tablet, Malazar will have a tough time ever finding this mine again."

"Why?" asked T.D. "They made it in last night."

Addison shook his head. "Malazar's men never solved the puzzle—they just followed our footprints. And our footprints are long gone." He gestured to the valley, glowing under the rising sun. Parting clouds of drifting sand revealed the land riddled with mines—thousands of mines—pocking the surface of the desert like craters on the moon. Each shifting dune looked alike in the sea of sand. There was no landmark and no way to tell a century from a millennium.

"What about us?" said Eddie. "Shouldn't we claim the treasure? All those rubies and diamonds and golden statues?"

Addison shook his head.

Eddie stared at Addison in dismay. "Well, why not?"

Addison swept sand from the sleeves of his suit jacket and the creases of his trousers. "Solomon is a prophet to the Muslims, a prophet to the Jews, and a saint to the Christians. Who will claim this treasure? What wars will they fight? There is enough wealth here to unbalance world economies. The treasure is safer underground for now." Addison gazed across the valley and nodded. "Our job is to protect this secret. We are not treasure hunters like Malazar. We are guardians."

"Relic guardians," said Molly. She rose to her feet to stand beside her brother.

T.D. climbed to her feet as well. "When I met you all in London, I thought you were fools . . ."

Addison nodded. It was understandable.

T.D. looked at each of them in turn. "I underestimated you. All of you." T.D. then did something Addison had never seen her do. She smiled. "I will see you again."

She shouldered her rifle to leave, but hesitated. "Oh

yes. I have something for you. I found this tucked under a rock by the Collective encampment. It is a letter."

T.D. pressed a folded scrap of paper into Addison's hand. She held his hand for a moment, squeezed, and then let go. Turning, she strode away across the flats and vanished in the gusts of sand.

Addison looked down at the note in his hand and quickly unfolded it. He squinted from the stinging sand and read . . .

Dear Addison and Molly,

If you are reading this, then you are still alive, and quite possibly, we are, too. Who knows if you will find this note—we can only have faith that you will. Perhaps it was faith that saved us in Mongolia, where we plunged into the white waters of that awful river and somehow failed to drown.

Malazar is searching for something at Kolossi Castle—something to help him with the prophecy. We are kept blindfolded, but have been shuttled between his strongholds from Russia to Spain to Cairo. He keeps us alive to help him find the Templar relics.

Stay strong, Addison and Molly! We love you and live on the faith we will be reunited again.

Aunt Delia & Uncle Nigel

Molly tugged at Addison's sleeve. "What does the letter say? Who is it from?"

Addison swallowed the lump in his throat and handed the letter to Molly. He could manage only two words. "They're alive."

Chapter Forty-Five

Hope

AS THE WIND DIED down, Addison's group hiked back across the desert basin. They were halfway across when Dax appeared out of the drifting sand, leading the team of camels. He beamed at the sand-caked crew. "Everybody still alive?"

"Yes." Addison grinned. "Even Aunt D and Uncle N." He handed Dax the letter.

Dax scanned it and broke out in a broad smile. "Your luck is turning, Addison. And mine is, too."

"Why, what happened?" asked Molly.

"Malazar left in a hurry. His helicopter's gone, but he left his entire camp full of equipment."

"So?"

"So I sold it all to a passing Bedouin caravan." Dax

winked, pulled out his wallet, and fanned a thick wad of Jordanian currency. "I'm back in business."

"What are you planning to do?" asked Raj.

Dax plucked the toothpick from his mouth and considered the question. "With this kind of dough I can be back on my feet again in Tanzania, hunting poachers."

"I thought there was a warrant out for your arrest."

Dax shrugged. "I'll just steer clear of Dar es Salaam."

Addison gave Dax a firm handshake. "I'm happy for you, Dax."

Dax clapped Addison on the shoulder. "You too, kid."

• • • • • •

Arriving back in London's Heathrow Airport, Addison and Molly gave farewell hugs to Eddie and Raj.

Addison turned to Eddie. "What are you going to do when you get back to New York?"

Eddie had clearly been thinking about this, because he answered immediately. "I'm going to start piano lessons again."

"Are you ready?"

Eddie nodded resolutely. "I played in that Turkish airport and it wasn't so bad. And after all, I faced Malazar and the pendulum of death. How much can an audience do to me?"

Addison smiled and turned to Raj. "And how about you?"

Raj had clearly been thinking this over as well. "I'm going to face up to my mom," he said. He took a deep breath, straightening his posture. "I'm going to tell her I'm rejoining the Boy Scouts. I'm well on my way to Eagle Scout. I enjoy it. I can help people. And you know what? I'm getting better at it."

"You are," Addison agreed. He and Molly hugged them one more time and waved as they boarded their flight.

······

By the time Addison and Molly were back at Runnymede, Uncle Jasper and Jennings the butler were already overseeing workmen removing Aunt Delia and Uncle Nigel's grave markers from the family plot. Addison watched the workmen's progress and smiled in satisfaction. He crossed to the grave of the very first Cooke—Adam Cooke—who had somehow escaped imprisonment in the Templar Fortress in Paris. Addison plucked a few nearby flowers— forget-me-nots—and placed them on Adam's grave.

Uncle Jasper stood by Addison's side and placed a hand on his shoulder. "We have to assume the Shadow knows your location now. It pains me to say we can't be sending you back to the Dimpleforth School in the spring. It's too dangerous."

Addison tried to hide his relief. "That," he said, suppressing a smile, "is a *terrible* pity."

"In fact," said Uncle Jasper, thrusting his hands in his

pockets and rocking back and forth on his heels, "I think we may need to send you and Molly abroad. Switzerland, perhaps. Or even Dubai."

Addison could no longer contain his grin. He broke out in a wide smile.

Uncle Jasper seemed not to notice. His face remained grim as he surveyed the misty Surrey landscape. "Malazar has yet another relic. He is that much closer to completing the prophecy. Maybe now the remaining Templars will see that we have no choice but to fight. Maybe this will drive them out of hiding."

Addison looked up at his uncle. "I have to tell you the last words Grand Master Gaspard spoke to me. He had a message, Uncle Jasper. He said to tell you the Order of the Templar must rise again."

"He is right," Uncle Jasper said. "There are very few of us left in the world. And many have not spoken to each other in a generation. It is time for a gathering." Uncle Jasper glanced up at the swirling clouds, portending rain. "The time has come. We will summon the last of the Templars."

••••••

That night, in Runnymede Manor, Addison was thrilled to be back in his own room and in his own bed. And yet he was not ready for sleep. He crossed his room barefoot in the dark to stand in the moonlight by the window over-looking the orchard.

He loved the stars and planets of the cosmos, and for years he had told people he wanted to become a cosmetologist until he found out what that word actually meant. Tonight he gazed up at the night sky—the Milky Way breaking out in a rash of constellations. And for once, all seemed well in the world. Or if not well, pretty close.

For it is only when the night grows dark, Addison reflected, that we can truly see the stars. Malazar now had the Ring of Destiny. Malazar now had the golden whip. But somewhere under those sparkling lights in the night sky, his aunt and uncle were still alive. And by those stars, Addison knew his true direction, his purpose. He had a score to settle. He had to make things right.

In these dark times, there is not always room for forgiving or forgetting.

But there is always room for hope.

Author's Note

THE KNIGHTS TEMPLAR ARE a real order of knights who fought in the Crusades during the Middle Ages. This group of knights helped invent the modern banking system and grew fantastically wealthy and powerful—even owning the entire island of Cyprus. This all came crashing down on Friday, October 13, 1307, when King Philip IV of France—deeply in debt to the Templars—ordered the Templar leaders to be arrested and eventually burned at the stake.

The "Temple" Fortress in Paris was built by the Templars in the thirteenth century, at the height of their power. It stood for centuries until Napoleon ordered it demolished in 1808. A Paris Métro stop now stands in its place.

The Paris Catacombs are entirely real and an amazing

spot to visit. They comprise more than two hundred miles of mines, tunnels, and ossuaries. The catacombs are mostly south of the River Seine, whereas the Temple Fortress was built to the north.

The massive reservoir of the Basilica Cistern is a real location in Istanbul, as is the Hagia Sophia. Kolossi Castle on the island of Cyprus is well worth a trip, but don't be disappointed if the actual castle is somewhat smaller, simpler, and less sinister than what I described in the book. As for 747s, they can indeed be boarded by climbing the front wheel ladder, though you probably shouldn't try this unless you have great health insurance.

The treasure of King Solomon is believed to be quite real, and includes Solomon's ring, the Ark of the Covenant, and a fabulous amount of gold. As of this writing, its location remains a mystery.

Acknowledgments

Cheryl Eissing, Michael Green, Laurel Robinson, Abigail Powers, Shanta Newlin, Nicole White, Brianne Johnson, and Christopher Adler.

THE ADDISON COOKE SERIES

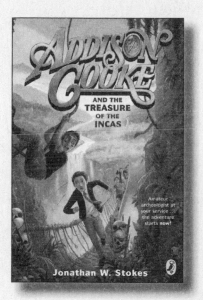

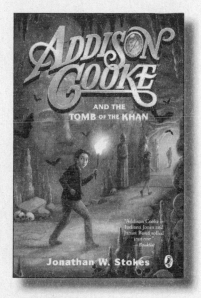

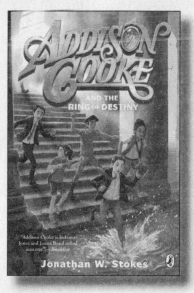

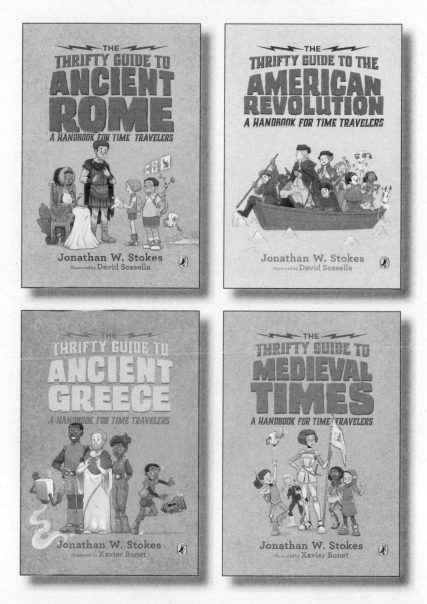

Author photo by Miles Crawford

Jonathan W. Stokes is a former teacher who is now a Hollywood screenwriter. He has written screenplays on assignment for Warner Brothers, Universal, Fox, Paramount, New Line, and Sony/Columbia. Inspired by a childhood love of *The Goonies* and *Ferris Bueller's Day Off*, Jonathan set out to create the world of Addison Cooke. Born in Manhattan, he currently resides in Los Angeles, where he can be found showing off his incredible taste in dishware and impressive 96 percent accuracy with high fives.

Follow him on Twitter
@jonathanwstokes

You can visit Jonathan at
jonathanwstokes.com

AddisonCooke.com